Steam

HOMECOMING HEARTS
BOOK FOUR

HJ WELCH

Also Available

BY HJ WELCH

Paddle Creek College (Daddies and kink)

#1 Heaven Sent

#2 Yes, Sir

#3 Little Pleasures

#4 Four Play

Pine Cove (Small town)

Complete Box Set

Homecoming Hearts (Former Boy Band)

Complete Box Set

Bears-4-U (Daddies and bears multi-author shared universe)

Keep Me

BY HELEN JULIET

Contemporary Fairy Tale Adaptations

The Fairy Tale Collection (Beauty and the Beast, Cinderella, Rapunzel)

Daddy's Fairy Tales (Daddies and kink – Goldilocks, Little Red Riding Hood, The Three Little Pigs, Puss in Boots)

CHAPTER

One

TRENT

All Trent wanted was a damn coffee.

It didn't used to be like this. Sure, he'd been in the limelight one way or another for the past eight years. But since his last film had hit the box office things had gotten so crazy he struggled to get anywhere without being hounded.

As soon as he ventured into the lobby of his apartment building in downtown LA, he knew he was in trouble. Camera flashes went off like the Fourth of fucking July, lighting up the night. Trent suddenly wondered if it wasn't too much to call his driver and ask him for a lift.

The coffeehouse was only around the block, though. A wave of resentment rose within Trent that he would be denied the simple satisfaction of buying his own damn cappuccino. So he shoved his hands in his leather jacket and continued walking out from the elevator.

Someone must have put up a new blog post or started a new rumor for there to be that many guys waiting outside his door like a pack of wild hyenas. They were already yelling and waving at him as he walked over the marble floor towards the wall of glass.

"I'm sorry, Mr. Charles," the reception clerk, Mario, called out to him from his desk. He was an older guy who had manned the building for as long as it had been standing, or so Trent had heard. Normally he was hard to rattle, but now he was wringing his hands. "I didn't know if I should have called the cops?"

Trent held up his hand and hunched his shoulders slightly as he neared the door. "It's okay," he grunted.

Goddamned freedom of the goddamned press. Today of all days Trent just wanted to hide away from the world. But his hangover hadn't dissipated from that morning and he'd gotten a craving for one of Java Jem's hazelnut brews. He couldn't make them in his apartment with his own machine and the shop didn't deliver.

Besides, if he turned around now, that would be letting those jackals win.

He tried to make himself look smaller as he released the door lock and stepped out onto the sidewalk. A difficult task at six foot three and two hundred and thirty pounds. But he dropped his head and let his shoulder-length hair cover his face as much as possible.

"*TJ! TJ!*" they bayed. There had to be two dozen guys flocking around him. The cameras were going off in a dazzling, continuous stream of flashes.

"TJ! Are the rumors about you and Elsie Hadden true?"

"When's the baby due, TJ?"

Baby? What *baby?* Trent tried his best not to shake his head. He just kept his gaze down and continued walking as they moved with him like a swarm of wasps. He'd discovered over his years of rising fame that the best thing to do was to ignore the shit the paparazzi spewed as much as possible.

He didn't want to be ungrateful for his achievements. So many people would give anything to be in his position. Not only a successful five years with one of the hottest boy bands on the planet, but then an action movie career that was only getting bigger. But with it came the bat-shit crazy lies which blogs and magazines were willing to print in order to get sales and views.

Trent hadn't even seen Elsie in years. They'd maybe crossed paths at a couple of awards ceremonies and parties. But generally, she moved in the music industry circles still, while he'd switched to the insane world of Hollywood.

Yeah, there had been that one time in New York in the bathroom of that club. And the weekend in Miami. But they'd never really been a thing. Much like most of Trent's lady friends, things had fizzled out before they'd ever gotten serious. Why were the paps bringing her up again now?

"How long have you been back together?"

"What does Penny have to say about it?"

Penny was yet another nice girl who had eventually gotten bored of Trent's lack of commitment and moved on. The press had liked her with Trent because she was an Instagram star and had a fitness program. Seeing her with a reprobate who apparently never stopped drinking made for a controversial visual, even if he was ripped.

She was better off without him. Trent was happy for her and her new guy.

Flash! Flash! Flash!

Trent was going to trip on the sidewalk if he wasn't careful. It was taking forever just to make a five-minute walk to the damn coffeehouse. He was going to have to buy a whole box of pastries as well to make this journey worth it. At least he could give one to Mario to try and apologize for making his night awkward by blocking the front of his building. Again. Trent was fully aware he wasn't the only tenant there.

"When's the baby due, TJ?"

"Are you guys going to get married?"

"What do you say to the rumors it's actually Reyse Hickson's?"

Trent snorted inwardly. His former bandmate fathering any babies would be news indeed. But it wasn't true. Trent knew that for a fact.

"Will you petition for custody?"

"TJ? TJ!"

This was stupid. If he didn't answer them, the truth would come out eventually, and the story would die out in a week. Because Trent would know for damn sure if he was the father of a baby. He'd never be that reckless. But it still grated that he couldn't defend himself.

"Don't you feel bad letting Elsie go through this all alone? Don't you feel you should be responsible, TJ?"

Trent risked a quick glance up to identify one of his most loathed regular stalkers. Scraggly goatee, navy baseball cap and thick black glasses. Dez Starr, self-proclaimed seeker of truth and justice. He'd say about anything to get a rise out of a famous face, then sell the photos to the highest bidder. Trent *definitely* needed to keep his mouth shut.

"TJ, look this way!"

"Did you plan on knocking her up, TJ?"

"Is the baby an accident?"

"Will you fight Hicks in court if he claims the baby as his?"

"Are you a homewrecker, TJ?" Dez called out.

The coffeeshop was in sight. Trent was so tempted to give these guys the double finger once he got there. But he'd only have to face them once he came out again to walk home. His manager had all but threatened him with castration if he caused any more trouble before they officially signed the contract for Fixer 2.

So he'd be a good boy for once and just keep walking. He already had enough on his mind that night. Once his coffee had straightened out his hangover, he fully intended on washing away any remaining thoughts with a serious amount of whiskey.

But of course, Dez wasn't going to let that happen.

"What would your mom say if she knew you'd knocked up a girl, TJ?" Dez asked. There was a nasty glint in his eyes. "Probably a good thing she's dead. Otherwise, the shame might kill her all over again."

Trent didn't even hesitate. It was like he disconnected from his body. He had no power to stop the fist that came flying up and punched Dez Starr right between the eyes, snapping his glasses in two, knocking his hat off and sending him crashing to the ground.

The camera flashes became a wall of light as Trent blinked back to his senses. He couldn't decipher a single question out of the dozens of voices now bellowing at him. He looked down at Dez who had plastered the perfect look of shock and horror onto his face.

"He hit me!" he cried, fumbling for his camera and his wayward baseball cap.

His voice sounded close to cracking as he pointed at Trent with a shaking hand. Then he scrambled backward, as if Trent was at risk of kicking him while he was still sprawled on the sidewalk. The other guys loved that. They were taking as many photos of Dez as they were Trent now. Trent, who was famous for portraying barbarians and hitmen and quarterbacks. And Dez, who looked like he'd weigh a hundred pounds soaking wet.

Trent had messed up, big-time. He needed to get out of there right away. But before he could make his feet move, the blip of a police siren alerted them to a squad car pulling up to the curb.

No, no, this couldn't be happening.

"Dez," one of the paps cried. "Are you going to press charges?"

"Is your nose broken, Dez?"

"TJ, do you hit Elsie like that?"

"Do you like to hit women, TJ?"

"What would you mom say about that, TJ?"

Trent grit his teeth, forcing down the rage that threatened to spill out. If he didn't behave, he would lose everything. That bastard had known what the date was and asked that question about his mom on purpose. Lashing out any further would only give him what he wanted.

So Trent just had to swallow it when the two cops got out of the car and the paps parted to let them through to cuff him. He closed his eyes as they read him his Miranda rights, cursing his stupidity.

How the fuck was he going to get out of this one?

CHAPTER

Two

ASHBY

Ashby no longer knew what time zone he was in, other than he had apparently been awake for half of his life.

He groaned and tried to stretch his long legs in the confines of the premium economy seat and cursed his past self. Why did he always do this? There was nothing noble about opting out of first class. Yes, he was convinced it was a ridiculous amount of money to waste on a flight he was probably going to sleep through. But then whenever he was actually *on* that flight, he remembered he was more giraffe than human and ended up too miserable to sleep.

Still, at least this was the last leg of his journey. The real hardship had been traveling from London to Chicago. His layover at O'Hare had been mercifully short and now he just had to get through a couple more hours until they landed at Jackson Hole, Wyoming.

The name didn't exactly inspire confidence. But Ashby pulled at his slender fingers and reminded himself that this wasn't some luxury getaway. The whole point was to disappear from the world for a while, and he could hardly do that at a popular resort during the ski season, even if it was the tail end.

If he'd wanted hot guys and parties he would have taken himself off to Aspen or the Alps. He would probably have flown first class while he was at it. But the whole point of booking last minute was to slip away somewhere quiet. Somewhere no one would think to come looking for him.

The Grand Resort in western Wyoming was a peaceful little place tucked away near the bottom of Yellowstone Park. It wasn't really renowned for anything other than being quiet, which was exactly what Ashby was craving. It had a spa for a bit of pampering and beginners' slopes if he felt like doing something crazy. Other than that, he was going to take a break from everything aside from a few good books.

All he needed was a log fire to read by and a bar that served hot chocolate during the day and drinkable wine in the evenings. No Michelin star restaurants or luxury apartments. Ashby wasn't going to be sharing a bed, so as long as he had somewhere to sleep at night, he would do just fine.

He sighed and reached down to his carryon to fish out his phone from where he'd stored it. It was on airplane mode, naturally, so the battery had lasted all this time. But Ashby had promised he would do this before they landed and he only had an hour or so to go.

Bracing himself, he unlocked the screen.

Well, the first thing that had to go was the wallpaper photo of him and Gordon hugging on the beach. That had been a long time ago.

Before Gordon had cheated.

Ashby swallowed the lump in his throat and refused to cry again. It was for the best. He'd known for a long time that he and Gordon weren't happy, that they weren't right for each other. He just couldn't believe it was finally *over*.

He deleted the photo entirely, squeezing his eyes shut as he pressed the little 'Yes' square. No point in keeping it in an album. Looking at pictures of when he thought he was happy would only make him feel sad. When the truth was, as that collection of pixels vanished, he remembered how *free* he was now.

He let out a little laugh, grateful that his neighbor was too engrossed in a film to notice. He'd known for almost a year that he wasn't really in love with Gordon. They had been together for two years in total, Ashby's longest relationship to date. But the cheating had given him the courage to finally end it. And here he was, crossing the Atlantic Ocean to mark the start of his new life.

Fuck, he was terrified.

"Um, excuse me," he said to the flight attendant as she passed.

She turned and beamed at him. "Why, don't you have the most adorable accent?" she said with a tinkling laugh. "Are you from England?"

Ashby blushed. "Well, I'm from all over really, but my father is English and I live in Chelsea, South West London now."

"Isn't that just wonderful?" said the young lady. "Keep talking. I love it."

Working on a small, local airline, she probably didn't get nearly as many Brits flying as Americans. She had shiny red hair tied in a neat knot and a smattering of freckles which made her look younger than she probably was. Ashby immediately felt comforted by her winning smile.

"I'll be happy to say anything you like in return for a gin and tonic," he said, clasping his hands together. "How about aluminium? Oregano? Or, oh! Caribbean."

She giggled over his strange pronunciations. "Oh, for that, hon, you can have a double."

Ashby smiled and tried not to let his melancholy creep back in. "A double sounds marvelous right about now."

Her returning smile suggested she picked up that he wasn't quite feeling his best. She winked and lightly tapped his shoulder. "I'll be right back with your drink. You just sit tight."

Ashby was being silly. This was for the best. It was what he wanted. *He* had been the one to put his foot down and end the relationship once and for all. He had forgiven Gordon for many things. But finding those messages on his phone from Dan or Sam or whatever the hell his name had been was the final push Ashby had needed. He was worth more than being messed around on. No matter what his doubts, Ashby had to believe that much.

So he made sure to keep taking deep breaths in and out and he cleared his inbox. He didn't want to see Gordon's name anywhere. In fact, Ashby would block him altogether to stop him from continuing his harassment. Gordon didn't love him. He was just pissed off that Ashby was defying him and walking away.

Every little thing he got rid of made Ashby feel that tiny bit better. He wasn't used to being alone. Actually, the prospect of being responsible and making decisions for everything by himself sounded god awful. But it was better than being undermined and second-guessed at every turn.

The flight attendant returned with his gin and gave him such a warm smile. It fortified Ashby enough to start the daunting task of deleting his photos. There were so many that gave him pangs. But every time he paused and asked himself if it would be okay to keep *just* this one, he remained strong. Yes, there were many nice photos of the two of them. But that period in his life was over now.

By the time the wheels touched down in Wyoming, Ashby's phone was sparse but healthy looking. As far as he could tell, all trace of Gordon was gone. The fact that there was so little left of Ashby's life on the device showed how much he had allowed his ex-boyfriend to dominate everything before.

That had to change as of now. No more men, at least for the time being. Ashby needed to work out who he really was. What his passions were. What made him happy. It might take him a month, a year or even longer. But he was determined that he was going to start treating himself as whole outside of a couple.

There was nothing quite like that first breath of fresh air after stepping off a plane, whether the flight had been one hour or twenty. He smiled as he inhaled deeply, then turned to his lovely redheaded attendant. "Thank you," he said, giving her a quick hug. She giggled again.

"Aw, shucks, hon," she said, swatting his arm. "You have a great vacation now."

He waved her goodbye then trundled onwards with the other weary passengers. It was midafternoon local time, but back home it was already creeping up to bedtime. He yawned and vowed to get a coffee as soon as possible. He'd much rather have a soothing cup of tea, but that would absolutely send him to sleep in the taxicab when he needed to stay alert and reset his body clock.

Once he'd reclaimed his suitcase and poured several sugars in his mocha he stepped out of the small airport into the snowy evening and immediately gasped in horror. It was *bitterly* cold, and he suddenly wished he'd changed into his thermals in the bathroom beforehand. The wind burned his face and he hastily dropped his suitcase to the ground and carefully placed his coffee beside it to rummage through its contents for extra scarves, a pair of gloves and a hat.

Slightly better protected, he zipped the suitcase back up with trembling hands and clutched his coffee to his chest like it might keep his heart beating if the cold tried to freeze it solid. "Bugger *me*," he said emphatically, stamping his feet and startling a middle-aged American couple as they walked past.

Evening was settling, so no wonder it was getting colder. If he stayed still much longer he was going to turn into an icicle. So he rallied himself and dragged his enormous suitcase over to the taxi line and tried not to shiver apart as he waited for his turn to slide into a car.

"Oh, thank god," he said as he was enveloped by the cab's blissfully warm interior air. The driver secured Ashby's suitcase in the back of the car then scurried around to get behind the wheel. "It's a bit chilly out there, isn't it?" Ashby commented with a laugh.

The driver looked at him in the rearview mirror like Ashby had lost his marbles. "It's snowing," he said, like Ashby might not have noticed.

Ashby chuckled quietly to himself as they pulled away from the curb. "It certainly is."

At home, he would have been alarmed by such weather. London may have survived the Blitz, but an inch of snow could cause utter bloody chaos. And where Ashby had spent most of his childhood growing up in Singapore, they didn't even *have* seasons. It was always just warm. So he couldn't help but press his nose to the window and look outside in wonder at the swathes of snow.

"You on vacation?" the cabbie grunted in a more-or-less friendly manner. He looked at Ashby in the rearview mirror again. There was a small dreamcatcher swinging from it with beautiful topaz blue stones woven into the design.

Ashby beamed at him. It tickled him that there were so many different words Americans used. He'd have to try and pick up as much of the lingo as possible and blend in. It wasn't his first trip to the States by far, but he'd forgotten a lot of the little intricacies of daily life here.

"I'm on holiday – vacation – yes," he said. "I've never been to Wyoming before."

The truth was he'd never been *skiing* before. He'd been to the Alps plenty of times growing up, but he had just indulged in the social side of things. He was always too afraid to fling himself down the side of a mountain. But he felt silly admitting that to a stranger.

Maybe this would be the holiday that changed his mind, though? He was here to find himself, after all. He needed to be brave and try new things.

"You're staying at the Grand?" the cabbie asked.

His voice had a bit of an accent to it that Ashby couldn't trace. But he spoke English very well, so Ashby admired him as much as he did anyone who attempted a second language. Unlike his mother, who spoke seven languages fluently and could immediately pick up phrases in any other she pleased, Ashby was hopeless. He could barely say hello in anything other than English.

"Um, yes," he replied. "I think that's what it's called. It should be the only resort in that region."

It was the only *anything* in that region. There were a few tiny towns if you drove out for half an hour or so, but other than that, the site was self-sufficient. Exactly why Ashby had chosen it. He needed to go somewhere free from distractions.

The cabbie didn't say any more after that. He just turned up the radio a little and Ashby continued to gaze out the window at the falling twilight as he sipped his coffee. He'd never been on holiday alone before. He'd always gone with family, friends, or, in the past two years, Gordon. Gordon liked booking everything and taking charge of the passports, wrangling Ashby like a sheep that needed herding. He often joked that Ashby could never go anywhere without him.

Ha! Well, Ashby would show him. He'd managed to get across a whole ocean on his own, find his own hotel, book everything online. He hadn't gotten lost or slipped up once.

That was, until they pulled up outside the supposedly Grand Resort.

Ashby looked out through the window at the dimly lit lodge. Several of the light bulbs over the main entrance were out and what little illumination there was allowed Ashby to see the peeling paint and cracked sign above the door.

His mouth slowly dropped open. No wonder this place was famed for its quietness.

No bastard had visited it since 1998.

CHAPTER

Three

TRENT

Trent walked down the brightly lit corridor with a sense of dread weighing him down. His legs felt hollow and his hangover was making his stomach roll and his hands shake. He'd really blown it this time.

His manager worked for an agency that represented actors in film, theater, television and anything else in between. They had some pretty big names on their books, most of whom had their portraits framed along the very corridor Trent was trudging his way down. He stopped at the print of his own face, his expression mischievous. The cultivated bad boy who ladies wanted to bed and men wanted to be.

Well, he wasn't so much bad boy now as borderline deviant. Thank fuck Dez Starr hadn't wanted to press charges. It made him look like the bigger, better man if he dropped his claim. But that didn't mean Trent wasn't still in a whole load of shit.

He knocked with a sense of trepidation.

"It's open," the gravelly voice snapped from beyond the wooden door.

Trent sighed and turned the handle, letting himself in.

Barry Barsky was a heavy-set man with a salt-and-pepper beard and a razor-sharp eye for detail. As was usual when he was awake, he was puffing on a cigar, the smoke from which had permeated every nook and cranny of his office, despite the supervisor giving him countless reminders that this was a no-smoking building.

Barry pointed the smoldering cigar at Trent as he closed the door behind him.

"Sit," he barked. "Now." His voice sounded like a cement mixer after so many decades of destroying it with smoking. The man was a cockroach though, or at least Trent had always affectionately thought so. He'd be here long after the apocalypse took the rest of the world out. There was no destroying Barry Barsky, god love him.

Although it felt some days like Trent was doing his best to try.

"What the actual fuck?" Barry rasped as loudly as his voice would go.

He jabbed the cigar toward Trent again, little flecks of ash drifting down onto the overloaded desk. Trent wasn't sure how he got any work done when his computer was buried under so many files and contracts and magazines. One of which he picked up and thrust into Trent's face. He winced at the front page, which showed a split image of him punching Dez and then him being led away by the cops in cuffs.

"The guy's a jerk," Trent mumbled into the back of his knuckles as he rested his elbow on the chair's arm.

Barry slammed the magazine back down again and blinked his big blue eyes at Trent. They stood out from behind the gray-black whiskers that encompassed the rest of his face. If it wasn't for the two-thousand-dollar suit, he could have passed quite nicely for anyone's lovable but slightly crazy unemployed uncle.

"A jerk?" Barry repeated. "Of course he's a jerk. This is Tinseltown, everyone's a fucking jerk. You're a jerk, all these guys are!"

He flung his arm out and indicated the many framed photos he had on his wall of all the talent he'd represented over the years and the A-list directors and producers he considered buddies. Four walls dominated by Barry shaking hands with Hollywood's best known from the last three decades.

Trent had yet to make it onto one of these particular walls. Barry was still unconvinced he had what it took to be a real name. And as it turned out, he was probably right.

"There's a difference between jerks with Emmys and jerks standing in lineups," Barry griped. "You feel me, kid?"

Trent grumbled again and folded his arms.

Barry sighed and leaned back in his gigantic leather chair, bouncing on the springs. "Look," he said, his voice gentler. He puffed on the cigar. "I'm not an idiot. I know what the date was. I can guess the kind of thing that prick Starr said. But you can't let him get under your skin."

Trent just shrugged.

Barry huffed. "Okay, look, I put out the Elsie Hadden fire. Turns out she's not even pregnant. She just gained a couple of pounds and a so-called gal-pal ran to the press thinking she had a scoop after she caught her drinking a soda instead of vodka for once." He rolled his eyes. "Some friend. No idea why they picked you to pin the bump on. But, whatever, it's over."

"Thank you," Trent muttered.

Barry toyed with his cigar for a few moments, flicking it against an already full crystal ashtray. "You wanna talk about it, kid?"

"No," Trent said immediately.

Barry sighed. "Well, if you don't want to talk to me, you

might have to talk to someone. Anyone. This shit was already getting out of hand before you got charged with assault."

"Dez dropped the charges," Trent countered. "I'm fine."

"No, you're not," Barry told him firmly, taking another drag. "For the past two years you've been drowning in booze and women, and it's not working."

"I've always done that," Trent argued.

He tried for his signature cheeky grin, but Barry's expression remained stony, so he dropped it. Seriously, though. What was the big deal? He'd been Below Zero's 'bad boy' when they were in the band, and that reputation had got him his first few film roles without even trying. Everyone knew he was a daredevil and did all his own stunts. After The Fixer had come out over Christmas, he was tipped to be the new Bruce Willis, Tom Cruise, Jason Statham.

He'd almost hoped that the incident with Dez might be *good* press if they could spin it right. But obviously, Barry wasn't seeing it like that.

"It was cute in the beginning," Barry said, shaking his head. "But that was before you started showing up on set drunk or hungover or somewhere in between. Before you picked fights with sound operators-"

"That guy was a lecherous prick," Trent interrupted.

Barry continued as if Trent hadn't spoken, "-and before you broke the heart of every girl you came into contact with. Actresses, runners, makeup artists. For fuck's sake, TJ. No one is stopping you from having sex. But, come on. Are all these girls so terrible you can't stand to look at them again the morning after?"

That was harsh, but Trent couldn't bring himself to argue. He'd tried to make it work with dozens of women over the past couple of years. But every time he'd talked himself out of it, sabotaging a good thing before anything could get too serious. He knew he was doing it. He just couldn't seem to stop.

"What do you want me to say?" he asked Barry, probably with a bit more growl than was necessary.

Barry wasn't where he was in this industry by being Mr. Nice Guy, though.

He leaned forward on his elbows, cigar still expertly balanced between two fingers even as he clasped his hands together. "I want you to admit that you've never gotten over your mom's death. And rather than deal with the shit with your dad, your toxic fury has seeped out into every other aspect of your life until you're in danger of destroying the lot." He took a long, slow drag on the cigar. "Am I close?"

"Fuck you," Trent mumbled, looking down into his lap. There wasn't any real venom to his words, however, and he knew Barry wouldn't take it that way.

Barry waited to speak until Trent pushed his hair back and glanced up at his manager again. "Kid," he rasped, his gravelly voice even heavier than usual. "You know there ain't a fire I can't turn into a bake sale. But I'm tired of this fucking shit. You're going to implode, and the sorry truth is I kinda like you. I'd rather not wake up one morning and read that you've OD'd or are serving life for killing some asshole in a bar fight."

Try as he might, Trent couldn't help but be touched by Barry's concern. He managed to twitch the corner of his mouth into a smile that he hoped conveyed his appreciation.

"So?" he prompted.

"So," Barry said, resting his cigar on the tray. He laced his stubby fingers together and rested them on his rotund belly. "I'm giving you a break. Three months. You don't have anything major planned until then, and you need to go get your head screwed on straight."

Trent frowned at him and pulled at a loose thread from

one of the rips in his jeans. "What am I supposed to do until then?"

Barry raised a salt-and-pepper eyebrow. "Go *home,*" he said, like it was obvious. "Go back to Wyoming and talk to your dad. Scream, hug, I don't give a shit. Get some fresh air and give your liver a damn break. *Stop* for a fucking minute."

That sounded horrendous. Trent narrowed his eyes at Barry and wondered if there was any way he was going to be able to wriggle out of this.

"You're not wriggling out of this," Barry drawled, deadpan.

Trent huffed and flopped back in his chair. "I haven't got anything to say to my dad," he said, pulling at the thread on his jeans again. "He's the one who wants to hide up in the mountains in that god-awful hotel."

"You make it sound like The Shining," Barry said. Trent raised a signature eyebrow at him and glowered. Barry held up his hands. "Hey, what do I know? It's not my fault your old man lives in the last place god ever created. If he lived in the Hamptons, would you have gone and hashed this out with him already?" Trent shrugged. "That's what I thought."

"So, I'm supposed to spend three months at a ski resort?" Trent grunted.

Barry shook his head, rolling his cigar around in the tray. It had gone out. "If it takes that long. If you're singing kumbaya and making father-son fishing trip plans after a month, I'd say you could come home. But I don't think that's likely, do you?"

Trent rubbed the stubble on his chin. Three months was a quarter of the year. He'd only just made a big name for himself. Fixer 2 wasn't a done deal. "You want me to sit on my ass and let the contracts go by?"

Barry chuckled. "Kid," he admonished. "Like I'd let you go cold. You can still do interviews over the phone and audition by tape if something juicy comes up. But you've got that goofball football-player-turned-spy film shooting in the summer, and Fixer 2's in the bag."

"Yeah?" Trent said, his hope rising.

Barry picked up his dead cigar and box of matches. "Yes. But *only* if we can reform your image. No more asshole TJ Charles. Lovable scamp, yes, great. Dickhead who doesn't care who he hurts around him is a much harder sell."

Trent chewed his lip. Forget his public image. He didn't want to become that person for real. He was tired of letting people down and breaking hearts. "Okay," he said.

Barry smiled as he relit the cigar then puffed out a couple of clouds of smoke. "Good boy," he said. "And who knows? Maybe you'll meet a nice local girl to calm you down. A bit of stability would do you the world of good."

Trent hated to admit it, but his heart ached at the thought. It wasn't that he hadn't liked most of the girls he'd hooked up with. Hell, he even thought he might have loved a few of them. But he was no good being in a couple. He always felt stifled after a while, scared that if he committed he'd just end up disappointing them.

But who knew? Maybe Barry was right. Maybe the Grand Resort, Wyoming, was where he'd meet the true love of his life.

He doubted it, but it was a nice thought.

CHAPTER

Four

ASHBY

For a split second, Ashby considered asking his driver to turn around and take him somewhere, anywhere else. But he looked a little closer at the resort and decided that, really, it wasn't that bad.

In fact, it had probably been utterly charming once upon a time. But it had obviously been a while since anyone had shown this place some TLC. That didn't mean it was bad. The reviews had been good, after all. It was just a bit run down.

Ashby was here to get away from his usual life, and that included the trappings of ridiculous wealth he'd known his whole life. He wanted somewhere peaceful, and if that meant his lodgings were less than luxurious, he could manage.

"It'll be like camping," he said to himself as he bundled back up in his scarves. His driver had already gotten out of the car to fetch Ashby's suitcase. So he glanced at the meter to get the right money out before he braved the snow again, adding a generous tip. "I'm sure everything will be fine once we take a peek inside."

His driver thanked him for the cash he handed over, then

hopped straight back in the car to escape the cold. Ashby took a moment to absorb the Grand Resort in all its glory before the wind got too much for him to bear.

It really could have been quite wonderful if it hadn't been allowed to fall into disrepair. There was a foot of snow over the triangular roof of the main lodge. The building itself was made out of timber. The resort's sign had a Scandinavian look to the lettering and the whole picture reminded Ashby of a Christmas card, despite it being early April. Icicles hung from the wooden beams and lanterns. If only the owners had kept up the replacement of blown bulbs, he could have over-looked the cracks and peeling paint on the door and window frames.

Ashby shuddered against the wind buffeting against him and decided he'd gawped at the outside of the building long enough. Time to check out the inside. At least there were a couple of cars parked outside, so he knew he wasn't the only guest. He disposed of his empty coffee cup by the entrance, then hauled his heavy suitcase over the snow and pushed against the door to let himself in.

He found himself inside a very bland lobby. A gust of freezing wind accompanied him inside, making the half a dozen people milling around turn and look at him as he struggled to shut the door again. He tried not to blush under their scrutiny. "Sorry," he whispered.

The guests on the floor went back to their business as Ashby unwound one of his long, woolen scarves. He used the moment to take in his surroundings.

Again, the place had probably been lovely a decade or two ago. There were wooden beams everywhere, a large fireplace, and although they weren't to Ashby's personal taste, he could see why the stuffed buck heads on the walls would suit the aesthetic. But they were dusty. The uphol-stery on the many sofas and armchairs littered about the room was faded and frayed. The plastic plants looked cheap and ugly.

But the fire was roaring in the fireplace. Ashby smiled as what looked like a couple of grandparents showed their small grandchild, wearing enormous glasses, how to hold their hands up to the flames to warm them safely. The architecture of the room was well thought out and the large windows probably showed the snowy mountains beyond to their full advantage during the daytime. Chatter filled the air as well as relaxing country music. He found himself smiling despite his apprehensions. It may not be the sort of accommodation he was used to, but he could certainly see beyond the slightly shabby surface and take the resort for what it was.

A getaway. A sanctuary.

"Hi there," said an extremely perky young woman as he approached the reception desk. She was in her mid-thirties and had her blonde hair in a short bob around her ears. Her uniform was an unflattering brownish red color with too-large shoulder pads, but it was pristine and she evidently wore it with pride. "Are you checking in?"

Her name badge read 'Kadie.' Ashby smiled and unwound another scarf. "Yes, thank you," he said. He pulled his reservation details out from his carryon. "The name's Ashby Wilcott."

Her green eyes sparkled. "Oh, wow," she said. "I love your accent. You sound like Harry Potter."

Ashby chuckled. "I never got my Hogwarts letter though, much to my dismay."

Kadie laughed. "Me neither. I would have made a great Hufflepuff."

Ashby gasped and placed his hand on his chest. "Me too," he proclaimed.

Kadie continued grinning as she brought up his reservation on her big, boxy computer. "Okay, Mr. Wilcott. Ah, it says you'll be staying with us for three whole weeks. That's wonderful!" She seemed genuinely delighted by the prospect as she fetched an actual key for his room. "There you go. Is it just yourself staying with us?"

"Yes, no boyfriend this time," Ashby said with a chuckle. Then he froze, horror holding him captive. What the *hell?* Why had he just outed himself to a total stranger? Panic threatened to overrun him.

Katie's eyes went wide, her hand hovering midair with the key she was still offering. "O-oh," she said, her cheeks going pink. "Oh, um, no, that's fine. Sorry, I've never met a, um, well, a *gay* man before." She whispered the last part like she was afraid they might be overheard. But she smiled broader at him and tucked her short hair behind her ear. "You know, I love that makeover show. The one where the gay guys come in and fix everything."

Ashby felt himself relax again as she flipped the key in her hand, presenting him with the circular end to take. "Oh, yes," he said nodding. "That's brilliant, isn't it?"

She laughed nervously and stared at him with wonder. "Well, okay, Mr. Ashby. You're in room thirteen on the first floor. You come find me if there's anything you need, okay? I'll be happy to help." She bit on her thumbnail and laughed again.

Ashby couldn't help but be relieved. Rather than treating him like a leper, she was practically enamored with him. Like he was something special when in truth he was just *him.* It was kind of sweet. He certainly preferred it to being asked to leave on account of him being a filthy pervert. He let out a breath and waved the key at her before turning to head toward his room.

There was no elevator and if there were any bell-hops they weren't around. So Ashby had to lug his enormous suitcase up the one and only flight of stairs to the first floor. The corners were extremely tight, and one of the steps was slightly uneven compared to the rest, causing Ashby to trip and fall onto the carpet. He lost his grip on the suitcase and it flipped backwards, sliding down several steps.

Ashby huffed and blew his hair out of his eyes. Despite being overly tired from traveling and generally on edge from the whole Gordon thing, he refused to get upset. So what if he fell over? No one had seen. He just needed to pick himself up and go find his room. Soon enough he could snuggle up in bed.

With renewed determination, he hauled the luggage up the last few steps and made it to the landing. But his troubles only continued as he dragged his suitcase down the hall, squinting at the numbers. Had he gone the wrong way? They seemed to start at twenty. But Kadie on the front desk had definitely said the first floor.

Once he got to the fire escape at the end and established there was definitely no room thirteen, he shook his head and turned around, determined to check again. He gritted his teeth. He just wanted to take his shoes off now and maybe brush his teeth.

"You okay there, sweetie?"

Ashby stopped and turned around to see a plump middle-aged woman in a big, puffy coat walking toward him. She had curly graying brown hair, multicolored horn-rimmed glasses and wore her bag slung over her shoulder like she was on her way out. Or home, perhaps? That looked like some sort of uniform under her coat.

"I, uh," said Ashby.

Suddenly his resolve not to get upset threatened to abandon him. He knew it was the jetlag overwhelming him, but Gordon's voice perked up in the back of his head telling him that he was so *useless*. He couldn't even find his bloody room!

Ashby swallowed that spiteful thought and tried his best to smile at the woman. "I can't seem to find my room," he said. "The lovely lady at reception said room thirteen was on the first floor, but I can't seem to see it. Is there another staircase, do you know?"

The woman with the multicolored glasses reached him and patted his arm. She was a good foot shorter than him. "Oh, honey," she said with a grimace. "That's because you're on the *second* floor."

"No, I-" Ashby began. Then he snapped his mouth shut as the realization washed over him. "Oh," he said meekly. "You see, in the UK, this would be the first floor and, well, downstairs would be the ground floor."

"Yeah," said the woman kindly. "That's really dumb. You want me to help you find your room? I just cleaned it not an hour ago. It's all spick-and-span."

Ashby sighed, ridiculously grateful. "That would be lovely," he admitted. "Oh, no, you don't have to!" he squeaked as the woman took ahold of his suitcase and began marching down the hallway.

"Come on, James Bond," she said. "You look dead on your feet."

Ashby had to chuckle as he trotted behind her. "I do feel like the back end of a bus," he admitted.

The woman barked out a laugh as she heaved the suitcase back down the stairs. She seemed to be doing better at carrying it than Ashby had been. "That's a hell of a saying. We don't get many Brits here, you know?"

"Really?" Ashby said. "Well, this place is-" he caught himself before he was rude "-very nice indeed."

The woman scoffed. "Oh, you're a charming one, all right," she said. She looked over her shoulder and grinned at him as they reached the ground – or first – floor again. "I'm Maeve," she said. "Worked here for over a decade, so you don't need to be polite."

Ashby glanced at the dingy walls as they walked along the hall. These rooms started at number one. "Well, I guess a lick of paint couldn't hurt," he conceded. Maeve cackled with laughter.

"You staying here for long, cutie?" she asked.

"Three weeks," he said as they approached his room. "So I guess I'll be seeing you around? I'm Ashby, by the way."

Maeve stopped in front of room thirteen and held out her hand. "Three weeks?" she said as Ashby dutifully gave her his key. "Wow, a pretty guy like you. What are you hiding out here in the mountains for?"

To his utter mortification, tears sprung in Ashby's eyes. *Damn* this jetlag. He didn't care about Gordon! He wasn't heartbroken. He was just reeling from all the sudden changes. He did his best to blink and clear his throat. "Just fancied a change of scenery," he said weakly.

Maeve didn't miss a thing, though. "Oh, hon," she said. Her shoulders dropped and her expression was one of sympathy. "Come on, tell me all about it."

She unlocked his door and shooed him inside before dragging his suitcase in after them. Ashby was ashamed to admit it, but he wasn't very good at being on his own. The idea of some company, even from someone he'd just met, was wonderful. "Aren't you on your way home?" he protested weakly.

Maeve blew a raspberry at him. "My cats can wait a while longer," she said, then pointed to the small table and chairs in the room. "Sit. I'd offer you tea, but I'm guessing it'll taste like dishwater compared to what you guys make. Something stronger?"

Ashby sniffed and wiped his eyes as he laughed and

plopped into the seat. "I wouldn't say no to a gin and tonic," he said.

Maeve shrugged off her old green coat to reveal a pink housekeeper's uniform underneath. While she rummaged in the minibar, Ashby looked around the room that was to be his home for the next three weeks. The walls were the same grayish white and the carpets the same brownish gray as the lobby. The faded pine table where he was sitting stood next to an equally starved-looking dresser with a clunky microwave on top. Above the table a small TV was mounted on the wall. Ashby was amazed it was a flat screen.

The bed looked comfy, though, and from what Ashby had seen he guessed, his window had a good view of the mountains. This would do just fine, he was sure.

Maeve placed a very full plastic tumbler of gin and tonic in front of him on the table along with bags of peanuts and some cheesy corn-chip things. She herself had a glass of neat whiskey in her hand as he sat down next to him. "So," she said, shifting on the pine chair to get comfy. "Who broke your heart?"

Ashby scoffed and downed half his drink in one glug. "Is it that obvious?" he asked. He winced as the alcohol burned his throat slightly, but in a sort of pleasant way.

"Yeah, hon," Maeve said with a nod. "A mom knows these things. Got four kids of my own, even some grandbabies. You wanna see?"

"Do I ever," he said with genuine enthusiasm.

She whipped out her phone, proud as punch. He oohed and ahhed in all the right places as Maeve flicked through her phone to show him some adorably chubby grandkids of indistinguishable gender. Ashby couldn't help but have a moment of melancholy, though. He managed to keep his smile in place, but his thoughts turned a little sad.

Would he ever have kids? It was so much easier for opposite-sex couples. But so many guys were just interested in fucking rather than settling down, let alone thinking about starting a family. At least in Ashby's experience.

He knew he had more than enough time to consider his options and find Mr. Right. He was only twenty-four, so hardly over the hill. But it was hard to imagine a future like that for him when he'd never even lived with a boyfriend before.

Maeve smiled at him and he wondered if he'd zoned out a little. "Sorry?" he asked.

"I asked what the bastard's name was who broke your heart," she said. She saluted him with her whiskey and downed the glass without even a pause. "He must be a real dick to let you go."

For the second time in an hour, Ashby was too scared to move. "H-he?" he stammered.

Maeve gave him a warm smile and patted his hand. "A mom knows these things," she said again. "You come here to get away from men?" Ashby didn't know what to say, so he just nodded. She snorted and opened up the peanuts for them. "Good choice. No men for anyone up here."

Ashby blew out a sigh of relief. It was bad enough he was scared of what Gordon might do once he realized Ashby really had left him for good this time. He didn't want to be starting anything unpleasant with the resort staff on the very first day of his getaway as well. "Thank you," he whispered as she pushed the peanut packet over to him. But he wasn't really thanking her for that.

She rubbed the back of his hand with her thumb. "I've been divorced ten whole years," she said firmly. "Best damn thing I ever did. Want to tell me about him?"

Ashby definitely didn't want to talk about Gordon. He wanted to forget they had ever met. He was embarrassed to think how stupid he'd been to ever allow himself to get involved with a man like that. He could see it all so clearly now.

"No," he said, managed a small smile. "He was a bad egg."

Maeve nodded as she refilled both their glasses from more of the minibar miniatures. "They are out there, sweetheart."

Ashby raised his glass. "To staying away from bad eggs," he said. She grinned and clinked her glass to his.

"Amen to that, sugar," she said. "Don't worry. You'll find a good one, one day. Someone who'll treat you like a superstar."

Ashby leaned his head back against his seat. The alcohol was already hitting his system and he felt his shoulders relaxing. He gazed at Maeve. "Is that what you did?" he asked. "Found a better guy after the divorce?"

Maeve scoffed and took another swig of her whiskey. "Oh, no, honey. That's what cats are for." She winked. "For company, I mean. All you need is a vibrator for anything else."

Ashby spat his drink back out into his glass and coughed so much Maeve had to slap him on the back, all while she continued to cackle wickedly.

"Blimey," he said once he could speak again. "Well, I guess I know what to do if I don't find Mr. Right."

But Maeve shook her head, her expression a little more serious. "Don't you worry. A nice boy like you? You'll be just fine," she assured him. "But some time alone up here will no doubt do you good."

Ashby wasn't so sure. Aside from his wealth and the looks he was born with, deep down he suspected Gordon was right. He was pretty unremarkable.

"I thought I might try finding myself," he admitted sheepishly. Maybe he would have something of substance if he looked hard enough.

But Maeve raised an eyebrow at him. "Hell yeah. You do that, baby."

"This didn't seem like the kind of place that drew a young crowd," Ashby said. "I was hoping to avoid a party scene."

Maeve sighed. "Yep, nothing exciting ever happens around here. You'll be safe."

She sounded sad. It was probably a little dull if this was your job. Considering how far away the towns were and how much she'd already drunk, Ashby wondered if she lived onsite, too.

Selfishly, safe, dull and a lack of men were exactly what he wanted. But maybe he could make a friend or two while he was here.

He held his glass up again for her to clink once more. "Here's to a good holiday," he said. "And new friends."

They tapped glasses. "I'll drink to that," said Maeve with a wink.

CHAPTER
Five
TRENT

TRENT LOOKED DOWN AT THE LARGE ST. BERNARD PUPPY squirming on his lap in the cab and wondered for the hundredth time if this wasn't the worst idea he had ever had. Over the years, Trent had indulged in some truly *spectacularly* bad ideas. But this could possibly make the top ten.

The puppy was wriggling and wagging his tail and licking Trent's hand like he had never been happier in his whole, short life. "How could I think you're a bad idea?" Trent mumbled into the little dude's fur. Or, not-so-little. He weighed more than Trent's luggage, he was almost certain.

Trent took a breath and reminded himself again that the fact that there had been a St. Bernard breeder in Jackson, Wyoming, with a litter ready to go and just *one* pup left the very week Trent had come home, was a sign from the universe he wasn't willing to ignore. Even if this was a dumb idea, the stars had aligned for him and there was no going back now.

He looked out at the weak midday sunshine reflecting blindingly off the endless fucking snow and sighed. The only good thing about this weather was that it meant snowboarding, something Trent intended to do a *lot* of while he was here. The resort didn't have a gym, so he was going to struggle to stay in shape during his stay. The best he'd been able to do was order a set of weights for his cabin.

His dad knew he was coming. Trent suspected that Barry had phoned Trenton James Charles Sr. in the couple of days it had taken Trent to fly out here and smoothed the way. Or tried to, at least. But in any case, Trent's dad had emailed him to let him know that the resort had a staff cabin he could rent for a reduced rate. Trent had wanted to write back and say he could afford the full rate, because he didn't want to come across as taking advantage. But he knew that kind of offer would be perceived as ungrateful.

He'd wanted some kind of peace offering to go to his dad with, though. Hence, the crazy idea of the puppy.

Trent looked down at the not-so-little guy and chewed his lip. He deliberately hadn't been back to the resort since the accident. He knew his dad was mad at him for that, but what could Trent do to make it better? He'd need a time machine to be able to say goodbye to his mom, and the longer he left it with his dad, the more awkward it became.

Two years was a fairly long time. Trent wasn't sure what he was even going to say when he saw his dad again. But he'd have to figure it out soon.

They were pulling up to the resort.

When Trent had been growing up, they'd lived in one of the actual towns about a forty-minute drive away. But when he'd left home at eighteen to chase his fame and fortune, his folks had quit their losses and moved into the staff accommodation. After over a decade here, Trent knew his dad felt like this was his home more than anywhere else had ever been. He *loved* the Grand Resort. More than he loved his son, Trent was almost certain.

Trent had never been all that close with his parents, but

they'd gotten along as much as possible with Trent being such a rebellious teen. They had at least tried to understand how stifling he'd found small-town life. Trent was meant for the big wide world, not Buttfuck, Nowhere, Wyoming. He had been happy for them to leave his childhood home as soon as he flew the nest. The resort was their home, their family.

Trent glowered at the shabby front entrance. It hadn't looked so dilapidated before. But it seemed appropriate to him. After all, this place had taken his mom from them all.

He didn't understand how his dad could stay here for two years with all those memories haunting him. But he had. Trent couldn't help but feel like his dad had forgiven the resort far quicker than he had Trent.

"Thanks, man," he muttered to the cab driver as he paid him.

He let the chubby puppy down in the snow where he immediately started tugging at his leash, attacking the powder with tiny growls as he pounced and dug a few holes. Trent looped the end of the leash over his wrist, then picked up his two bags to take them toward the front door. Despite wearing sunglasses, Trent still squinted up at the lodge. Wow, the place had really gone downhill. What had happened?

Due to the state of the building and the fact it was nearing the end of the season, Trent wasn't surprised there were only about a dozen people milling about in the lobby, including the staff. That didn't help him feel any more comfortable when all twelve of those people turned to look at him as he and the puppy and his massive suitcases clattered through the door.

He cleared his throat and pulled off his glasses. Damn. At least his dad wasn't out here.

"Oh – my *god*," a voice declared in jubilation. It immediately caught Trent's attention even before he identified who had spoken. The last thing he'd been expecting to hear out here was an English accent.

He looked around to the guy who was standing by the reception desk to his left. Then Trent blinked. Wow. That guy was beautiful. There was no other way to describe it, even if he was a dude. Tall, slim, pale blond hair that flopped over in a neat side part, high cheekbones and a bright, open smile. Designer jeans clung to his narrow hips and a cashmere sweater hung off his torso and arms.

Model, Trent thought immediately. But he immediately reconsidered when the guy threw up his hands, then dropped to the floor with absolutely no regard for his couture and opened his arms up for Trent's puppy.

"Who's a good boy? You are, yes you are!" the Brit cried, letting the puppy scramble and slobber all over him. "Good *lord*, he's adorable. What's his name?"

Trent looked down into a pair of teal-green eyes, wide with excitement. This guy was completely uncaring of the fact everyone was looking at him. He just smiled at Trent like he was the only person in the room.

Trent frowned. He didn't have the energy for this. Did the guy recognize him? Was he flirting? He was obviously gay and Trent didn't feel like breaking any hearts before he'd even had the inevitable row with his dad.

He glanced up at the rest of the room. Luckily, the same old country music was playing quietly over the sound system, so it wasn't completely awkward with no one talking. He gave a tight smile to the people loitering around. Strangely, he wasn't sure *anyone* recognized him. There were a couple of grandparents with a bespectacled kid under five making their way to the restaurant, probably for lunch. A dude in a white Stetson turned to a bellboy to ask a question, and a group of three middle-aged women in skiwear was sitting around the fireplace on sofas with hot drinks. They were all looking because this Brit was causing a scene and, to be fair, the puppy was adorable enough to grab anyone's attention. But Trent didn't spy that hungry look of recognition he usual got from fans.

He relaxed just a fraction, then looked down at the Brit. He was still gazing up at Trent as he played with the puppy.

Oh, right. He'd asked Trent a question. "No name, yet," he said in a low rumble. "Excuse me."

He knew it was rude, but he was so on edge he thought he might lash out or fall apart if he had to deal with any unnecessary distractions. He just needed to speak to his dad, then he could think about other people. If the Brit did know who he was and blabbed on Twitter, Barry could sweep that kind of thing away easily. Trent wasn't here to make friends.

He tugged the puppy away from the guy and dragged his suitcases over to the desk. Luckily, the conversations around him were picking up again, so he didn't feel everyone was listening in.

"Trent!" the girl behind reception said in delight. "So nice to see you again!"

Trent glanced down at her tag. He felt awful that the name 'Kadie' rang absolutely no bells for him. But it had been, what? Four years since he last came here? She looked to be in her mid-thirties, so probably had been here when he'd visited as a teen with his head in the clouds.

Trent smiled, though. He didn't want to be an asshole, after all. He'd promised Barry he wasn't going to turn into that person.

"Hi, Kadie," he said. "My dad said he'd organized my accommodation. Do you have the key?"

Kadie obviously knew exactly how famous Trent was, but she was doing her best to be professional. Her smile was so wide it looked painful, and she was a little breathless as she spun around to get Trent what he needed.

"Yes, of course," she said. "It's Cabin Three and you've got it for as long as you need. The usual tenant left a couple of months ago. We love you – I mean – we'd love to have you as long as you like. Here. Really."

She went pink and pressed the key into his hand. "Thanks," Trent said. He couldn't help but smile at her and she giggled softly.

No. He wasn't even going to think about messing around with that sweet girl. No more broken hearts. So, he dropped the smile and pocketed the key. "Dad in the store?" he grunted.

"Um, yes, I think so," said Kadie, her smile only faltering a little. She was a professional, after all.

Trent nodded. "See you later, Kadie," he said.

He turned to find the Brit standing behind him, patiently waiting to presumably speak to Kadie again. He had his hands in his pockets and the dazzling exuberance from before was gone. He looked downcast, only offering Trent a small twitch of his lips.

"Sorry I petted your puppy without asking," he said, stepping around Trent to get to Kadie.

Trent opened his mouth to say there wasn't any need to apologize. But the guy was already speaking to Kadie in soft tones about something, the spa possibly? He laced his long fingers together on the desk and hunched his shoulders.

Urgh. Trent hadn't meant to upset him. He just didn't feel able to navigate a conversation with *anyone* right now. He simply needed to get through this first meeting with his dad. Then he could maybe act normal again.

Maybe he'd see this guy around later to apologize. Unless he was checking out? Well, then Trent wouldn't have to worry about him again.

Except, he didn't like the idea he had made such a seemingly nice person sad.

Feeling more of a jerk than ever, Trent yanked his suitcases forward. The puppy scampered by his feet as they crossed the lobby of the main lodge and went down one of the corridors toward the gift shop. Okay, this was it. Whatever happened now, things would be better afterward. Right?

His dad was behind the counter of the jumbled gift shop, fiddling with the scuffed radio and drinking coffee from one of the green-and-silver-striped mugs that immediately brought Trent back to his childhood. It was like no time had passed at all. Except so much had changed in the years since he had last set foot in this place.

"Hi, Dad," he said softly.

Trenton Sr. looked up. Then he looked back down again.

Trent swallowed and eased his way further inside the shop, leaving his luggage out in the corridor. It was difficult enough to maneuver himself and the dog inside due to the fact that the place was an Aladdin's cave of junk and crap.

Stock teetered haphazardly in towers that defied physics. Ashtrays and maracas and creepy wool dolls. Magnets and shot glasses and miniature wooden clogs that Trent had never thought had a place in an American ski lodge. Poorly painted Christmas baubles rattled as Trent passed, trying to restrain the puppy from sniffing at the yo-yos on the bottom shelf they were passing.

"Um, it's good to see you," Trent tried again.

Trent's dad was a weather-worn man in his fifties. His skin was tanned and starting to wrinkle, his dark hair beginning to gray. He wore the same style of chunky knit cardigan he had worn to this store every single day for over two decades. His glasses had a smudge that Trent saw reflected from the fluorescent lighting above.

"What's that?" his dad asked, jutting his chin toward the St. Bernard puppy.

"Uh," said Trent. Fucking hell. He performed for a living.

He made blockbuster movies and had sung in front of eighty thousand people numerous times. Yet his old man made him tongue-tied. "He's for you."

He bent down to pick up the puppy, who naturally squirmed and wagged his already quite powerful tail. A tail that swiped off a whole row of china bells with *'Visit Wyoming!'* painted cheerfully all over them. Trent cringed as they clattered to the floor, breaking several in the process.

He looked over at his dad whose jaw was tense. "Um," said Trent and cleared his throat. "I'll pay for those," he muttered sheepishly, trying to minimize his large bulk. He held up the puppy. "He's, uh, well. I thought you could call him Merlin. Or Arthur, I uh…"

He knew he'd fucked up as soon as the words left his mouth. His dad's scowl intensified and he picked up his coffee to take an aggressive swig. "He's not Lancelot."

Trent gritted his teeth and moved closer, narrowly avoiding the display of pint glasses with the wrong mountains engraved on the sides. Honestly, he didn't know why his dad still cared so much when the company gave him such shit to sell.

"I know he's not, Dad. But I thought you might like a new friend. He's a cute little guy."

Lancelot had been an old dog when he'd passed away peacefully last summer. But after Trent's mom's sudden departure the year before, Trent suspected his dad had taken that heartbreak even worse. Trent missed the big old dude, too, but there was only so long someone could wallow in grief. Trent knew his dad well enough to think he'd appreciate the company a new puppy would bring.

Except, he wouldn't even look at the poor puppy.

"You can't just *replace* people, Trent," his dad said, settling the radio channel on a soft rock station.

Coldness more bitter than the snow outside cut through

Trent. Why the fuck had he ever let Barry talk him into this? The entire endeavor was doomed to fail. Trent's dad didn't want to talk through their shit any more than Trent did.

"Fine," he said, doing his best to keep his hurt hidden. "I'll just take him back."

He made to turn when his dad slammed the coffee cup down so hard on the glass counter Trent thought it might crack. It didn't. But his dad's expression was still angry. "You can't take him *back.* Just…leave him here." His eyes flicked over the dog. "Merlin," he said, like he was trying it out.

Trent licked his lips. He was almost certain his dad would love the puppy – Merlin – if he just gave him a chance. If Trent left them alone and his dad could forget where the dog had come from. He had adored his St. Bernards all his life.

So he carefully placed Merlin on the carpet and offered the leash to his dad over the counter top. His dad narrowed his eyes at it, then managed to take the end without making skin contact with Trent.

Trent shoved his hands in his pockets and walked as fast as he could back out of the shop. He paused to grab the handles of his two suitcases again, maneuvering them so he could wheel them away toward the exit that would lead to his cabin.

He thought he might have heard a small 'thank you' as he left. But he was probably imagining it.

CHAPTER

Six

ASHBY

ASHBY HAD SO DEARLY WANTED TO ASK KADIE ABOUT THE grumpy guy with the puppy. She clearly knew him from the way she smiled at him, although Ashby stayed back far enough that he couldn't hear what they were saying.

He had reminded himself sternly that this was to be a man-free holiday. Maeve had promised him there would be no hunks around to tempt him. So whoever he was, Mr. Tall, Dark and Rude probably wasn't sticking around for long, despite getting a key for a room.

Ashby resolutely put him from his mind as he finished chatting to Kadie about the spa treatments available, then went back to his room to change. After a couple of days, he was getting the hang of his jetlag, so he'd gotten lunch from the resort's restaurant at a reasonable time, then felt like a bit of pampering was long overdue.

Still, it might have been nice if the gorgeous guy hadn't been in such a hurry to get away from Ashby. He was obviously straight, so Ashby had no doubt scared him off with his unapologetic fem-ness. Well, screw him. Ashby didn't want to have anything to do with someone if they didn't like him for who he was. Not again.

He couldn't help but dwell on the mysterious stranger, though, as he pottered from his room to the spa facilities in his robe and flip-flops. Those muscles. Those dark eyes, like deep pools. The shoulder-length hair that was so thick and glossy, it was positively begging to be grabbed during a really good f-

"And this is you shutting down that thought and forgetting *all* about him," said Ashby firmly and out loud. The couple approaching him along the corridor raised their eyebrows at him. He cleared his throat. "Good afternoon," he said. They walked past warily and Ashby sighed. "No need to scare the locals," he muttered quietly to himself.

The spa was in the same state as the rest of the resort. It had probably been bang on trend twenty years ago, but now just looked a bit sorry for itself. The paint wasn't peeling, but the color had faded somewhat from the walls and the familiar beiges and creams looked tired. But there were actual live plants in pots injecting a much-needed shot of color to the reception area and the scent of lavender greeted Ashby as he walked through the doors. He inhaled deeply, enjoying the sound of soft panpipes that drifted through the air from a CD player in the corner.

A woman in her early-forties came out from behind the desk. Styled chestnut curls tumbled to her shoulders and her shiny lips were painted red. The technician's blouse she wore was an immaculate white and unbuttoned just enough to show off her perky breasts. Her gaze raked over Ashby as she clasped her hands in front of them. At least her perfect French manicure gave Ashby some hope that this wouldn't be a wasted visit.

"Well, hello," she said, her voice husky.

"Hello," Ashby said cheerfully. "I was going to book an

appointment, but lovely Kadie at the front desk assured me it wasn't necessary."

The technician's heavily mascaraed eyes lit up at him. He probably looked like someone who spent a lot of time at spas, because he did. If she was hoping he was going to take his break-up frustration and sexual longing for the stranger he'd just met and channel that energy into indulging in as much pampering as he could muster, she was in luck.

"No appointment necessary," the technician purred. "Not for a pretty thing like you."

"Oh, goody," Ashby squeaked, wondering if he was going to get eaten alive. "That's, um, wonderful."

She beamed at him. "Anything in particular?"

Ashby eyed up the board with the list of available treatments. "All of them?" he joked.

The technician laughed. "Aw hun, in need of some TLC are you? Don't worry. My name's Skye and I'm going to fix you right up. How does a back massage sound to start with?"

Ashby sighed. "Heavenly." He offered her his hand, which she shook. "I'm Ashby, by the way. I'll probably be bothering you an awful lot over the next few weeks."

Skye clicked her tongue and beckoned him to follow her. "Oh, that accent. You can come in as often as you like, sugar," she said, winking over her shoulder at him. "Business slows down this time of year, so you feel free to come keep me company any time."

"You're very kind," Ashby said, following her into the treatment room. The low-level lighting helped this particular area look slightly less run down than others and the scent of lavender intensified. Ashby sighed and got himself settled on the massage table.

For an hour, he drifted in and out as Skye's hands worked their magic. He could tell by the tender patches she found that he had a lot of knots, but she didn't comment until they were finished and she was eagerly laying him down for a full mud facial.

"You got a lot on your mind, hon?" she asked, cleansing his skin before applying the mask. At a glance, Ashby would guess the products they were using were about a decade behind current skincare trends. But that would make them cheaper, so it made sense. This place, for whatever reason, was clearly on its knees.

"Trying not to," he replied with a sigh. The clay felt cool as she smoothed it over his cheeks with a brush. "The Grand looked like an ideal place to come and forget everything," he admitted.

She snorted and clicked her tongue again, like she was popping bubble gum. "That's because everybody else went and forgot this place, too," she said. Ashby looked up to see her shake her head upside down at him. "Swish young fella like yourself would have loved it round here in its heyday. Why on earth you'd want to come here when you could go to Aspen, I don't know."

"Peace and quiet," Ashby said simply.

Skye hummed. "There's peace and quiet, then there's tumbleweeds in a graveyard," she said frankly.

Ashby chewed his lip as she brushed the clay between his eyes. "Why *is* it so run down, if you don't mind me asking?"

Skye chuckled ruefully. "Well, you didn't hear this from me," she said, clearly eager to gossip. "But you come across Bob yet, the manager? He's the sad-looking fella you'll find propping up the bar most evenings. Balding, same old gray tie every day."

Ashby shook his head, but Skye waved the brush at him, dangerously close to flicking clay on his white bathrobe.

"You'll spot him soon enough," she continued. "So, rumor has it his wife's putting him through a nasty divorce even though their kid's coming out the other side of chemo." She tutted and dabbed more of the face mask onto Ashby's chin. "Some people. Anyway, I don't think his heart's in it anymore. We can only work with what he gets the owner to give us, and lately, that ain't been a whole lot."

Ashby hummed. That was a real shame. He listened to Skye chatter on for a while about how things used to be, thinking of what Maeve had told him as well. The more he saw of the Grand Resort, the more he was convinced it just needed a little love.

Ashby's fears that Skye was going to pounce on him were further allayed when she inspected his hands. "Urgh, you gay boys do keep your nails so nice," she said. "Would you like me to tidy your cuticles and do a quick oil massage?"

Although it was a little presumptuous that straight guys couldn't have nice nails, Ashby knew she meant well and accepted the compliment. "That would be wonderful," he said sincerely.

While she busied herself moving her nail treatment station, Ashby chewed his lip. Surely, it couldn't hurt to *ask?* Skye seemed to know so much about the resort.

"I made a friend this morning," he lied as she began filing. "But I didn't catch his name. Tall, dark hair down to his shoulders, big muscles. He didn't seem like a guest." Or at least, Ashby assumed from the familiar greeting Kadie had given him.

Skye's perfectly penciled eyebrows slowly climbed up towards her hair. "Trenton Charles's boy?" she asked. "No way. He's back?"

"Um," said Ashby. "Maybe? He had luggage with him. And a puppy. He was wearing a black leather jacket despite it being arctic outside." Even *thinking* about that jacket put Ashby in danger of popping out of his robe.

"Dreamy eyes, muscles for days?" Skye sighed. "That's

him. Oh my god, I can't believe he's here. I'll have to get an autograph."

Ashby frowned at her. "Autograph?"

Her eyes went wide. "Uh, yeah," she said. "You did recognize him, didn't you?" At Ashby's blank face, Skye gasped. "He's *TJ Charles!* The movie star. It's, like, this place's only claim to fame."

Ashby blinked. "TJ Charles?"

Oh no.

Yes, he was aware TJ Charles was a film star, but Ashby had not caught on that he was who he'd dropped to the feet of a couple of hours ago. He really *should* have realized he'd been flirting with a former member of Below Zero, though. How had he *not* registered it was one of his teenage crushes he'd been babbling to?

"Ah," he said, shame washing over him. "Well, that's embarrassing."

Skye snorted. "Come on. Tell me all about it, babe. Then I'll tell you how I once fell into the lap of Zac Efron at a Bar Mitzvah."

"No?" Ashby said, scandalized and delighted all at once.

She nodded. "He's a friend of a friend. So, come on, what did you say to our little TJ?"

Ashby sighed and recounted the whole cringe-worthy story from the lobby. But as he was describing it, he realized it wasn't all that bad. It was TJ's fault if he was too miserable to take delight in a puppy. Ashby promised himself he wasn't going to let himself worry about it any longer.

Even if TJ Charles was still just as hot as when Ashby had stuck his posters on his bedroom wall. Hotter, even, now he was a fully grown man.

Ashby warred with himself as he bid farewell to Skye with the promise to come back soon. He needed to banish TJ from his mind. Yeah, he was hot. But he was also rude. Ashby had no time for that. Besides, he was probably just passing through the resort and Ashby wouldn't have to see him ever again. At least, not in the flesh.

With that bittersweet thought in mind, he made his plans for the evening. After a short nap – he blamed the massage as much as the lingering jetlag – he showered and took himself over to the restaurant for dinner with a book. He would rather have had his old, paperback copy of Pride and Prejudice to keep him company, but if he'd packed all the books he wanted to read this holiday, there would have been nothing else in his suitcase. He begrudgingly admitted that his eReader was actually pretty brilliant.

He people-watched while he read about Lizzie Bennett for the umpteenth time and ate, enjoying a glass or two of a rather nice Malbec wine. As Skye had mentioned, there was a gentleman at the bar who appeared quite down-in-the-dumps. Bob, Ashby guessed, the manager of the resort. He would probably be quite handsome for an older man if he didn't look like he had the weight of the world on his shoulders. Wearing a frayed ski jacket and worn jeans, he picked at his beer bottle label and dispassionately watched baseball on one of the TV screens.

For a brief, horribly selfish moment, Ashby worried if that was how he was going to end up. Then he mentally slapped himself. Yes, he'd been through a tough breakup, but it was of his choosing and undoubtedly for the best. He was half this guy's age and wasn't facing anything nearly as bad as seeing a child through a long illness. Skye had assured Ashby the boy was out of the woods now, but a divorce on top of that was bound to be exhausting. No wonder the resort looked in dire need of love. *Bob* was in dire need of some love, too.

"Carpe diem," Ashby reminded himself for the hundredth time since he'd left Gordon. He was only twenty-four, and he needed to start seizing the day more so he didn't end up lonely and unfulfilled.

Starting with a nighttime swim.

He'd fancied the idea since he'd arrived, and after his third glass of wine, he decided now was the time. The hotel's heated, outdoor pool was open late so guests could enjoy a warm paddle surrounded by snow. It sounded scandalous to Ashby. Something that surely should have been against the rules. Which is precisely why he wanted to do it.

Feeling tipsy and naughty, he went back to his room and put on his favorite tight swimming trunks. As it was dark and the hotel was low on guests, he figured he'd get away with no one seeing how skimpy they were. They left absolutely nothing to the imagination. Then he wrapped up in his robe once more and stuck his feet in his fluffy boots to head outside.

The shock of the cold cleared out the cobwebs and sobered up Ashby immediately. He giggled in shock at the sharp contrast of temperature between indoors and out, scampering over to the coat hooks to shuck off his robe and step out of his boots.

"Fuck, fuck, fuck," he hissed, hopping and dancing his way across the snow into the warm waters of the pool with another laugh. It was more like a large jacuzzi with pressurized jets creating bubbles and currents around the edges. Ashby sighed as he sank down until only his head remained in the frigid air. "Magic," he said softly to himself as the steam rose from the water all around him.

There was a sauna house to the left that had a foot of snow on its roof. Ashby was looking forward to giving that a go soon. Trees rose up beyond the fence, encircling the back of the resort. Pointed pines that climbed up the start of the mountainside, hinting to the summit lost in the darkness. Ashby sighed, feeling blissfully peaceful.

Until he realized he wasn't alone.

As he turned and glanced to the right, he realized there was someone else bobbing in the corner of the rectangular pool, hidden initially by the steam. Someone familiar.

"Oh, hello?" Ashby spluttered. Obviously, he wasn't going to be able to play it cool, no matter when or where he saw TJ Charles. "Sorry, I didn't see you there. I didn't splash you, did I? It's damned cold getting from the clothes rack to the water."

TJ was staring at him. His dark eyes were wide enough that Ashby could see a fair bit of the whites despite the gloom. "Uh…" he said.

Fuck. Ashby had forgotten he was wearing the skimpiest damn swimwear ever invented. It was practically a thong. He blushed, wondering how much of his junk TJ had seen bouncing around when he'd run over the snow.

"Sorry, I'm bothering you again," Ashby mumbled.

His knee-jerk reaction was to get out of the pool as fast as possible and take himself far away from TJ's judgmental stare. But his pride refused to bow down to that. His body was also extremely against the idea of getting back out into the snow any time soon.

So instead, he swam over to the opposite end of the pool, by the pine trees, and rested his hands on the stone edge. He stared up at the side of the magnificent mountain, trying to ignore TJ's presence and enjoy himself.

Only when he heard the splashing of water and the door to the main lodge swinging shut did Ashby finally relax again.

Well, it seemed his unfortunate crush hadn't left the resort just yet, after all.

CHAPTER
Seven

TRENT

IT WAS LIKE THE IMAGE OF A CERTAIN ALMOST-NAKED-BRITISH guy was seared into the back of Trent's eyeballs. Every time he closed his eyes, his lithe body dashing across the snow appeared. Normally, Trent noticed other guys' bodies in an abstract sort of way. Like, he thought about how much they did or didn't work out to get their physique. But the Brit was like an otter or mythical elf. Lithe, slender, but with enough muscular definition so his body didn't look skinny. Trent's mind kept drifting back to him simply because he was incredibly attractive to look at.

Which was weird, right? Trent could understand it if it had been a gorgeous girl in a bikini, her breasts bouncing as she jumped into the water, squealing in delight. But something about this guy's ridiculous dash across the snow along with his willowy body clad only in the tightest, tiniest Speedos had taken up space in Trent's brain and refused to leave.

Maybe it was just unusual? He had an ethereal, androgynous sort of look about him, further tempting Trent to think he might have been a model. But his dorky nature didn't really add up with that.

It had annoyed Trent that he'd taken forever to get himself to sleep the first night in his cabin as he'd been so preoccupied with random thoughts about a strange dude. What was that about?

By the time morning came, he felt like he hadn't slept at all. It didn't help that when he wasn't thinking about the stranger he'd now crossed paths with twice, he was thinking about his dad. Yesterday's reception had been far from ideal. But Trent would be willing to try as many times to smooth things out between them so long as his dad was looking after Merlin well enough.

That was stupid, he told himself as he made coffee downstairs in the open kitchen part of the lodge. His dad would never mistreat any animal, let alone a dog. But Trent still wondered if he was feeling brave enough to visit his dad again so soon to check up on them both and allay his fears.

He leaned against the kitchen counter in his sweatpants and hoodie, taking in what was going to be his home for the next couple of months. The cabin was starting to warm up now with a fire going in the fireplace. Trent was hoping he wouldn't have to swaddle himself every night just to avoid freezing to death. He was used to sleeping in the nude.

It would also mean he wouldn't have to resort to evening swims to warm up in future. It would probably be best to avoid the pool for a while if that was where the British dude was going to be hanging out. Trent had embarrassed himself twice in front of the guy now, and he didn't look forward to doing it a third time. He probably thought Trent was a total monosyllabic asshole.

Aside from being freezing when he'd first entered yesterday, Trent had to admit he liked the staff cabin he'd been allocated. It was becoming cozier as the temperature crawled up, and Trent had to admit he'd always been a sucker for a log fire having grown up around snow. It happily crackled now as he padded around the main room of the cabin.

The open plan of a kitchen, den and dining room all rolled into one made it feel even more intimate. The floors, walls and furnishings were all made of the same dark wood, but the sofa coverings, throw pillows and big fluffy rug by the fireplace were a pleasant cream. The lampshades and dining chair covers were a deep forest green. Artifacts from the local Arapaho tribe decorated the walls in a tasteful way. Trent was part Arapaho on his mom's side, so he appreciated seeing her culture being treated respectfully. He suspected whoever lived here last had taken it upon themselves to spruce the place up, rather than relying on the resort to do it for them.

Off from the main room was a bathroom and a single storage closet filled with spare bedding and cleaning products. Creaky wooden stairs led up to a half floor above where his double bed sat. There was a balcony that looked down on the rest of the cabin making the whole place feel connected. Trent kept finding himself idly walking over to it whenever he was getting dressed or undressed.

Yes, he could see himself being happy enough here during his stay. At least there was internet and the TV had Netflix. If his dad refused to talk to him, he'd veg out and eat junk for a change. If Barry didn't like what that did to his body, he'd just have to shove it.

Not that Trent was planning on staying put for three months. In fact, he was already gearing up for his first snowboarding session. He felt electric with anticipation. Having spent a good chunk of his youth on the slopes when he wasn't on a stage, he'd missed the simple joy of throwing himself down the side of a mountain over and over again.

Being near the end of the season on what was already a

quiet resort, the slopes were sparsely populated when Trent headed out midmorning. He'd bought his own snowboard and gear, ordering it to be delivered to the cabin along with his weights. If he was going to be at the resort for three months, he wasn't going to mess around borrowing kit. He knew what the best brands to buy were thanks to his previous experience. As he took the lift up the side of the mountain to one of the medium slopes to ease himself back in, he felt comfortable blending in with the other skiers. Just an ordinary guy for once.

The same could not be said for all the guests out on the snow.

As the ski lift slowly brought him upward, Trent glanced down at the beginners' slope. His eyes were immediately assaulted by a riotous jacket of a hot pink camouflage pattern, hot pink trousers, goggles and gloves, contrasted with a black snowboard and toque, complete with fluffy pom-pom. Trent would have assumed it was a woman, but the lift was close enough to the ground that when the person took off their hat and glasses, looking up as they took a breath, he could recognize them.

It was the British dude.

Trent sighed and looked away. Was he cursed to keep running into this guy everywhere he went? For some unfathomable reason, as soon as Trent realized it was the same guy, his mind went straight back to the image from the night before of his svelte body disappearing into the outdoor pool, tight black Speedos barely concealing his junk.

"For fuck's sake," Trent muttered to himself.

He'd seen countless guys in various stages of undress on numerous tours and sets. Hell, he himself hardly bothered to cover up if it was inconvenient and he was among friends. His Below Zero buddies had seen it all, he had no doubt, and more to the point, no shame. He wasn't judging this guy for practically skinny dipping, especially when he obviously had thought he was alone. So why was the image burned into Trent's retinas?

He shook his head and tried to push the issue aside. So what? He was a creative person, he found appeal in all kinds of different things. There was evidently something about this guy that had captured his imagination and that was it.

Hurtling down the mountain on his first run in years helped to push all unessential thoughts from Trent's mind. It was just him and the snow and it was blissful. His heart was pounding by the time he had ridden his way to the base again, despite it not being a tricky route. There was nothing quite like snowboarding.

The distraction didn't last though. When Trent rode the lift up a second time, the Brit was still struggling on the same patch of snow, falling over himself. And the third. By Trent's fourth ride up, the guy had his phone out. From the way he was looking at it, Trent would have to guess he was watching online tutorials on how to ride a goddamned snowboard.

He didn't know why, but the sight irritated him. The guy was evidently clueless, but every time Trent rode past, he was doggedly trying again. It was obvious he hadn't even attempted a dry slope before he'd brought himself out onto actual fucking snow.

However, as much as Trent wanted to be annoyed by this guy, he couldn't stop himself being impressed at his single-minded determination. He wasn't letting that damn board beat him. It was endearing.

Which is probably why Trent couldn't stop himself on the next journey upward catching the lift to the beginners' slope instead of the advanced one he'd been intending to try out.

He felt bad for being a complete jerk to this guy, twice. He hadn't deserved it either time. Trent wasn't an asshole, he *wasn't.* He was sick of the press and Hollywood and even his own dad making him out to be that way. Barry was right. He needed to start behaving more like himself before he ruined his reputation completely.

It was more than that, though, he argued to himself as he dismounted from the lift and made his way over to the Brit. He *wanted* to help this guy. He seemed nice. And no other fucker out here was offering to give him a hand.

"Hey," Trent grunted as he approached.

The Brit spun around in a small wave of snow and stumbled backward. Unfortunately, he had one foot attached to his board, so he pinwheeled his arms as he started to fall.

Trent was too quick for that, though. He lunged forward and grabbed him by one of his gloved hands and his waist, still slim despite being clad in numerous layers of skiwear. He was so close, he could see the guy blink through his tinted goggles.

"Oh," he said, his breath coming out in a little puff of white condensation. "It's you. Hello."

He looked completely bemused and a tiny bit scared. Trent cleared his throat and released him so they were both standing upright once more.

"Sorry," he said. "Didn't mean to scare you."

For a beat, the guy just stared. Then he broke into a truly beautiful smile. *Model,* Trent's brain suggested again. "No, you're all right," he said, a little breathlessly. "You just made me jump."

Trent licked his lips and squinted against the bright sunshine. Fuck, this was awkward. What was he supposed to say? *Hi, I can't stop thinking about you almost naked. You suck at snowboarding, so in a moment of spectacular arrogance, I decided to come down here and offer to teach you. Oh, did I mention I'm a movie star?*

"Hey," he said again. "Um. I'm Trent. We met the other

day." That was nice and vague. He didn't think it wise to bring up the pool.

The guy smiled wider, however. "I remember," he said cheerfully. "I'm Ashby. I'm sorry. I think I startled you both times."

"Nah," Trent said with a sigh. Might as well be honest. "I was an asshole. I'm not usually that rude. Thought maybe I could make it up to you."

Ashby's eyebrows rose under his goggles. "Is that so?" he squeaked.

Trent indicated the board. "You seemed like you were struggling. No offense."

Ashby glanced down at where his foot was still attached to the board. For a second, Trent thought he'd just been a rude asshole again by pointing out the obvious. But after a second, Ashby laughed with genuine mirth.

"Oh, you spotted that, did you?" he asked with a chuckle. "Yes, I'm a hapless beginner at real risk of breaking an ankle or a wrist or both. Never tried snowboarding before."

"I guessed." He gave Ashby a half smile, and for the first time since they had run into each other, he didn't feel quite so awkward. Ashby grinned some more and rubbed the back of his head. "You want a hand?"

Ashby blinked. "You – you'd teach me?"

Trent shrugged. "The basics," he said. "Get you on your feet. It's the least I can do after ignoring you twice. You seem like a nice guy."

Ashby's smile became bashful. "Thank you," he stammered. "I – that would be lovely. Although," he added, touching Trent's arm briefly, "I didn't think you were an asshole." Trent arched an eyebrow. It was a look he was famous for. It was intimidating and smoldering all at once, or so he was told. Ashby bit his lip. "Okay. Maybe a *tiny* bit of an asshole. But I can see that's not true, now."

Trent grunted and dropped his board down on the snow. "Haven't started teaching you, yet."

Ashby fell to his ass and unclipped his boot from the board, ready to start from scratch. "Nah," he said cheekily. "I can already tell. You're a big old teddy bear."

Trent didn't know why that pleased him so much. But it did.

CHAPTER
Eight
ASHBY

Ashby was still too stunned to really process what was happening. His default was to smile and joke and generally flirt a little. But the truth was, he was still unsure as to why Trent had come over to talk to him.

'Talk' might have been a bit of an exaggeration. The man seemed allergic to chit-chat. But Ashby nattered along enough for the both of them to fill up the awkward silences.

"So, I get skating with one foot," he said. "But how do I then stop? Sticking my free foot into the snow? Because I was doing that before but then I would just trip and fall and, well, I guess that's what led you over here to save me from myself."

Trent did that thing again where he arched his eyebrow. Ashby hadn't seen any of his movies, but according to the internet that was a 'thing' he did. It certainly had an effect on Ashby's insides. Although whether that effect was good or bad, he really couldn't say.

"Use your boot to stop you," Trent said. He had his own board with only one foot strapped in, so he demonstrated by skating a few feet, then stopping.

"You make it look so easy," Ashby said weakly.

Trent shrugged. "Because it is."

Ashby bit his lip and tried not to feel ashamed. But the truth was, he'd had a silly notion that he would be amazing at snowboarding. Like it was a hidden talent he'd been sitting on all this time. Of course he was useless at it, just like everything else.

"Oh," he said softly. "I must be doing it wrong. I, um, I guess I'll try again."

Trent nodded. "You can do it," he said.

Ashby breathed the cold mountain air in deeply. Trent was probably already regretting offering to come over. But the sooner Ashby got this, the sooner Trent could leave.

Which would undoubtedly be for the best. As mega-hot as Trent was, Ashby didn't need to be crushing on any straight boys right now. This was supposed to be his man-free getaway.

But then Trent moved over to him and touched his arm. "Hey," Trent said. "You've got this. Just give it a try."

He smiled and Ashby's heart came to life. "Oh, okay," he said, smiling back at him. "Yes, you're right. How hard can it really be? I'm just letting my giraffe legs get the better of me."

Trent stepped away and nodded at him. So Ashby took a breath and pushed himself off with his free foot, resting it on the back of the board while the strapped-in foot at the front steered him.

"Now, stop," Trent instructed.

Ashby didn't think, he just put his foot down. And stopped. Without falling.

"Ha!" he cried, throwing his hands up. "Amazing!"

Trent smiled. That did dangerous things to Ashby's heart.

But just because Trent was being pleasant now didn't mean he wasn't generally rude and moody by nature. Ashby had to be wary. He'd been swayed too many times in the past by a handsome face and brooding ways.

He needed to find a nice, happy fellow. One who was into men. Trent was neither of those things, so Ashby needed to calm down and focus on the snowboarding.

"Okay," Trent said. "Next step. Let's strap you in."

Ashby gulped. "Oh, sure, okay."

Trent chuckled. "It's not that scary."

But Ashby wasn't so sure. "How do I stop without a foot free, though?" he said. It made him think of those bicycles which you rode with your feet strapped in. The thought terrified him. He'd be mashed into the pavement in no time if he tried to use pedals like that.

Trent shook his head. "I'll be right here. Just do what I do." He dropped his backside to the snow and made fast work of strapping both his feet to the board. He gripped the middle of the board with one hand, then pushed off the snow behind him with his other. "See? No big deal."

Ashby chewed his lip. *Come on,* he urged himself. This was what he'd come on holiday for. To try new things, to challenge himself. So he copied Trent and sat down on the ground, snapped the clasps around his boots, then pushed himself back up again, focusing on keeping his balance.

He stood, hands out in anticipation. But he didn't fall or slip. "I'm starting to believe you when you say this isn't that hard," he said sheepishly.

Trent laughed. Fuck, if his smile made Ashby's heart flip over, his laugh made it flutter like a butterfly.

"Dude, you just need a bit of confidence. That's all any sport is, really. You gotta believe in yourself."

"Natural aptitude and athletic prowess do tend to help as well," Ashby said with a grin. Trent grinned back.

"All right, smartass," Trent said, lightly slapping Ashby's arm. "You're not competing at the Olympics. You're just trying to have fun. Show me what you got. *Believe* you can do it."

Trent shuffled forward by raising his toes over and over again, encouraging the board forward. Then he looked over his shoulder at Ashby, raising that eyebrow again, challenging him.

"Fine," said Ashby haughtily. "Anything you can do," he said, mimicking the move, concentrating on keeping his core muscles solid.

But he was stunned when he accomplished the motion with little trouble at all.

Trent whooped. "Hell, yeah, man. You're getting it."

Ashby didn't dare speak until he shuffled his way over to where Trent was standing and came to a halt. "Whoa," he said. "That was pretty cool."

"You feel up for some sliding?" Trent asked, wiggling his eyebrows.

Ashby almost balked. But, no, he could do this. "Yes," he said, nodding. "Show me."

Trent turned so he was facing down the small slope. "Best to do it together," he said, shuffling next to Ashby. "Just reach with your hand in whichever direction you want to go, lean into it and let gravity do the rest." He waited until Ashby set himself up like he had, then together, they leaned.

"Oh my god," Ashby whispered as they began to move. "Bloody hell, this is brilliant," he said excitedly.

"Okay, now lean the other way," Trent said. Ashby did and they changed direction. Ashby whooped.

"You know," he said, "you're a very good teacher."

Trent didn't say anything to that, but he did have a small smile on his face when Ashby glanced over. "Let's stop there," Trent murmured.

"Stop?" Ashby squeaked.

He lost his concentration and flailed. Before he could hit the powder, though, Trent caught him. Again.

His hands were firm on Ashby's waist. "Sorry," Trent said with that same small smile. "Should have covered stopping first."

"Oh, it's fine," Ashby said. "This way I get to sneak in another hug." He laughed, but Trent raised his eyebrows. "Fuck, sorry, that was a stupid thing to say. I didn't mean to make you uncomfortable."

Trent was still holding onto him, however. His body felt so solid against Ashby's. "Nah, man. Most of my best buds are queer. I'm the odd one out. Takes more than that to scare me off."

Ashby licked his lips. "Good," he said. Then he took a breath and stood up straighter, making sure he was stable. "Right, okay, then. How do I stop when I *don't* have a dashing hero to come to my rescue?"

They worked on basic techniques for a little while longer. Ashby was gob-smacked to discover that not only did he have a wonderful time, but it wasn't only down to Trent's company. He thought maybe he could get quite fond of this snowboarding malarkey.

After another hour, Trent suggested they try one of the actual slopes. "Just a baby one," he assured Ashby.

Ashby was keen to do anything to keep Trent in his company. He knew it was a bad idea, but they were having fun, so why couldn't he enjoy how hot Trent was at the same time? Trent never needed to know.

It felt incredible to be achieving something for once. The more Ashby progressed on the board, the less conscious he was of Trent's proximity to him. As he tipped over and slid down the slope for the first time, everything went from his mind except how this was possibly the closest anyone could get to flying.

"Yeah!" he yelled most of the way down, dizzy with exhilaration. He'd done it. He even stopped by himself at the bottom and stood waiting for Trent to come down and meet him. "That was fantastic," he said, bobbing up and down as much as he could while secured to a heavy board. "Can we do it again?"

"Sure," Trent said. Then he checked his watch. "Although, I'll have to head off soon. I've got to go see someone."

Ashby's good mood dropped in a flash. "Oh, of course," he said contritely. "You probably have friends waiting for you. I'm sorry, I've taken up half your day."

But a slow smile spread across Trent's face. "No, actually. I have to see my dad about something. He works at the gift shop here. I'm just visiting. I'm not here with friends. In fact, I'm on my own."

Was that...some sort of hint or invitation? Ashby couldn't tell. "Oh, that's all right then." He rubbed the back of his neck with a gloved hand. "Uh, well, I'm by myself, too. If you wanted to hang out again." As soon as the words left his mouth, horror washed through him. "I mean, you know, as friends. Or – could-be-friends. I know you're not, um. That wasn't me asking you out on a date."

Trent laughed and shook his head. "Dude, chill," he said. "It'd be nice to hang. See you at the bar later, maybe?"

"S-sure," Ashby said, doing his best to recover.

His heart was racing at the idea of seeing Trent again. He thought this snowboarding lesson would be the only chance they'd have to spend together. Even if it was purely platonic, Ashby couldn't deny he was excited by the possibility of getting to know him better.

How could he not have recognized Trent right away when they'd met in the lobby? He hadn't been obsessed with Below Zero exactly, but he'd watched enough of their videos.

His teenage self would lose his mind if he knew that one day he would be asking TJ Charles out for a drink.

"I'll probably have dinner down in the restaurant," he babbled. "I normally go down about six o'clock. Although my jet lag is all but gone now, so I could go later if you wanted? Did you want food or just drinks or…you know what, don't worry. I'll just…see you when I see you, yeah?"

Trent rubbed his chin. "After six," he said, nodding. "I'll be there. Catch you later, Ashby."

With that, Ashby watched him slide away, expertly handling his board. Ashby sighed. Well, that wasn't how he planned his day to go. He had to be firm and not let his imagination run away with him. But Trent was a lot nicer than he'd come across the day before, and Ashby couldn't help but look forward to spending more time together that evening.

CHAPTER
Nine

TRENT

Trent was surprised by how much he'd enjoyed hanging out with Ashby. He was a nice guy, but he was also really fun. As Trent made his way back to the main lodge, he felt lighter somehow.

It had been years since he made a new friend. Someone who was genuine, not a work colleague or a fan or some blogger looking for a story. Ashby was easy company. Trent was glad he'd swallowed his pride and approached him to make amends for his initial behavior.

Ashby reminded Trent a little of his buddy Joey. Not just because they were both obviously gay, but he felt like Ashby wore his heart on his sleeve just like Joey did. He was surprised to realize he was actually looking forward to meeting up again later.

Now, if only he could have a civil conversation with his dad, Trent could relax. But all the work he'd done forgetting his troubles on the mountain was undone as soon as he stepped inside the resort again.

Fuck, he didn't want to have this conversation.

But he hadn't wanted to have this conversation for two

years and nothing was getting better. Maybe knowing he had a friendly face to see later would fortify him. It was certainly more appealing than going back to his cabin by himself. Besides, the whole point of him being here was to try and bury the hatchet with his dad. Barry would have Trent's hide if he didn't at least try.

When Trent went around to the shop, it was packed. Or, at least as packed as such a tiny place could get. The couple of aisles between all the tightly stacked souvenirs were filled with half a dozen geeky guys who looked like they were barely out of high school. Trent guessed this was maybe the first vacation they had taken by themselves from the way they were goofing around taking photos on their cameras wearing anything they could from his dad's stock.

Trent didn't want an audience for this little chat, so he lurked a little way down the corridor and took off some of his layers from where he'd been out in the snow. With his jacket unzipped, his gloves shoved in his pockets and his board propped up against the wall, he fished his phone out from where he'd secured it deep within one of the pockets.

When he saw the messages waiting for him, he almost put the phone right back.

Not because he didn't want to talk to his friends. But because of what they wanted to talk about.

Trent had forgotten all about the wedding.

Jesus, he was a shitty friend. How could he forget that was this weekend? Groaning, he unlocked his phone to face the music.

Since Blake, Joey and Raiden had all got themselves boyfriends, they had started a new band group chat, this one including their other halves but leaving out the fifth and final member of Below Zero, Reyse Hickson. Hicks wasn't really in the loop anymore, what with being one of the most famous pop stars on the planet. It made Trent sad that there were some inevitable hurt feelings that the label had dropped the rest of the band to pursue solo prospects with Reyse. Trent had never cared, but it had left a rift between them as their lives all moved on.

So now he mostly talked to the guys in this chat group. There wasn't the time to ponder that, though, because Blake and his partner Elion had very specific questions on their mind. Questions for Trent.

Hey TJ! Blake had written an hour or so ago. *How's the vacation? Meet any hot girls? Maybe one you'd like to take to a wedding this Saturday???* He followed it with several winking emojis.

Dude, we're not playing around here! came Elion's message next. Trent sighed, imagining the happy couple sitting next to each other in their appartment in Cincinnati, tag-teaming their efforts to tie Trent down to an answer. *I'm printing the place cards at home, but there's still so much to do!*

Elion had recently qualified as a Licensed Practical Nurse and had taken a position at one of the city's ERs. The stress of that on top of wedding planning meant he had apparently been bursting into tears regularly over the past few weeks.

He was a charming guy. Trent was very happy for him and his buddy Blake. But damn if they weren't making this huge fucking deal over Trent picking a girl to come to their big day with.

They kept saying that Trent could bring anyone. He never had a shortage of ladies in his life, after all. But Trent couldn't help but feel like this wasn't a 'bring any old girl' type of situation.

Blake had met Elion almost as soon as the band had broken up. Joey had met his guy Gabe a few months after that, and they'd gotten married last fall in a beautiful cere-mony that Trent actually remembered most of, despite the free-flowing tequila. Then Raiden had surprised everyone last year by getting together with his beast of a bodyguard. Although Trent maintained he had felt there was something brewing between them when they'd met in Philadelphia.

However, now it meant the pressure was on him. Why did happy couples always want to see everyone else settled down as well? All that shit he'd been feeling in Barry's office came crawling back, causing his throat to get tight. Trent knew his friends meant well, but their incessant pestering for him to find The One was just making him feel even crappier for all the incredible women he had let go over the years. Because when it came to commitment, apparently TJ Charles was a big fucking chicken.

How did you know when you met the person you wanted to spend the rest of your life with? Trent had fallen for so many girls over the years. Some he even thought he'd been in love with. But he'd never felt that 'struck by lightning' moment, where his heart ached so much it was physically painful to be apart from that special someone. Wasn't that how love was supposed to feel?

This plus one situation with the wedding felt like the guys were trying to get him to commit, really commit. Like they'd all ganged up on him and decided he needed to find his soulmate, now, or he would never be happy. What if he wasn't ready yet? He could bring a girl to the *next* wedding. Maybe she really would be The One.

He certainly wasn't going to produce a girl in time for the flight out on Friday. Let alone someone truly special.

Fuck it, they'd just have to get over themselves.

Sorry, dudes, he typed out. *Looks like I'll be going stag again. Invite some hot girls for me to meet. Maybe I'll get a date by the end of the night?* He added a winking and kissing emoji, hoping he wouldn't upset them that much. But he just wanted to enjoy one of his best friends' special day. Trent felt like he'd had enough attention on him for now.

The little dots bounced to show that Blake was writing something. Sure enough, a new message popped up within thirty seconds.

Hey man, no worries. It's gonna be a blast. Can't wait to see you.

Definitely! Joey piped up, making Trent smile. He'd always had a soft spot for the youngest and undeniably sweetest member of the band.

See you soon, Trent typed back. He'd missed his friends a lot. No one understood their crazy lives quite like each other.

He slipped his phone back into his pocket thinking about how he'd have to cancel the flights to Ohio he'd had booked via LA and get new ones sorted from Jackson. But at that moment, the gaggle of teenage boys left the gift shop. Trent knew he needed to go face his dad right now before he lost his nerve. He could rearrange the flights later.

Sighing, he picked up his board, damp with melted snow, and trudged over to the gift shop. He thought for the nth time how he wouldn't mind so much that his dad devoted all his energy into this place if the resort actually gave him decent things to sell. But this stuff was all so tacky.

It was a good thing at the moment, though, he realized as he entered. Because an excitable Merlin saw him come in and immediately went berserk. He started barking, his tail going crazy and sweeping off whatever was on the bottom shelves along the aisle between him and Trent as he charged over to greet him. Trent gasped, throwing his hands up to try and calm the little fella before he wrecked everything.

"Hey, hey," he said, grabbing him by his collar and pulling him away from the glass ashtrays. At least he'd only knocked down some wooden, poorly painted boomerangs. This time. Trent risked glancing up and making eye contact with his dad, who was scowling at him from behind the counter. "Sorry."

His dad gave a shrug with one shoulder. "He's better when you're not here."

Trent gritted his teeth and tried to keep his cool. It hadn't always been like this. He knew his dad loved him. He'd always been supportive and happy for Trent, even if he didn't understand his chosen careers.

"Dad, can we talk?" Trent asked, rising to his feet. Merlin dutifully followed as he approached the counter, thankfully going behind it to Trent's dad where he couldn't cause much mayhem.

Again, Trenton Sr. gave half a shrug, his attention on his laptop. "We're already talking."

Trent sighed and propped up his board against the counter, wincing when he realized the snow was already dripping onto the wooden floor. It was only water, but he didn't want to give his dad any reason to kick him out of the store before they'd at least tried to clear some of the air.

Trent decided to keep things plain and simple. "I know I didn't come back here when I should have," he said.

He couldn't bring himself to look his dad in the eye, so he picked up a keyring from the display on the countertop and ran his thumb over the design. It was a cactus. What the hell did a cactus have to do with a ski resort in Wyoming?

"No, you didn't," his dad agreed.

Trent winced, yet he still couldn't bring himself to look up. "I just...I see her everywhere here." It was one of the reasons he liked his staff cabin. He'd never been in there before, so it had zero association with his mom.

His mom, who had been skiing like she always had, when one day something went drastically wrong. She'd lost control of her skis and slammed into a tree. She'd died instantly.

Not that Trent had known that at the time. It had taken him almost seventy-two hours to hear the news. He'd been too busy partying in Prague to notice his phone had died. By the time he'd recharged it, his dad had been coping with the death of his wife, Trent's mom, for close to three days. Alone.

"It's a good thing you see her here," his dad said stiffly. He was scrolling on the mousepad, but his eyes were fixed when Trent risked glancing up. He doubted he was looking at anything on the screen. "This was her home. She loved it."

"I miss her," Trent said softly around the lump in his throat. They'd never been the closest of families. He'd always been far too different from his parents for that. But he had loved them regardless. He still loved his dad, even if he didn't exactly like him right at that moment.

His dad harrumphed as if to challenge the idea that Trent missed his mom. Trent swallowed down his hurt. Fuck, he'd been a jackass. This wound had been festering for too long. He'd only come back to Wyoming long enough for the funeral. He should have made much more of an effort.

But it was always so much easier to get drunk, throw himself into work, and fall into bed with a girl. Literally anything to distract him from his hurt. Except his work had been suffering from how much he'd been drinking, and no girl ever stuck around long enough to build anything meaningful like a relationship.

"I miss Lancelot, too," he mumbled.

His dad hadn't called when their old dog had passed. Trent hadn't gotten the chance to say goodbye before he'd been put to sleep. Trent knew it was his dad's way of protecting himself after Trent hadn't been there when his mom had died, but, fuck. He would have come. He would have supported his dad then. He would have liked to tell that old mutt he was a good boy one last time.

Trent squeezed his eyes shut. He hadn't cried over his mom or his dog. Not once. What the fuck was wrong with him? Was he even human? What kind of dickhead didn't grieve for his family?

"The puppy doesn't replace Lancelot," his dad grumbled.

Trent smacked the glass counter, making his dad jump. Finally, they looked at one another. Trent curled his hand into a fist and took a breath. He wasn't going to lose his temper. He wasn't that guy.

"Merlin isn't supposed to replace anyone," Trent said, his voice heavy as he deflated. "I just thought he'd be a good friend for you. That…that he'd be better at looking after you than I've been."

That sounded like he was letting himself off the hook, but that really wasn't it. He wasn't ever going to have a life at the Grand. The best he could do would be to repair things with his dad to call every week or two, like they used to. Merlin could be with his dad every damn day. Trent didn't want him to be lonely. Sure, his dad had friends at the resort and in the nearby towns. But Merlin could be with him all the time. He'd never judge him.

"Look, Trent," his dad said. He rubbed his eyes under his glasses. They had a different smudge on them today. "I appreciate what you're doing. But I don't know what you're expecting. Maybe you should just go back to California."

The words hit Trent like a sucker punch. "No," he said carefully. "I want to try and make things right." Besides, Barry wouldn't let him come back so soon. Trent had to stick it out in the mountains for as long as his manager said.

Trent's dad clicked his fingers and managed to get Merlin's attention long enough to attach his leash. "Some things," he said slowly, "you just can't fix. Too much damage has been done. You can stay as long as you like. Just…bear that in mind."

Trent watched silently as his dad placed a 'Back in ten minutes' sign on the counter, then led Merlin and his wagging tail out the door. Trent sagged against the counter, his stomach rolling.

Goddamn it. He would give anything to change what had happened. He wished his mom hadn't gone on the slopes that day. He wished he had charged his phone. He wished he'd swallowed his own shit and just come back to be with his dad two years ago, no matter how difficult that was.

But he couldn't alter any of that. All he could do was keep trying and hope that eventually, he and his dad might have some sort of breakthrough.

In the meantime, he was going to go back to his cabin, change his clothes, then hope that Ashby really did want to hang out tonight. Because if ever Trent needed a stiff drink and a friendly face, it was right then.

CHAPTER

Ten

ASHBY

When Ashby plugged his phone in to charge back in his room, he had a momentary ice-cold wash of panic that he hadn't called Gordon yet today. Then he remembered he no longer had to do that.

He sat down on the bed and took a few long breaths. He knew he hadn't been in love with Gordon for almost a year now. But undoing the damage of his controlling behavior, which had sunk its claws into Ashby in so many different ways, was going to take longer than overcoming any heartbreak.

It took a long, hot shower to get rid of the chill which the prospect of talking to Gordon had instilled in him. He needed to shake that off and enjoy his damn holiday like he was supposed to. That included meeting his new friend Trent for dinner and drinks.

Feeling like Gordon had crawled under his skin again meant Ashby experienced several twinges of guilt before he was finally able to truly convince himself he was single now and could do whatever the hell he liked. Not that this was even a date. But Gordon wouldn't have liked Ashby hanging out with another guy one-on-one, no matter the circumstances.

But he could do what he wanted now. He just needed to be brave. Ashby knew there wasn't enough that scared him in his life.

When you were born privileged, it was easy to numb yourself to the world. There were never any real consequences for failure. In Singapore, he'd been in a bubble of other ex-pat Brits, all very well off and sheltered from the Asian culture around them. Like glorified tourists with maids and nannies and cooks, like that was real life.

It took Ashby years to realize what a disadvantage that gave him. The most shocking development in his life had been to discover he was gay, a fact he was sure of by the tender age of thirteen.

But even that wasn't the great catastrophe he knew so many other people faced in their lives. His parents hardly blinked an eyelid, telling him they loved him no matter what, and honestly, had always sort of known. Therefore, his fear had developed very late when he'd stepped out from his sheltered life into the real world and finally been subjected to the true prejudice of someone who was so effeminate and obviously queer.

It was only as he hit his twenties, a few years ago, did he learn how cruel people could be. So he did the only logical thing he could think of.

He stayed out of the 'real' world as much as he possibly could.

Money could get you all kinds of magical places. His stunning good looks, although hardly rugged or masculine, still opened all manner of doors. Ashby knew he was a coward. That was why he stayed on the peripheral, where things were shiny and simple. As much as possible, he stayed within his comfort zone.

But deep down, he knew that as much as there was a part of him which craved that safety, there was also a darker side of him that pushed him up the side of that damn mountain that morning.

Because try as he might, Ashby could never seem to stay away from the bad boys.

He thought maybe he had broken that cycle with Gordon. Ashby never wanted to be with anyone like that again for as long as he lived. But Trent had a reputation. Only last week he had gotten in trouble for punching a photographer and from what Ashby had seen in person, Trent definitely had some issues rolling around. But as much as he cautioned himself, he couldn't help but be tentatively happy as he picked an outfit to wear down to the bar. Because Trent was also sweet. And kind.

Ashby looked at the clothes he had hanging up in his little temporary wardrobe. He touched one of the prettier tops he'd brought. As much as he felt like getting a bit dressed up to meet Trent, he didn't want to scare him off. Besides, it was difficult to gauge how people here would react.

So he played it safe with a super comfy, huge cream cable knit jumper – or sweater as the Yanks called it. He smiled, enjoying adapting to the different lingo again after not being in the country for a few years. He paired the jumper with a pair of black leggings and black fluffy boots – the same ones he'd worn to dash out to the pool the night before. He chuckled as he put them on. That sight obviously hadn't sent Trent running, so maybe Ashby could risk being a little flamboyant.

He decided to go for a bit of makeup. Nothing too extreme. But foundation and concealer, a hint of contouring and a touch of pencil to fill in his brows. The most outrageous thing he put on was a slick of pale pink gloss, just enough to give his lips some shine. It wasn't like he was going to be kissing anyone tonight, so he could indulge in a little glamor.

His hair ruffled and aftershave applied, Ashby sauntered out the door leaving everything behind. He didn't need his phone because he was taking a break from everything. It felt wonderful. He could charge all his food and drinks to the room, so all he needed was his key, which he slid into the side of his boot once the door was locked. He also brought his lip gloss with him, which he dropped down into the other boot. He felt remarkably free as he sashayed down the corridor toward the lobby.

As he was making his way to the restaurant, he spied a familiar furry face. "Oh!" he cried as he approached Trent's puppy for the second time. Looking up, he quickly confirmed the person holding the leash was not Trent. But there was enough familial resemblance for Ashby to guess this was Trent's dad that he'd mentioned was working here. "Hello," he said as he got closer to the older man. He held out his hand. "You must be Mr. Charles. I met Trent and your lovely puppy here yesterday."

The old man narrowed his eyes. Ashby got the sudden feeling that maybe he'd put his foot in it. "You know Trent?" Mr. Charles asked. His eyes raked over Ashby and Ashby got that familiar prickling anxiety when he wondered how much he was being judged. He was very glad he hadn't gone for a more outlandish outfit, but he did try and lick the gloss off his lips as subtly as he could.

"Yes," he said brightly. "I'm by myself on holiday and he's taken me under his wing, somewhat."

For a second Mr. Charles continued to stare. Then his face lit up with a tentative smile that Ashby also recognized from Trent's face. "That's nice," he said quietly, nodding to himself. "I'm glad he's being good to you."

Ashby hadn't been expecting that, but it felt reassuring. Like Trent's dad approved of him or something. "He's been very kind," he assured him. "He taught me how to snowboard in, like, an afternoon. Which shows he has the patience of a saint." Ashby chuckled, then looked down as the puppy scratched at his leg. "Do you mind if I pet him?" he asked. He'd learned his lesson the day before about making assumptions with other people's dogs.

"Sure," Mr. Charles said. "It looks like he likes you." The puppy had flopped onto his back, demanding belly rubs.

Ashby crouched down and obliged. "Oh, that's because he's a good boy, aren't you? Yes, you are. What's his name?"

"Merlin." Ashby looked up. Mr. Charles sounded sad for some reason.

"That's a great name," he told Mr. Charles.

"Very English," Mr. Charles commented with a rueful laugh.

Ashby tilted his head and smiled as he continued to rub the pup's fat belly. "It is indeed," he said warmly. Reluctantly, he stood back up. It was getting close to six o'clock. "I'm actually going to meet Trent now. You'd be more than welcome to join us, if you'd like?"

But Mr. Charles got that sad look on his face again. "That's very kind of you," he said, pushing his glasses up his nose where they'd slipped a little. "But we'll let you boys have fun. Maybe…you could tell him I said to have a nice night, though?"

Ashby beamed at him. "Of course," he assured him. He gave Merlin one last rub on the head, then watched the two of them walk away.

He sighed. There was a story there, he was sure. But he

wasn't going to pry. Perhaps Trent would elaborate when Ashby relayed his dad's message.

While no one else was in the corridor, Ashby sneakily pulled his gloss out from the side of his boot and reapplied it to his lips. Feeling buoyed from his brief chat with Mr. Charles, Ashby walked toward the bar, wondering if Trent had beat him there.

Eleven

ASHBY

THERE WAS NO SIGN OF TRENT, SO ASHBY TOOK ONE OF THE many spare seats at the bar's counter and smiled at the bartender. The guy nodded, drying a glass with a towel as he approached. His name badge read 'Darnell' and he barely looked old enough to be serving alcohol. He was, however, very cute with light brown skin, dark curls and a dimple when he smiled back at Ashby.

"Hi, there," he said. He put the clean glass under the counter and the towel over his shoulder. Then he automatically placed a folded napkin and a small bowl of pretzels in front of Ashby. "What can I get you?"

"Do you have a menu?" Ashby asked. He was in the mood for a fun cocktail.

Darnell gave him a slight frown. "I'm afraid not." He indicated the bottles of spirits stacked up behind him. "What you see is what you get."

"Oh," Ashby said, a little disappointed. "No chance of a Long Island Iced Tea, then?"

Darnell glanced at Bob, watching the baseball at the other end of the bar as usual. Then he rubbed his fingers together and nibbled his lip. "Um, well…I *could.* I'm just not supposed to. Management says things like that are too 'foofy.'" He used air quotes to show what he thought of the word 'foofy.'

Ashby grinned, feeling devilish. He pulled out his key and winked at Darnell. "Room thirteen. I'll sign for a twenty-dollar tip. I'm game if you are?"

Darnell's eyes lit up, looking at the key like it was something scandalous. Tentatively, he glanced at Bob, then back at Ashby's hand. Ashby gave it a little wave, hoping to tempt him. Darnell exhaled, his face lighting up with a grin as he swiftly nodded then rang up a completely different drink on the register with the tip.

Ashby did very well not to clap in delight. This guy was clearly keen to whip up something interesting, rather than pour the same old wines, beers and spirits. Ashby watched as within seconds, Darnell was pouring and stirring with a flourish. He splashed the different spirits together with confidence, although he did glance nervously every now and then at Bob. But he never stopped grinning and poor Bob was too engrossed with the television. Ashby couldn't help but gasp when Darnell threw the bottle up in the air and caught it again like a juggler.

"You're *really* good at this," Ashby enthused as Darnell finished off the drink with slices of lemon and lime. He pushed it toward Ashby, then took a little bow.

The bartender looked bashful. "I did a mixology course after school," he said. "I'd love to do more interesting things."

Ashby tasted the drink and let his eyes flutter closed. "You *should.* Yummy and pretty. My favorite combination."

"Thanks," Darnell said. But his face dropped somewhat as he pulled the towel from his shoulder and began rubbing down the perfectly clean counter.

Ashby frowned and stirred his drink. It tasted so good he was tempted to drink it fast, but that would be a bad idea before eating. Instead, he glanced around at the other patrons, many of whom were women. "I bet you could get away with serving more cocktails, you know?" he said in what he hoped was a supportive manner. "Those ladies there," he said, nodding toward three middle-aged gals all glammed up. "They'd love cosmopolitans, I bet you anything."

Darnell shrugged. "We'll see," he said.

The couple Ashby had startled previously in the corridor approached the bar, so he left Darnell to it. It wasn't his place, after all. But he couldn't help but feel like the guy's wings were being clipped and that upset Ashby. Life was too short to dance around what you really wanted.

As if to prove his own point, he felt a hand on his lower back. A thrill shot through him as he turned to face who he assumed would be Trent.

It wasn't.

Ashby immediately flinched, but years of well-trained good manners kept the smile plastered on his face.

The hand belonged to a stranger. He was tanned with a mouthful of straight white teeth and the beginnings of laughter lines crinkling around light blue eyes. He might have been handsome, but there was something predatory in his gaze that set Ashby on edge.

He tipped a gleaming white Stetson Ashby's way, slipping onto the bar stool beside him. "You look like you're celebrating," he drawled in a smooth southern twang. "What's the occasion?"

His hand graced over Ashby's hip before he touched his lower lip briefly. His eyes danced as his gaze skimmed over Ashby's face.

"Um," Ashby said. Alarm bells were going off in his head. He wanted to get away from the guy but couldn't see a way do so easily without causing a scene. "Just waiting for my friend," he said, hoping Trent wasn't far away. If he was even coming at all. They'd made very loose plans.

"How rude of him to keep you waiting," the guy said. He flicked two fingers towards the bar, not even looking to see if Darnell was paying attention. "Lucky I'm here to entertain you." He held out his hand. "Kiefer Burton. Nice to meet you."

Ashby felt like he had little choice but to reciprocate the shake. "Ashby Wilcott," he said, pulling his hand back as soon as possible. Kiefer's skin was awfully dry.

A quick scan of the man's attire revealed at least seven designer labels as well as manicured nails and a watch that probably cost more than some small countries made in a year. Being from money himself, Ashby wasn't intimidated. But someone that flashy immediately set his nerves on edge.

"Ashby," Kiefer said, like he was rolling his name around on his tongue. "Well, I can safely say we don't get gentlemen of your caliber around here very often. Your accent's as delightful as your name is, darlin'."

Ashby shifted uncomfortably in his seat. "You come here on holiday a lot, I take it?"

Kiefer snickered quietly, like Ashby had said something hilarious. It made him feel self-conscious. "Naw, darlin'," he said, sliding his gaze over Ashby's form. "I own this little establishment."

Ashby's eyes went wide despite himself. He almost asked why on Earth someone with his obvious wealth and style had let the place get so terribly dilapidated. But he found he didn't want to engage this man in any further conversation than was absolutely necessary.

Instead, he glanced at Bob. He hadn't acknowledged Kiefer's arrival in any way.

"Oh, I'm not usually here on the ground," Kiefer said with a chuckle. "Not really my scene. I see what you're thinking, though." He wagged his finger toward Ashby. "This place ain't exactly looking its best. I let certain things-" he glanced at poor old Bob "-get out of hand. But I'm taking care of that now."

He paused while Darnell placed two drinks in front of them. One was a whiskey. The other was another Long Island Iced Tea. Ashby felt his eyes widen at the prospect of a second strong cocktail before eating anything. "Oh, is that for me?" he squeaked.

Kiefer winked. "I said I'd entertain you."

He picked up the whiskey Darnell had known to make him without actually saying any words. While he sipped it, he continued to observe Ashby over the rim of the tumbler.

Ashby swallowed. "Thank you," he said, not really meaning it.

"So," Kiefer said. He was leaning in just a little too close for Ashby's liking. "Who's this friend of yours?" A finger from his free hand touched Ashby's knee.

Ashby ground his teeth. He should tell this guy to fuck off. Who cared if he owned the place? Ashby wasn't impressed by money. His family was probably just as rich as this guy was, for crying out loud.

But where could Ashby go? He wanted to meet Trent, but more to the point, he needed to eat and there wasn't anywhere else in the resort to go.

"Just a friend," he said, keeping his voice pleasant. He couldn't really risk pissing off this guy if he was going to be hanging around for the time being. If Ashby was lucky, this was just a quick visit. Then hopefully their paths wouldn't cross again. But he had to be careful.

He recalled how earlier he was lamenting that not enough in his life scared him. How he wished he could take that back now. He got the feeling that this was the kind of man who could not only find out what room Ashby was staying in but possibly also get himself a key.

The only thing he could think to do was to smile sweetly at Kiefer and take another sip of his drink. His head was starting to swim.

"*Just* a friend," Kiefer repeated. "Well, that's good to hear. How many of these friends are you on vacation with?"

"Oh, no, I'm here alone," said Ashby before he could really think about lying. Damn that drink.

Kiefer's smile grew another few millimeters on one side. "Is that so?"

He took another swig of his whiskey, licking his lips as he carefully placed the glass back down. He then shifted even closer and Ashby could feel his breath on his cheek as Kiefer placed his hand on Ashby's knee again. This time it stayed there. He tilted his head so the Stetson blocked their faces from the view of the rest of the bar behind them.

"Why don't I whisk you off somewhere worthy of your gorgeous lil' self, huh?" he murmured. "We could hit the Aspen scene, have some real fun. I can guarantee I'll show you a good time. The best."

Get off, get off, get off! Ashby screamed in his mind. He tried his best not to tremble and show how repulsed he was, but he couldn't help but grimace and shut his eyes. He had to get out of this situation as fast as possible, but he had to be clever and safe about it. How could he refuse though?

"Babe!" a warm and glorious voice called out over the bar. Kiefer pulled away. Ashby released the breath he'd been holding and opened his screwed-up eyes to take in the most welcome sight of Trent striding towards him and Kiefer. "I'm so sorry I'm late." He marched right up to Ashby, ignoring Kiefer, and leaned in to kiss Ashby on the cheek. He briefly caressed Ashby's neck, and only then turned to look at Kiefer. "Hi?"

Ashby tried not to sag in relief too much. He felt dizzy from Trent's intimate touch but more off-kilter from the surprise rescue. "Hello, sweetie," he said, doing his best to sound like he said that every day. "This is Kiefer Burton. He owns the resort."

Trent remained standing, hugging Ashby close to him. Ashby wrapped his own arm around Trent's waist, squeezing his hip in what he hoped was a silent signal. *Thank you! Get me the fuck out of here!*

"Mr. Burton," Trent said flatly. He glanced down at Ashby's two drinks. "You ready for dinner, babe?"

Ashby sighed, trying to disguise his relief as remorse. "I am so sorry," he said cheerfully to Kiefer, "but we've not seen each other all day. I hope I'll see you around." His smile was probably veering toward simpering, but he didn't care. He stood, intending to leave his cocktails behind. He'd just order more from Darnell to make up for it over dinner. "Thank you so much for keeping me company."

Kiefer looked coldly at Trent's arm wrapped firmly around Ashby's back. "Not so alone, after all?" He raised an eyebrow before turning to knock back the rest of his whiskey. "See ya around, English."

Ashby was thoroughly glad to see the back of him.

CHAPTER
Twelve

TRENT

As soon as Trent had seen Ashby and that guy Kiefer, he'd known something wasn't right. He probably should have checked the situation before going barreling in, but the way Ashby was recoiling from the dude's touch made Trent see red.

He knew he didn't have a stellar record when it came to heartbreaks, but he would *never* creep on a girl who was clearly not interested. Despite his face being hidden behind Kiefer's white Stetson, Trent could still tell from Ashby's clenched fists and ramrod straight back that he was very unhappy.

He wasn't sure what the hell possessed him to act like Ashby was his boyfriend, but it was the first idea that popped into his head and ran with it. Thankfully, Ashby responded like it was exactly what he'd needed.

Still, when they'd watched Kiefer leave, Trent had turned uncertainly to Ashby as he gently let him go. "Sorry," he said. "Seemed like that guy was an asshole."

Ashby rubbed his eyes with the heels of his hands. "Yes," he said thickly. Then he took a gulp from the half-finished cocktail in front of him. "He was. And I'm deeply grateful for the dashing rescue. I hate when things like that happen. It would be nice not to have to rely on a friend to bail me out, but…" He trailed off and gave Trent an apologetic smile. "I hope you were planning on dinner after all, because it's my treat after that. I insist."

Trent opened his mouth. He was so used to covering the check when he went out with friends. But Ashby's eyes were glassy and it seemed important to him to pay Trent back.

"Okay," he said. "But let me buy you a new drink." Kiefer had obviously bought the fresh one for Ashby and a petty part of Trent didn't want him touching it.

A strange emotion played across Ashby's face. "Deal," he said softly. Then he leaned against the counter, catching the bartender's attention. "These were simply wonderful, Darnell," he said with a genuine air. "But I think we're going to switch to wine now." He glanced at Trent. "Unless you prefer something else?"

Trent shook his head. He'd drink anything, quite frankly. "Sounds good."

He watched while Ashby amiably chatted with Darnell, shaking off his fright at having that douchebag's hands on him. He just loved people, or so Trent was starting to think, as he asked Darnell his opinion on the best red wine they had. Darnell, in turn, brightened up at being asked about something he was clearly passionate about.

By the time the two of them moved into the restaurant area, Ashby happily knew which wine to ask their waiter for and seemed fairly recovered. But Trent was perturbed.

"That happen a lot?" he asked once they were seated with their menus. Trent slipped his leather jacket off, noticing Ashby's gaze lingering on it as he did.

Then Ashby looked questioningly at him before understanding what he had asked.

"Ah, yes," he said, toying with one of the prongs of his fork. "I'm always too scared to tell them to fuck off. I bet you think I'm pathetic."

Trent frowned at him. "Not your fault dickheads get all pervy."

He glanced up and realized Ashby was looking intently at him. "I suppose," he said. "But I'd like to stand up for myself a little bit more. I'm sure you've never suffered from unwanted attention in your life."

Trent thought back to the paparazzi that had hounded him until he'd snapped. Dez Starr's face probably disagreed with that statement.

Ashby seemed to realize he'd said something off. "I mean, I doubt you've felt very afraid," he said quietly, looking down at his menu. He blinked a couple of times. "You're so big. You could scare anyone off."

He was clearly disturbed by Kiefer's advances and Trent felt furious all over again. It was true he could handle himself. Ashby looked so much more delicate. "That sucks," he said, unsure what else to offer. "Glad I could help this time."

Ashby relaxed a little. Then he reached over to squeeze Trent's hand. "Me too," he said. "Thank you. Now, enough of this moping. Let's act like we're on holiday."

He offered his dazzling smile to the waiter so he could order their wine as well as olives and bread. He was extremely confident asking for what he wanted but not patronizing to the staff. It made Trent feel like he'd been brought up with both money and manners.

"So, I met your dad," Ashby said, sipping his wine once their waiter delivered it. "He was walking Merlin. He seemed nice."

Trent blinked at him. "You…talked to my dad?"

Ashby nodded. He didn't bite into his bread, rather ripped

off little bits, then buttered them individually before popping them into his mouth to chew slowly. "He said to tell you that he hoped you had a nice night. I invited him to join us, but I think he felt like he'd be intruding. It was nice to say hello though. Do you visit him here often?"

Ashby was so innocent, but Trent couldn't help but raise his hackles. His dad wouldn't talk to him, but he'd talk to Ashby? Fine. "No," he said. "I've not been here in a while."

He didn't want to go into why he was back or talk about his mom. He didn't want to admit that Ashby had probably exchanged more kind words with his dad than he had in years. So instead he sipped his wine and mustered up his best smile.

"It's nice to be back," he said. He wasn't entirely lying. His cabin was nice and quiet, and he hadn't expected to make a friend. Even if Ashby was so completely different from him. Trent leaned his elbow on the table and rested his chin in his hand, arching an eyebrow. "What about you? You seem like the kind of guy to have lots of friends. Why come here alone?"

Ashby closed his menu. Their eager waiter spotted the gesture and zipped over to ask if they were ready to order. Trent already knew he wanted the steak, so he let Ashby go first as he was also decided, choosing the ravioli. The waiter took their menus once they were done, leaving them one less thing to fiddle with.

"I do," said Ashby. "Have a lot of friends, I mean. I went to school abroad and didn't really stay in touch with a lot of those people. But I've met loads of people on the London scene." He laughed and rolled his eyes. "The trouble is, you meet each other through partying and dating and shagging. Then you're in this strange bubble where most of you know what everyone else looks like when they orgasm." He smiled and touched his thumb to his lower lip before knocking back the rest of his wine. "They are a lovely lot, though," he concluded while he topped up both their glasses. "Sorry, that was probably more information than you were expecting."

Trent shrugged. It took a lot to surprise him. "So, what? You got bored of them?"

"Oh, no," said Ashby, his eyes wide and earnest. "No, if anything, they were sick of me, and, well...I guess I just needed a break from everyone." Trent raised an eyebrow at him and he sighed in response. "I was dating this guy for a while. Gordon. He was absolutely rubbish, but I was too stubborn to see it, even when my friends tried to save me from myself. I...may have said some unkind things to them."

Trent could sympathize with that. He'd accidentally burned far too many bridges in his life. It was a miracle he was still as close with Blake, Joey and Raiden as he was. "But you broke up with the asshole?" he prompted. He found he was curious to know.

Ashby's eyes darkened and he took another big gulp of wine. Did he realize how the altitude would affect him up here? He'd get drunk pretty fast if he kept that up. Normally, Trent was the first to start a party, but he was strangely worried for Ashby's well-being. So he took a sip from his own water, hoping to drop a hint.

"Yes," said Ashby firmly. "I should have done it ages ago. He...well, I found him cheating on me. So I finally got enough backbone to break it off." He sounded disgusted with himself.

Trent scowled. "It takes a lot of guts to end a long-term thing," he said. His co-star on The Fixer had been in the midst of a divorce during filming and Trent had supported her through a lot of shit. Hell, Barry had been divorced three times. Trent knew what kind of toll that could take on a person.

Ashby offered him a small smile. "I guess," he said.

Their food arrived and distracted them for a few minutes while they ate. Trent kept glancing at Ashby though, just every now and again. Who could cheat on such a nice guy? He was gorgeous, too, objectively speaking. His ex must have been a real piece of work.

"You feel like more boarding tomorrow?" Trent asked before he could consider the implications. But as soon as he said it, he thought he'd like that a lot. Who else was he going to hang out with, after all? He'd just spend the rest of the week getting more annoyed that he didn't have a date to Blake and Elion's wedding.

Ashby blinked, then grinned. "I'd *love* to," he said. He placed his cutlery down on his ravioli and drank a little more of his wine. "I can't believe how much I enjoyed it! I was actually not half bad, I thought, once we got going. You're a pretty good teacher, you know." He frowned. "But you're sure you don't mind?"

Trent took a drink, not wanting Ashby to feel like he was the only one enjoying the wine. He and Darnell had certainly picked a good one. "What else am I gonna do?" he asked, although the question was kind of rhetorical. He already knew he didn't have much else other than his TV to keep him entertained. Plus, Ashby was fun. He didn't mind spending time together. In fact, he thought he could maybe call Ashby a real friend if they gave it time. He got a good vibe from him despite them only knowing each other a day.

Ashby's smile was somewhat coy. "Well, I'd love to, in that case," he said. Then he sighed, swirling his wine around in his glass. "I never thought hurtling down a mountain would be so peaceful at the same time as being so exhilarating. That's a contradiction, isn't it?"

"It's right, though," Trent pointed out. That was exactly how he'd always felt about snowboarding.

For a second Trent held Ashby's gaze as they grinned.

Then Ashby swallowed and blinked rapidly, a pink tinge rising on his cheeks. "Yes, um, I'd love to meet up again and practice. If you really don't mind."

"Sure," Trent said. It was no big deal. In fact, he was looking forward to it.

They ate the rest of their food in companionable silence until Ashby asked the waiter for more wine and the dessert menu. When had they gotten through the first bottle?

Trent felt pleasantly buzzed, but he was slightly concerned that Ashby was going to make himself sick. "You know the altitude messes with your system up here," he said gently.

But as soon as he spoke, Ashby's face fell. "Oh," he said. "Should I have not ordered any more? I just felt so on edge after, well, you know."

He looked guilty and Trent regretted not choosing his words more carefully. "Hell, no, man," he said. "You said it yourself, you're on vacation and that asshole tried to ruin it. Let's do this." He nudged one of the water glasses toward him. "Just maybe hydrate as well, for me."

Ashby looked at him a moment and licked his lips. A slow smile crept onto his face. "Of course," he said. Using his long fingers, he plucked the glass from the table and drank it all in one go. Trent watched his Adam's apple bob elegantly as he swallowed. He wasn't sure why the sight was so mesmerizing.

A drop remained on the lip of the glass and Ashby licked it before placing the glass back down. "Done," he said cheekily.

Trent shifted in his seat. "Thanks," he said. "You'll feel better."

He wasn't sure what had just passed between them, but he couldn't help but be relieved when their wine showed up.

After lecturing Ashby on not accidentally getting too wasted, he found he might be in need of some relief himself.

He'd never spent time with anyone like Ashby before. It wasn't that he was gay, he was just…unique.

Urgh, Trent knew he was getting weird. They'd lapsed into a slightly awkward silence. He needed to un-weird it. If Ashby were a girl, Trent knew he would have been able to just give her a smoldering look and ask her about herself. That always set his dates at ease.

Well…this wasn't a date, but he still wanted to set Ashby at ease.

"So, um, you've been to the States before?" he asked. He ran his thumb and index finger up and down the stem of the wine glass.

As he'd hoped, Ashby's face brightened. "My father and I are British citizens, but my mother is actually American," he said. He wiggled his fingers, getting animated. "She's a translator for the UN, speaks several languages, *very* exciting. Traveled all over the world, met my dad in London, he's an engineer. Then they settled down in Singapore while I grew up. I mean, they were always traveling still, but I got to go with them in school holidays and it was all rather grand."

"That's awesome," Trent said.

Ashby nodded, then sighed. "A lot to live up to," he admitted.

"So what do you do?" Trent asked, genuinely curious.

Ashby gave Trent a tight smile and flipped his blond hair. "I'm just gorgeous, *dah*-ling," he said with a giggle. "No, I…go to parties and date idiots and have an Instagram with ten thousand followers for no other reason than I'm rich and pretty and go to parties and date idiots." He rolled his eyes. "Spoiled trust fund baby, you see. My grandfather was a stockbroker on Wall Street," he added. "You can see why I'm such a catch. Utterly useless. Shallow." He laughed and drank more wine, but Trent didn't think he was joking.

Trent frowned, licking the wine from his lips. It was genuinely very good. "I think you're cool," he said. "You don't need to have your whole life mapped out already. Especially if you don't have to worry about money."

Ashby sighed. "You're right," he said. "I can't complain. I'm just in the post-breakup blues, maybe."

Trent scoffed. "The guy was clearly a Grade A jerk," he scoffed. "You're way better off without him."

Ashby lifted his glass toward Trent. "I'll drink to that," he said emphatically. "Cheers!"

They talked a little about what Ashby's life had been like in Singapore and ordered some dessert. The food here was actually pretty damn good, Trent had to admit. As much as Trent had been isolated in the mountains growing up, Ashby had been in a bubble of European migrants, not really experiencing the Asian culture around him. Trent thought perhaps as nice as having staff and an enormous house had been, Ashby felt like something was missing from his life.

Love?

Trent blinked. Yeah, probably. Wasn't everyone looking for love? Ashby deserved to be with a nice guy. Not someone like his cheating asshole ex.

They managed to skirt around the topic of what Trent did for a living, which was the first sign that alerted him that maybe Ashby knew more than he was letting on. But it was so nice for a change to just pretend he wasn't a fucking movie star or pop star. He felt like he could enjoy himself for once. There was always a chance another guest might recognize him and put a photo up on Twitter. But as they made their way to the end of the bottle, Trent found he didn't care.

He had enough wits about him to ensure they each drank another couple of glasses of water. But Ashby was so much smaller than him and by the time they charged the meal to Ashby's room and the wine to Trent's, Ashby couldn't stop giggling.

It was endearing. Trent couldn't help but smile at him. "Come on, trouble," he said. For the second time that evening, he wrapped his arm around Ashby's waist as they walked through the restaurant and out of the bar. "Let's get you home."

"Shh," said Ashby, pressing his fingers to his pale pink lips. "People will think we're a couple."

"They already do," Trent assured him, grinning back down at him. "Why, are you ashamed of me?"

"Oh, do be sensible," Ashby slurred. "You know, I actually had your posters on my *wall* growing up." He snorted. "I can't believe I didn't recognize you when we met."

Something strange fizzed through Trent's insides. So, Ashby *did* know who Trent was. The idea of Ashby having Below Zero posters up as a teenager made Trent's insides tingle. Not that he hadn't made friends with fans before, but he just hadn't expected it of Ashby.

"It was probably because I was a dick to you," Trent grumbled. "Supposed to be all smiles, all the time. Every girl's dream."

Ashby blew a raspberry as they walked through the lobby towards his room. Or at least, Trent assumed. Ashby was leading the way, tugging Trent along with his arm still around his waist. "You're not a dick. You're a teddy bear." Ashby patted Trent's chest. "Maybe make that a grizzly bear. Dear lord, you're so buff. It makes me weep."

For some reason, the compliment made Trent feel a little flushed. "You're hot, too," he said without really thinking it through.

Ashby giggled, then stumbled free of Trent's arm. "Don't be silly, silly," he said. "I'm not..." He waved his hand up and down. "You. Anyway, this is my room." He patted the door affectionately. "Me. I sleep here." He sighed and leaned against it, pulling a key from out of the side of his boot. Then he looked up at Trent through his eyelashes. "I know I'm totally barking up the wrong tree. But…I do sort of wish I could invite you in." He smiled and pressed the key to his lips, his eyes half-closed and sleepy looking. "You are very lovely, Trent Charles. If ever you need a pretend boyfriend in return for tonight, you know who to ask."

With that, he hummed and unlocked his door. Waving, he bade Trent goodnight, then went inside his room.

Trent stood there for a good twenty seconds before he realized he should walk away and go to his own cabin.

Ashby wanted to invite him in. Well…that was extremely gratifying. It was natural that Trent be flattered by the compliment. In his reasonably drunken state, he grinned and wondered what that might be like. To sleep with a guy.

Having so many male queer best friends, it wasn't like the concept was totally alien. But as Trent let himself inside his cabin and stripped for bed, he found his mind wandering for the first time, perhaps ever. Normally the idea of going with another guy left him feeling a little perplexed. It did nothing for him. But the good wine and good mood were urging him on.

What if he'd said yes to Ashby's offer?

It wasn't like they would see each other again after this vacation. They lived in different countries. Trent could have accepted the invitation into Ashby's room and explored where the night might take them.

By the time he got into bed, he was half-hard.

It was just a fantasy. It wouldn't do any harm. So he spat in his palm and took himself in hand. Ashby had such a pretty mouth. The image of him touching the key to his lips fueled Trent as he massaged his balls with one hand and jerked off with the other.

He pictured Ashby sucking him off and loving it. Trent would hold onto that beautiful blond hair and moan like he was now, loudly and with abandon. He gnashed his teeth as his climax built quickly.

All too soon, he was gasping and spilling into his hand, quivering as the orgasm rippled through his body. He hummed in contentment, draping his arm over his eyes as he caught his breath. He barely had enough energy to pull a couple of tissues from the box and mop himself up before sleep claimed him, the smile still on his lips.

The last thought that drifted through his mind was that maybe he *should* have said yes.

CHAPTER
Thirteen

ASHBY

Ashby was definitely dying. It was a scientific fact.

He moaned and whimpered as the knock on the door roused him from his sleep. "Bugger off," he wailed, stuffing his throbbing head underneath his pillow.

He felt a weight make the bed dip, then a finger poking at his ribs. "You appear to still be in bed," Maeve commented.

Ashby grumbled and pulled his pillow down tighter over his head. "Go away," he mumbled.

"But then who am I gonna gossip to?" Maeve asked, her voice a pesky singsong. The poking continued.

"I should have you fired," Ashby threatened.

Maeve snorted. "I've been fired four times from this place. *Come on,* you're killing me! You had a date with TJ Charles and now you have to tell!"

Coldness washed through Ashby. He risked peeking out from under the pillow. "It wasn't a date," he mumbled.

Because he had to keep telling himself that, apparently. Fucking hell. He'd been a bit of a mess by the time he and Trent had finished dinner. But he hadn't been so trashed he didn't remember inviting Trent into his room. Into his bed.

Urgh, even if it had been a joke, it was grossly inappropriate. He'd probably made Trent feel horribly uncomfortable. He wanted to go back to sleep and pretend the whole thing had never happened.

Except…they'd had a truly wonderful evening until that point, hadn't they? He'd felt so at ease and relaxed. Trent had opened up a little from his usual gruff self and really made Ashby laugh. When Trent looked at him, he felt worthwhile.

He was so fucked.

The poking finger returned.

"Darnell from the bar seemed to think it was a date," Maeve said. "Come on, Ashby. I can't torment my own kids anymore. Entertain an old woman with some juicy details!"

Ashby removed the pillow and batted her lightly with it. She was wearing her uniform and was obviously here to clean. Or, at least, that was her excuse. Normally she didn't come in until at least after midday.

"You're not old," he said.

A yawn took him by surprise as he rubbed his thumping forehead. Glancing at the clock, he realized it was already ten thirty and he should probably crawl out of bed soon if he wanted to catch the last few minutes of breakfast.

"Yes, I am," Maeve said, tapping his arm and laughing. "I need amusement. So, if it wasn't a date, what was it?" She nodded in an all-knowing manner. "That boy is quite a hunk if I recall."

Ashby could feel himself blush. He tried to blow over it by sitting up in bed. Thank goodness he'd worn pajamas, or Maeve might have given herself a bit of an eyeful.

"He's straight," he said, trying not to sound defensive.

Maeve raised an eyebrow. "My daughter informs me that the majority of people are at least a *little* bit gay. I think that's because she has a hopeless crush on her yoga instructor. But, really, in this day and age, more people are open to it than you think. Darnell told Kadie at the front desk who told Skye in the spa who told *me* that TJ Charles had his arm around you when you left." She leaned back and kicked her feet like a small child as she looked around the room. "Did he come back with you?"

Ashby couldn't stop the flush burning on his cheeks and he pulled awkwardly at the bedsheet. "Actually, I *did* tell him it was a shame I couldn't invite him in." He cringed. "I told him he was lovely."

Maeve's eyes went wide and she placed her feet back on the carpet. "And what did he say?"

Ashby shrugged. "Nothing. I came inside and closed the door. It all seemed quite funny last night." He covered his face with his hands. "People aren't going to be awful to him, are they?" he whispered. He felt like bile was crawling up his throat. "They won't…think he's gay or bi, not really? They know him."

Slightly callused fingers gently pried his fingers from his face. "Hey?" Maeve said with concern. "No, nobody's gonna be a jerk. And if they are, I'll slap them silly. They know how it is. Why would you think they'd get crappy?"

Ashby shrugged. Because he lived in the real world? But he managed to give Maeve a small smile. It felt good to have her on his side, at least. "Well, I would hate for him to have any trouble when there was no reason," he said. "We're just friends." *Sadly,* he thought to himself.

That was if Trent still wanted to be friends after Ashby's inappropriate behavior. He felt even sicker at that idea. Ashby would hate to ruin their relationship in its early stages, even if they were only going to have this holiday to see each other.

The stupid thing was he hadn't thought to get Trent's phone number at any point. So, he couldn't text to ask if he was feeling equally rough or if he wanted to meet Ashby on the slopes again or if he was going to totally avoid Ashby for the next three weeks. Ashby bit his tongue and blinked against the prickling at the back of his eyes.

Trent had saved Ashby from that toad Kiefer hitting on him. Then Ashby had repaid Trent by hitting on him just the same way. Fuck, he was a shitty person.

Maeve squeezed his thigh through the blankets and got to her feet. "Come on," she said. "I'll do next door first, give you time to get your wits together. Then you head to breakfast and I'll fix your room." She stood with her hands on her hips. "Stop moping. It's no fun if you mope!" she cried, getting a tiny smile from Ashby. "Look. Did you have fun last night? Was he nice to you?"

Ashby nibbled on his lower lip. "Yes," he admitted, somewhat reluctantly. "And, yes."

"Then he's not going be a bag of dicks to you now, is he?" she said, arching an eyebrow. "Especially if he's anything like his dad. Trenton Sr. is a *good* man." She sighed wistfully for a moment, just enough to make Ashby wonder what she meant. But then she snapped her attention back to Ashby. "So, make sure you look stunning, then when you bump into him today, he can see exactly what's being offered if he's feeling brave."

Ashby rubbed his nose and gave her a small, bashful smile. "Okay," he said.

She was definitely barking up the wrong tree. Trent would never be interested in Ashby sexually. Romantically. But it was nice of her to think he might.

Taking her advice to heart, he threw some clothes on to grab a bite of breakfast, then took himself off to the sauna outside. Twenty minutes sitting in some glorious steam would sort his hangover, he was sure. Then he could come back and get a bit glamorous in case he did bump into Trent somewhere.

It was another beautiful day in Wyoming. The sky was cobalt blue and the sun was shining, reflecting off the picture-perfect snow piled around the swimming pool and on the sauna's roof. There was an indoor changing area with lockers and towels stacked up neatly. Ashby helped himself to one and wrapped it around his hips before walking through the door into the sauna room itself.

Except, there was already someone in there.

"Oh," he said as horror consumed him. Stupidly, he waved at Trent, who was sitting in the hot, dark room, also with nothing but a towel wrapped around his waist. A short towel at that. "Um, hello."

Ashby was suddenly aware of how slim and willowy he was. Trent was all muscle.

His pecs and abs were gorgeously defined with bumps in places Ashby wasn't even aware there could be bumps. Diagonal rivets pointed like arrows to what lay beneath Trent's towel, and tendrils of his damp hair clung to a neck that begged to be kissed. His skin was a light brown, whether by tan or heritage, Ashby wasn't sure. He was too mesmerized by all the body art he could see in any case.

Trent had tribal designs in black ink and quotes in various languages and images of dolphins, dragons, skulls, butterflies and clocks. The one that caught Ashby's eye the most was a single word over Trent's heart: Bulletproof. He wondered what that was about.

For a split second, at least. Because then he remembered he was mortified and should probably run away very fast.

"Sorry," he stammered. "I can leave you alone."

"No, no," said Trent, holding up his hands. He shifted like he was uncomfortable, but then he smiled. "It's good to see you. How's your head?"

Ashby wasn't sure how to interpret the mixed signals. But

he closed the door and sat down on the bench opposite Trent. He didn't think he should get too close.

"Wonderful," he said, answering Trent's question. His smile was a little shaky, but it was the best he could muster when he was feeling unsure and nervous. Was Trent mad that Ashby had hit on him? Uncomfortable? "I love feeling like there's a pneumatic drill inside my skull."

Trent laughed and Ashby finally allowed himself to relax a fraction. "Tell me about it. We went a little nuts on the wine, huh?"

Ashby laughed. Maybe this was going to be okay. He made damn sure to keep his gaze focused on Trent's face, not his chest, so he wouldn't feel like he was being objectified again.

"I flirt with everyone, it's kind of a defense mechanism," Ashby confessed, swallowing around the lump in his throat. He did really like Trent and wanted things to be cool between them. "I know you don't swing that way, so I'm very sorry if I put you in an awkward position." Ashby took a deep breath. "I, um, know who you are. Out in the world. I don't care about any of that," he added quickly. "But I just want you to know that I wouldn't take advantage of that or flirt just because, you know, you're famous. I just think you *are* lovely, as a friend, and I got a little carried away."

Again, Trent shifted, adjusting his towel, but he also smiled. "It was cute," he said, meeting Ashby's gaze. "Don't sweat it." He licked his lips and glanced around the room. "I was just heading out. Don't wanna get too dehydrated. But you still wanna hit the slopes later? Try something a little higher?"

"Oh, y-yes, p-please," Ashby spluttered. If Trent wanted to forget about the whole thing, that would be amazing. Ashby knew he would never be able to get him into bed, but he would love to be friends. In fact, the prospect of hanging out with a nice guy without the pressure of shagging was extremely appealing. "When do you want to meet?"

Trent's smile became bigger. He stood up, keeping careful hold of his towel. "One?" he suggested. "By the base of the ski lift?"

Ashby nodded. "Fantastic," he said. "See you there."

He watched Trent go out the door, then took a long, deep breath of the hot, damp air. He could already feel his headache clearing. He was so glad things were okay between them still. Now he could look forward to snowboarding and a few more of those TJ Charles smiles.

He was still as on track for his man-free holiday as he was before.

CHAPTER

Fourteen

TRENT

It was typical that just as Trent had been trying to sort out his thoughts from the night before, Ashby had showed up almost naked. Again. Trent was still trying to convince himself not to feel guilty. He'd jerked off to the image of plenty of girls he knew before. This was no different because it was a guy. It was just a fantasy. Trent conjured up all kinds of dubious things in the privacy of his mind when he got off. Everyone did.

So why did he still feel rotten, even after leaving the sauna? He and Ashby had cleared the air, not that it had been totally necessary. The fact that Ashby had gotten upset over a perfectly innocent bit of flirting made Trent sad. He didn't want such a sweet guy getting himself in knots over Trent. He was done making people feel like crap.

But Ashby was still his friend and he never needed to know that Trent had made himself come picturing the idea of them making out. Objectively, Trent could appreciate that Ashby was gorgeous. There was a femininity to his beauty which was probably why Trent had been able to take a leap and wonder 'what if' they'd gone to bed together. It wasn't like he was planning on doing anything in real life about it.

Trent wasn't queer. He had absolutely nothing against being gay or bi or whatever. It just wasn't him. He'd know that about himself by now, at twenty-eight. He was just turned on by the prospect of a new sexual experience, was all. He'd done almost everything he could think of with all his lady hookups over the years. The novelty of doing something different with a guy was most likely what had awakened his cock last night.

Trent realized he'd been standing in front of his wardrobe after his shower for goodness only knew how long. Five minutes? His feet were starting to get cold. With a sigh, he picked out some clothes and dropped his towel to the floor. He glowered at his temporarily free cock to behave itself until he got some boxer-briefs on. If his body could only cooperate, he wouldn't need to knock one out thinking about his new friend again.

It occurred to him that because he didn't want to face his dad, his mind was running off on tangents. But Trent had made up his mind that he was going to see him again today and try to talk. The trouble was he was ashamed to admit he couldn't remember where exactly his dad *lived* nowadays. It was staff accommodation somewhere, but Trent was damned if he could recall the details. So that left him in the uncomfortable situation of only being able to approach him while he was at work in the gift shop.

He wasn't giving up, though. He was going to ask his dad if he wanted to visit his mom's grave together at some point. He was also determined to ask if there was a memorial to her somewhere in the resort. This place had been her home and his dad certainly felt like she was still present within its walls. If there wasn't a bench or a pond somewhere for her, Trent thought he could offer to have one built.

He knew it would more than likely fall under his dad's category of 'too little too late' but Trent had to try. He knew he didn't want to visit a lonely grave to feel he was close to his mom again. It was almost certainly one of the reasons he had avoided coming home during the past two years. She deserved somewhere beautiful, here on the grounds of the place she and his dad loved so much.

As he walked through the snow from his cabin over to the main lodge, Trent swung between musing on his parents and trying not to worry about Ashby anymore. Normally, if something was beyond his control, he just forgot about it. He didn't chew over it for hours. But making amends with his dad was eating him up, and for whatever reason, Ashby was occupying almost as much space in his thoughts.

He pinched the bridge of his nose and pushed through the door into the warmth of the resort. The temptation to be reckless and just start drinking niggled at the back of his mind. But he swore he wasn't going to do that anymore. There was a vast difference between a little too much wine at dinner and all-day boozing for no damn reason other than he was feeling sorry for himself. He had to stop running away from his problems. That was the whole point of coming here.

Unfortunately, luck wasn't on his side.

As soon as he reached the gift store and saw the middle-aged lady behind the counter, he remembered it was Wednesday. Wednesdays and Thursdays were his dad's weekend, so he wouldn't be back now until Friday, when Trent was flying off to Ohio for Blake and Elion's wedding on Saturday. He wasn't going to be able to speak to his dad until at least Sunday night now.

Fuck. He scratched his chin and scowled at the shop from just outside the door. Now that he'd made up his mind he really didn't want to have to wait. But this wasn't the kind of conversation he wanted to have over the phone. Besides, with his dad as grouchy as he currently was, he'd probably just hang up on him.

Trent shoved his hands into the pockets of his leather jacket. Typical. He was trying, he really was. But Barry would lose his shit if he knew how little progress Trent had made. At least he had three months to try and fix this mess. Barry didn't need to know how badly he was doing just yet.

He had just turned around to leave when the sound of crashing and clattering made him snap back around. To his horror, he saw Merlin come tearing down one of the shop aisles toward him. His leash was trailing behind him, knocking half the contents of the bottom shelves off in its wake as it whipped back and forth. He'd obviously been behind the counter but had smelled Trent or something and come bolting out.

"No!" the part-time woman cried in horror, leaping to her feet. "Bad puppy!" An older guy looking at a map of the local area had to jump back to stop his legs being taken out from under him.

Trent dropped to his knees and tried to calm the puppy when he reached him. "No, shh!" he cried as the little dude barked and barked, his yelps earsplitting. "It's okay, buddy, calm down."

"He was tied up, I swear," the woman said as she hurried to try and grab Merlin's leash. "Your dad is out of town for today, so I said I'd watch him. But my dogs aren't like this one!"

Trent felt bad he didn't recognize the woman, but at least she knew he wasn't a customer who was going to complain. Trent wasn't so sure about the guy who had been looking at the map, but fingers crossed even if he did find Bob to moan at, Bob wouldn't care.

That Kiefer Burton might, though, Trent realized. If he

was still around. He seemed to have his wits about him. Trent couldn't remember his dad ever mentioning an owner above Bob before. If he wasn't such a sleazeball, Trent might have hoped Kiefer was visiting in order to do up the place. But Trent couldn't help but worry Kiefer was intent on doing the opposite.

Knowing how much the resort meant to his dad, Trent would rather not have him made aware of any extra issues he couldn't already see for himself.

Between him and the part-time lady, they managed to wrangle the chubby puppy so he wasn't near anything breakable. Trent cringed and wondered how many other broken bits of useless knickknacks he'd end up paying for after this particular destructive outburst. He was going to have to set up a running tab at this rate.

"Dude," he lamented as Merlin finally calmed a little. Trent rubbed his ears and sighed. "Can't you cut me a break for like five seconds? I swear, my dad will like you more if you do."

Merlin gave another bark and wagged his tail. Trent wasn't really mad at him. The poor pup didn't know any better, and besides, it was nice that he was so happy to see Trent again. But wrecking his dad's store was not the way to win his heart.

The part-time woman ran her hands through her light brown hair and sighed as she surveyed the damage. Luckily, it looked like Merlin had only wrecked a few salt-and-pepper shakers. The rest was just strewn across the floor.

"Hey," Trent said, standing to look her in the eye. "Would it help if I took him for a walk while you clear up?"

The woman broke into a relieved smile. "Oh *would* you?" she asked. "I think it might be a good idea to burn off some of his energy."

Trent assured her it was no trouble and left her to it.

Merlin seemed more than happy to trot about the resort for a little while, sniffing at everything. Trent figured he could walk him around the outside of the main lodge and hopefully the little guy would do his business out there rather than the lobby's carpet.

"Well, look who it is," an unfortunately familiar voice drawled.

The Texan twang alerted Trent even before he turned around and registered the bright white Stetson. Kiefer Burton was sauntering down the hall toward Trent, possibly on his way to the restaurant behind him and Merlin.

Kiefer had two other guys in cowboy hats and boots walking either side of him. They were both older than Kiefer, one with a substantial belly and the other tall and gawky, all three wearing enough gold between them to open a bank. Rings and watches and spurs on their boots. One look at them told Trent they wouldn't be the sort to tip their waiter, though. These guys got their wealth by stepping on other people's heads.

"Jim, Marv," Kiefer said, not bothering to look at his companions. "This here's the Grand's local celebrity. TJ Charles himself." He sniggered. "Ain't we lucky?"

Trent wondered if Kiefer had recognized him when he'd recklessly gone in and claimed to be Ashby's boyfriend. Damn it. Forty-something dudes from the Midwest didn't used to be his demographic. That was before The Fixer had made him more of a household name, though.

"Mr. Burton," Trent said curtly. "Good to see you again." They both knew he was bullshitting, but Trent smiled nonetheless.

"Where's that cute little boyfriend of yours?" Kiefer asked, biting his thumbnail and spitting the bit he'd torn off away. "I would have imagined he would be the one on the leash." He glanced down at Merlin and Trent's hackles rose for more reason than one.

He didn't like Kiefer getting anywhere near his dad's puppy, and he definitely didn't like him mentioning anything to do with Ashby. "He's around," Trent said curtly. He felt bad continuing the lie that they were dating, but he wasn't exactly going to admit they'd made the whole thing up. That would leave Ashby vulnerable to this asshole.

Kiefer gave him a mock show of concern. "Trouble in paradise?" He licked his lips and leaned in toward Trent. "I should have just fucked that sweet lil' ass anyhow. Maybe I still will. Clearly, you haven't got the kind of hold on him a boy like that needs."

Jim and Marv, whichever was which, suddenly looked extremely uncomfortable as they shifted from foot to foot behind Kiefer. Their disgust no doubt came from homophobia. Trent, on the other hand, was completely appalled that Kiefer would talk about Ashby in such a vulgar way. He could feel his anger rising.

He jabbed a finger toward Kiefer. "You *stay away* from Ashby. You hear me?"

He was somewhat undermined as Merlin chose that moment to pounce on Kiefer's boot and chew it, his tail whipping back and forth as he issued little growls that he clearly thought were terrifying. Trent cleared his throat and tugged Merlin's leash, trying to encourage him back.

Kiefer regarded Trent coolly, ignoring the puppy's attack. "Or what?" he drawled. Then he laughed. "Sugar, this is my little kingdom. I'll do what I want. Although I am curious. Are you serious enough about this cute lil' twink to go public with him? I'm sure your fans would be pretty devastated to find out you don't like fuckin' pussy no more."

Trent ground his teeth. "That a threat?" he bit out, arching an eyebrow.

Merlin dropped his ass on the carpet and scratched his ear.

Kiefer shrugged. "Depends," he said slyly. "Are you ashamed of him? See-" he placed a hand on his chest, showing off his bling "-I'm a real man. Everybody knows I'll fuck all the cute twinks I like and fuck up anybody who thinks that's some sort of weakness. But you?" He sneered, his eyes dancing with malice. "I know your history. You run at the first sign of trouble."

Once again, his companions became extremely interested in the bland, outdated décor of the corridor. Merlin gave a noisy yawn and batted at the laces on Trent's boots.

Trent couldn't help but hesitate in the face of Kiefer's accusations. It was one thing to say he was dating Ashby to keep this fucker away from him. But it was another entirely to risk the public finding out and the homophobic backlash that might cause.

But when Trent thought of sweet Ashby's face, his innocent smile and sparkling eyes, he couldn't bear the thought of hurting him. Was an easier life with the tabloids and bloggers worth putting before Ashby?

Fuck anyone who thought less of Trent if he dated a guy. Blake and Raiden had both thrown their sexuality in people's faces. Blake very publicly so.

No. Trent was going to choose his friend over anything, even if they were telling a little white lie.

He leaned into Kiefer, looking him unflinchingly in the eye. Trent quirked the corner of his mouth into a sneer. "Go find another cute twink who isn't repulsed by you," he said softly. "Ashby is nobody's property. He's not interested in you, so leave him – and us – the fuck alone."

Marlin yapped in agreement.

Trent didn't bother looking back at Kiefer or his cronies as he marched away, heading for the door to take Merlin to his cabin for a while. Trent was aware that Kiefer had the power to make life difficult for his dad, but Trent knew first-hand what a stubborn old bastard his dad could be. Let Kiefer try and pick a fight with him.

But if Trent was going to be serious about this whole 'dating Ashby' thing, he had a real decision to make.

Because you brought your other half to weddings. And if he didn't take Ashby this weekend where there would be press coverage, there was a chance Kiefer could find out. Let alone the idea of leaving Ashby alone for three days with him around made Trent very nervous.

He let himself into his cabin and took a deep breath. It looked like if he was going to keep up this charade, he was going to have to go whole hog with it.

The question was, what would Ashby think of this idea?

Fifteen

ASHBY

"I'M SORRY, BUT YOU WANT TO DO WHAT?"

Ashby blinked at Trent across the table. Trent had been unusually quiet during their snowboarding session that afternoon, even for him. Then he'd suggested they grab a hot drink to warm themselves up again, where he'd casually asked Ashby to be his date at a wedding.

Well, not really. He'd explained about running into Kiefer again and how the lie had gotten out of hand. But Ashby couldn't help but think it would have been easier to come up with another solution.

Trent shifted his bulk in the slightly too-small chair. "I know, it's crazy," he mumbled, twisting his coffee cup around. "You don't have to."

The thing was, it was nothing for Ashby to buy plane tickets at the last minute. He could pick up a new suit and afford a hotel room. It was more the implication that Trent was willing to lie, not just to Kiefer, but the world at large.

"You want to pretend to your friends?" he said.

Trent quickly shook his head. "No," he said. "I was going to say that we were friends. That's, um, true. Right?"

It was adorable to see a normally big, confident hunk look at Ashby like he was at his mercy. His trust and respect after such a short amount of time put Gordon and Ashby's other exes to shame.

"Of course we're friends," Ashby said, laying a hand on Trent's hand for a second. "But it's a big deal to even flirt with the idea of coming out of the closet. You won't be able to undo this if people get wind of it."

Trent shrugged. "So?" he said. "I don't see anything shameful in being bi. If people want to flip their fucking minds over it, I don't care. I'm the dumb idiot who pretended to be your boyfriend. If we have to keep that up to keep you safe, I'd love to have you be my plus one." He gave Ashby a tight smile. "Besides, this way you get to meet my best buds. If we're going to be friends, that would be cool, right?"

Ashby was dumbstruck. Trent wanted to be friends for real? Not just for the next week or two? And he wanted him to meet his friends? More to the point, he didn't care if people called him gay or bi?

Well, he wasn't. He could ride out the rumors, then go back to his real life. He wouldn't really be coming out of the closet.

Ashby wasn't sure how he felt about being a part of such a large fib. He couldn't help but feel it would make a mockery of him and other queer people. However, Trent was only doing it to try and keep him safe from that repulsive creep.

"So," he said slowly. "We'd just be going as friends? Well… that could be fun, couldn't it?" He smiled, warming to the idea. Because Trent wasn't asking him as a cruel joke or anything after all. "I do love weddings."

"Yeah?" said Trent, brightening. "So, you'll consider it?"

"Sure," said Ashby. "Why not? You only live once, right? But won't your friends be put out by a last minute extra guest?"

For some reason, Trent laughed. "They've been desperate for me to bring a date, so there's a place for you," he said. "But, to be honest, the idea of bringing a friend is so much better. We can dance and eat cake and drink Champagne."

An unhelpful thought crept into Ashby's mind that maybe…just *maybe*…if Trent was willing to go further with this fallacy, there could be a grain of truth to it. After all, if he was repulsed by the idea of holding hands and cuddling with a guy, he wouldn't do it. Right?

Ashby decided to be as honest as the situation allowed. He smiled and took a sip of weak tea. "If you really don't care about people gossiping, I'll be honored to come along as your friend. I actually think it's pretty admirable that you wouldn't care what people think of your sexuality."

Trent gave him one of those rare kilowatt smiles he kept hidden away. "You know what? Fake boyfriends or not, I'm happy you're coming along. You're fun to hang out with, man." He clapped Ashby on the knee, sending sparks through Ashby's body where his hand touched him. "Besides, it's a gay fucking wedding. If anyone has issues with that in this day and age, they can eat my ass."

Ashby was momentarily completely sidetracked with the idea of eating out Trent's delicious ass. It was a filthy thought and something he hardly ever did. But the image burrowed into his brain and he had to shift in his seat before his cock got too excited.

Then he realized what Trent had said. A gay wedding?

"Hang on," Ashby said. "Whose wedding is it we're going to?"

Trent smiled again, but this time it was pure wickedness. "Who do you think?" He winked. "I hope your inner fanboy is ready."

———

It turned out that Ashby's inner fanboy was in no way prepared for the prospect of going to a Below Zero wedding. Now, if he had bumped into Blake Jackson on the street, Ashby would have known right away. His dance school reality TV show was a guilty pleasure of Ashby's. He'd been so moved to see Blake's relationship with Elion Rodriguez unfolding on his screen, and Blake's passionate speech about coming out as bi at the Nickelodeon awards had actually made Ashby cry.

Now here he was, flying out to attend their wedding. Ashby went to enough A-lister parties back in London to admit he'd met plenty of celebrities over the past few years. But Blake and Elion *meant* something to him. As did Joey Sullivan and Raiden Jones. For a time, Below Zero had made young Ashby feel less alone. There had always been something inherently queer about the band to Ashby's mind.

"Are you okay?" Trent asked as they sat in their seats on the flight from Chicago to Cincinnati. Unfortunately, there wasn't a direct route from Jackson, Wyoming.

"Yes, fine," Ashby said. He sat on his hands so he would stop scratching at the armrests. "I meet my teenage heroes all the time."

Trent leaned a bit closer and waggled his eyebrows. "Come on," he said, his voice a low rumble. "You met me, and I'm nothing to get flustered over, am I?"

Ashby managed a sort of squeak, then looked back toward the small TV in the back of the seat in front of him. The miniature airplane was tracking their progress in the air across the screen. Luckily, he had his jumper folded over his lap, so he didn't have to squirm to hide just how flustered Trent was capable of making him.

He sipped his gin and tonic that he'd ordered from the in-flight service and tried to relax. But he was going to be meeting mega-successful people and what would Ashby tell them he did for a living when they asked? That he was essentially an it-boy? That he went to parties and put photos on Instagram? It was almost too cringe-worthy to bear.

"Um," he said, swirling the drink around. "I guess I'm nervous that they might not like me," he said.

Trent frowned, the playfulness gone from his face. "You're one of the nicest people I think I've ever met," he said, as if that was obvious. "Why wouldn't they like you?"

Ashby sighed and placed his drink down on the little tray. Then he turned to look Trent in the eye. "Because you guys all earned your fortunes," he said. "You're talented. My parents did all the hard work and I…I've never strived to do anything much with my time. It's embarrassing."

Trent's frown deepened. "I know labels can be important," he said eventually. "But you're more than just a job title. You're kind and funny and really stylish. The guys aren't dicks. They'll like you for you. I promise."

Ashby momentarily forgot how to breathe. Trent thought he was kind and funny and really stylish? That was…a lot to take in. "Um, thank you," he said bashfully.

Trent tilted his head, his gaze questioning. "You just haven't discovered what you're really good at yet," he said. Then he lay back in his seat and closed his eyes. "That sounds like a challenge. Before you fly back to England, we're gonna work out what makes you tick."

"We are?" Ashby said. He hadn't managed to discover his true passion in twenty-four years. He doubted Trent was going to come up with anything in a little over two weeks.

But Trent smiled, his eyes still closed. He folded his large hands over his stomach and snuggled down a bit further. He looked like he was going to take a nap. "Yup," he said. "But first, we'll have wedding fun. Then we can fix your life."

"Just like that," Ashby said with a disbelieving laugh.

Trent cracked an eyelid and looked at him. His gaze sent tingles over Ashby's skin. "Just like that," he agreed.

TRENT WASN'T USUALLY THE KIND TO GET ANXIOUS OVER things. What was the sense of worrying about what might happen? If it was out of his control, he let it go and went with the flow. That applied to filming, singing, parties, dates. Chilled out was his response to almost everything.

But pulling up to the large colonial manor house turned hotel on the outskirts of Cincinnati where Blake and Elion were tying the knot, Trent suddenly felt a rush of apprehension.

Was this the dumbest idea he'd ever had? If he'd thought buying a puppy for his dad was madness, then pretending to be bi with his new gay best friend who Trent *knew* was into him had to be insanity. Was he seriously ready to deal with the ramifications of this? Was he risking ruining his and Ashby's friendship before it had even really got a chance to thrive?

Trent knew he'd been quiet during the drive over and he could feel Ashby looking at him as they got out of the cab in front of the hotel. He was aware he needed to say something and break the tension that was growing between them, but he couldn't seem to find anything to say.

Luckily, Ashby was ready to chatter away and soothe both their nerves.

"Oh goodness, isn't this charming?" he remarked.

They stood in front of the three-story building, admiring its yellowy-cream wooden façade, slate-gray roof and pristine white windows, shutters and columns out front. The American flag hung above the front door, fluttering gently in the breezy afternoon sunshine. A short concrete path led up through a white picket fence that surrounded the property. Lush green grass stretched out around the fencing and towering oak trees stood either side of the approaches. Gleaming white verandas were nestled beside the house, under the trees, and out back beyond those, Trent could just see where the staff were setting up the white gazebo for the wedding tomorrow.

"I've never been to an outdoor wedding," Ashby continued as they made their way up the steps in between the fence, heading for the door. "It would be more than a little ambitious to predict the weather anywhere in the UK with that kind of confidence. You'll almost certainly get rained on or freeze your arse off or even get sunburned if it was summer. Generally, on the whole, we regard the weather as a sort of enemy to be treated with complete mistrust." He laughed as Trent opened the big, heavy front door for him. "Oh, thank you," he said and hopped up the last step into the cool interior of the house. "Ahh, this is so pretty."

They were greeted by gleaming oak floors and large floral rugs. The walls were sage green with white trim and adorned with bronze-gilded mirrors and paintings. Crystal chandeliers hung from the ceiling and there were potted ferns in every corner that Trent could see in the small lobby as well as the two rooms either side through the open archways. The room to the left had rows of dark wood chairs, presumably for a conference or maybe the wedding reception if the weather turned on them. A large fireplace stood in the room to the right with packed floor-to-ceiling bookcases.

"I can see why your friends would pick this place," Ashby said quietly as they stood and took everything in. There were people already at the front desk, so they had a moment to appreciate the decor. "Grand, but still intimate."

Trent had noticed that Ashby kept referring to Blake and Elion as 'his friends' despite knowing who they were from TV and being a fan of the band. He was probably trying to normalize them. Trent didn't blame him. He was so used to being famous, meeting celebrities didn't faze him anymore. But it was sweet to see Ashby so conscientious of being polite and not freaking out. Despite his nerves at inviting him for his own personal ramifications, he trusted that Ashby wouldn't embarrass him when he met the guys.

Which was a good thing because at that moment they were greeted with a cry of delight.

"TJ!"

Trent and Ashby both looked up to see Joey Robinson running down the central staircase, his blond curls bouncing as he sprinted toward them. Ashby would know him by his previous name, Joey Sullivan, as that was still his stage name. Joey's husband, Gabe Robinson, came down the steps at a slower pace, smiling at Joey's enthusiasm.

For someone so petit, Joey still packed quite a punch, barreling into Trent at top speed. "It's so great to see you!" he cried. He squeezed him tight, then turned to Ashby.

And paused.

Trent shifted on his feet as Gabe joined them. Tall, dark, handsome, and always the more sensible of the two, he didn't hesitate to stick his hand out for Trent and then Ashby to shake. "Good to see you again," he said convivially. It was easy to see he was the firefighter working with the community and that Joey was the excitable actor.

But Trent knew full well he had only given Blake and Elion Ashby's name. He hadn't explained Ashby was a guy.

"Hi," Joey said, evidently finding his voice. "Are you…here with Trent?"

Ashby had obviously picked up on the slight atmosphere, but unsurprisingly to Trent, he just gave them one of his big, gorgeous smiles. "I am," he said as Joey finally got his wits back and shook his hand too. "Ashby Wilcott. I'm just thrilled to be here."

"Sorry," Gabe said, shaking his head. "I think we were just assuming you were a girl. I've not met an Ashby before. We didn't mean to be rude."

"Oh," said Ashby with a wave of his hand. "Girl, boy, what's the difference?" He chuckled.

"And you're…" said Joey. "TJ's date?"

"We're just friends," Ashby said quickly. For some reason, that made Trent feel bad. Probably because he knew that Ashby would have quite liked to be here as his actual boyfriend. "It's a bit of a complicated story, but I owed Trent a favor and making sure he wasn't at a wedding alone seemed like a great opportunity to pay him back."

"You're from England?" Gabe asked, slipping his arm around Joey's waist. Joey was still looking between Trent and Ashby with a slightly open mouth and wide eyes. He was definitely putting two and two together and getting five.

"I am," said Ashby proudly. "Well, lately. I spent my childhood in Singapore, but lately, I hale from London, specifically. I'm on holiday at Trent's dad's resort and we made friends. He's been teaching me to snowboard."

That got Gabe off on a snow sports tangent. He and Joey had been skiing over Christmas and being the natural athlete he was, he'd loved it. But Joey's attention was still on Ashby, alight with curiosity.

Trent caught Ashby's eye. "I'm just going to go check us in," he said.

He hoped Ashby wouldn't mind talking to his friends for a minute, but the front desk was now clear. Trent didn't want to stand here getting grilled for hours, even if it was by his best friends. He'd rather they escaped to their room for a bit and minimized awkward questions. Because, yes, they were here as friends. But Joey was absolutely going to want to get to the bottom of why Trent had pretended to be Ashby's boyfriend in the first place, and Trent didn't have a good enough answer.

Which was probably exactly why Joey peeled off and joined Trent as he walked toward the desk. Trent glanced back at Ashby standing with Gabe and all their luggage. "I'm just getting the room key, little man," he said to Joey, using his old nickname for Below Zero's youngest member.

"So, you're sharing a room," Joey prompted, his eyes twinkling.

Trent sighed. "There are only so many rooms in this place," he said, trying not to get irritable. It wasn't a usual hotel, after all. Even though it was a big manor house, there still weren't enough rooms for them to go side by side. "We had to share, but it's a double. It's fine."

The truth was, even with two beds in the room, Trent was slightly nervous. It was a lot to share a space with someone for one night, let alone two. But he was sure he and Ashby would survive.

Trent could feel Joey grinning up at him as they approached the desk. "What?" Trent all but snapped.

"Nothing," Joey said in a singsong voice.

Trent was aware of his friend continuing to watch him as he checked in and gave the girl behind the desk his card.

Trent ignored him until he had his and Ashby's keycards in hand. Then he moved halfway between the desk and where Gabe and Ashby were standing.

"Seriously, dude," Trent growled. "Don't make this weird. I know he likes me, but I'm not bi, am I? So don't make him uncomfortable. He's been a great friend to me."

Rather than look sheepish, Joey just narrowed his eyes at Trent. Being with Gabe had done wonders for his confidence. Ordinarily, Trent would argue that was a very good thing. But not when he was keenly aware he was about to get that grilling he'd been trying to avoid anyway.

"He likes you," Joey said. "And you've brought him to one of your best friends' wedding as a plus one...and you're telling me you don't feel even a teeny tiny bit curious if there's something there?"

Trent glanced at Ashby who was happily talking to Gabe, fluttering his hands about. Trent bit his lip. Joey gasped.

He grabbed Trent by the lapel of his leather jacket and yanked him closer. "You *do* like him," he hissed as excitedly as he could while keeping his voice down.

Trent glowered and batted Joey's hands away. "Yes, he's a nice guy," he told him firmly. "Really nice. But I'm not into dudes. It's nothing personal."

Joey gave him an infuriatingly smug smile. "I just think you shouldn't shut yourself off to any possibilities, that's all." He patted Trent's arm, then skipped back toward his husband.

Trent tried not to grind his teeth. When Ashby glanced over to him as he approached, he forced himself to smile. "I've got our keys," he said, holding them up. "Shall we go freshen up?"

"Absolutely," Ashby said. He wheeled Trent's carryon over to him before taking the handle of his own. "Flying leaves you feeling so *urgh*, doesn't it?" he said to Gabe and Joey who both frowned and nodded in complete agreement. "Gabe was saying they were planning on meeting for dinner with some of your other friends," Ashby said, raising his eyes at Trent.

"Levi and Raiden are here," Gabe explained. "I think Levi and I were going to entertain Elion in his room while Joey met with Rai and Blake." He nudged Joey affectionately. "Getting the band back together and all that."

"Why don't you two join us?" Joey asked. "Respectively, I mean."

Trent paused, glancing at Ashby. He really wasn't sure about leaving him at the mercy of his overenthusiastic friends. "We'll let you know," he said quickly, not wanting to hurt anyone's feelings. He'd see how Ashby felt first. "For now, we'll make ourselves more human, then drop you a message."

"Good plan," said Ashby, still smiling. He turned to Trent's friends. "It was lovely to meet you," he said, betraying his first small hint of being star-struck as he glanced at Joey. "See you soon."

His sweet and earnest nature managed to thaw out Trent's irritability somewhat as they made their way up the stairs. It was hard to be pissed off when he was near such a joyous soul.

"It looked like you and Gabe got along," Trent commented.

Ashby nodded. "He seems a very nice chap. I'd be happy to spend the evening with him and the other boyfriends if you wanted to meet with your band friends." Ashby gave him a genuine smile. "It must be so nice for you to be back together after the rough time you've had."

Trent frowned slightly as they walked along the corridor to their room on the third floor. The wooden boards creaked beneath their feet. "I don't want to abandon you," he said.

But Ashby shook his head. "You wouldn't be. Besides, it's

a sort of stag do thing, isn't it? Um, bachelor party, I mean. The grooms can't see each other the night before, so it's the friends' job to entertain them."

Trent nibbled his lip as they approached their room at the end of the corridor. They must have taken the very last reservation. He *was* going to be spending the whole morning with Blake and the other groomsmen tomorrow. It would be good for Ashby to have already gotten to know some other people so he wouldn't be lonely.

He smiled at Ashby and swiped the key. "Yeah, that could be fun," he admitted. "So long as you don't mind?"

Ashby laughed. "What's the worst that could happen?" he asked as the door swung inwards.

They both paused.

There was only one bed.

CHAPTER
Seventeen

ASHBY

IT WAS FINE. THIS WAS FINE.

At least, that was what Ashby kept telling himself.

Trent had shrugged the whole 'only one bed' thing off and immediately said he was fine taking the sofa. Ashby protested that this was *Trent's* friends' wedding and Ashby should be the one put out. But Trent wouldn't hear of it. Literally. He took himself into the shower, then said he was going to go meet Joey and the others as planned.

Before he left though, he gave Ashby his phone and allowed him to copy not only Gabe's but Levi's and Elion's numbers into his own phone so he could arrange where to meet. Trent was still obviously freaked out over the bed thing, but Ashby thought it was extremely kind and trusting of him to do that.

Gordon would certainly have never handed over his unlocked phone, despite the number of times he had snooped through Ashby's without permission. Ashby was happy that although Trent didn't want to share a bed with him, he did at least trust him with whatever personal information was on his phone. Not that Ashby snooped. He gave it back as soon as he had Gabe and the others' numbers.

The boyfriends didn't want to meet until another hour or so as Elion was still fretting over last minute wedding details. Gabe messaged Ashby privately and said they were crashing Elion's room at seven o'clock regardless. At some point, Gabe argued, Elion would need to be saved from himself. Being included in these plans made Ashby feel included already despite hardly knowing these people. It gave him a warm feeling inside.

Which was lucky, because he felt slightly sick every time he thought of Trent's face upon seeing the bed they were supposed to share. He couldn't have made it clearer that being anywhere near Ashby in a sexual way was repulsive to him. Ashby tried not to blame him. But he couldn't help being hurt just a little.

Trent was straight, though. Ashby had to be fair. If Ashby was more masculine, his gayness might be easier to ignore. He didn't exactly make it easy on Trent. So he would do everything he could to make him comfortable during the wedding. Then they could go back to having separate rooms when they returned to Wyoming. He hoped they could still continue being friends, at least.

It meant Ashby had to work very hard at suppressing any excitement he'd felt at sharing a room. It was tantalizing for him to be this close to Trent. Not because he was some age-old teenage crush of Ashby's, but because he was a real-life interest. Ashby saw Trent for who he was now, not who he was to him then. But seeing as Trent was obviously finding the situation difficult, Ashby would be a proper dickhead to take advantage of it in any way, so he went for a walk around the grounds while Trent showered and changed.

There were other people milling about the venue when he

went outside, presumably also here for the wedding. Ashby didn't recognize any of them, and they didn't know him either, so he was left in peace to stroll across the veranda and amble down toward the recently decorated gazebo, ready for tomorrow's ceremony.

White chairs stood on the grass in neat rows facing the gazebo's entrance. Pink and purple flowers had been arranged in an archway at the front opening as well as on the chairs standing alongside the walkway. Petals were strewn on the steps and either side of the aisle, and white gauze curtains were pulled and tied either side of the gazebo's archways. Green trees swayed behind the structure, creating a picturesque image.

Ashby sighed. He *loved* weddings. Two people, committing to love and support one another, to spend the rest of their lives together, forsaking all others. It was beautiful. He always cried, regardless of how well he knew the couple in question.

He had only been to one or two of his own friends' weddings. Mostly he'd attended ceremonies or receptions for his parents' acquaintances or even their own kids. This would be his first official same-sex wedding. He looked up at the gorgeous flowers curving over the top of the gazebo entrance and couldn't help but be filled with hope. Even a decade ago, this wouldn't have been possible for him. Not in the same way it was now. Love was love and having that now recognized by law made him swell with pride.

Before he could get weepy, he shook himself and headed back inside. Trent would have had plenty of time to get himself together by now. Sure enough, Ashby returned to an empty room.

He showered quickly and picked out a simple, conservative outfit of jeans and a T-shirt. He wasn't sure how these other guys would receive him, so best to play it safe. He did put a little basic makeup on, however, just to even out his complexion.

At five past seven he stood outside the door that was allegedly Elion's and bit his lower lip. He had no reason to be nervous. He was very good at socializing, after all. These weren't even the very famous members of Trent's friendship group. But they were still part of Trent's inner circle and Ashby was keen to have them like him.

He smoothed down his T-shirt and took a steadying breath. Then he raised his hand and after a beat, knocked twice.

"Come in!" a chorus of voices rang out.

Ashby swallowed his nerves, mustered up a smile and opened the door that had evidently been left off the latch.

He was greeted by three guys, two of whom he recognized and one he'd never seen before. Muscular Gabe with his dark brown hair was currently hugging a laptop to his chest by the double bed. An even bigger blond guy Ashby didn't know was standing next to him, holding his hands out at a pouting Elion Rodriguez, who looked like he was trying to grab the laptop.

Elion was even more gorgeous than he was on TV, Ashby realized with a jolt, with light brown skin and big brown eyes. The hot pink tips of his dark hair looked to have been freshly dyed. His frame was slender but still defined with muscle in a way Ashby never seemed to manage. As pretty as he was, it was hard to take him seriously while he was stamping his foot and waving his hands in front of him.

"Gabe!" he whined, making the word last several seconds just like a child having a temper tantrum. "I need it back! I need to double-check the table plans and the music for the pre-drinks reception and make sure I transferred the money for the florist. *Gabe!* Levi, tell him!"

The big guy, Levi, chuckled and pulled Elion into a hug.

"It's all done and you *know* it." He let Elion go and squeezed his shoulder. "You and Joey are enough to put anyone off weddings, jeeze. Let's have some fun already."

Gabe put the laptop under the pillows on the double bed occupying half the room and held up his finger in warning. "No more work, guys," he said. "It's time to party. On which note, I'd like you to meet someone." He walked over to Ashby, smiling and extending out his arm. "This here's Ashby Wilcott, Trent's friend."

That got Elion's attention, judging from the slack look that suddenly occupied his face. "But…" he said, "Ashby's a girl. I've got…I thought…"

He made to go get his laptop, but Levi caught his hip and steered him away to the dresser. "Nuh uh," he said, handing him a Champagne flute. "Fun, now, remember?"

Ashby nibbled on his lip as Gabe ushered him into the room. It was much like his and Trent's, with cream walls, wooden floors with a large floral rug under the bed and a large bronze-gilded mirror on the wall. Ashby and Trent's had an impressive writing desk that was missing from this room, though. Ashby had been admiring it before he came over. It looked like the kind of place you'd sit and write legal documents. Or love letters.

It was a tiny bit crowded with the four of them standing between the bed and the couch, but Ashby soon also had a cold glass of bubbly pressed into his hand which soothed his nerves somewhat.

"Cheers," Levi said, holding up his drink and eyeballing Elion, who sighed and offered him a weak smile.

"All right," he grumbled. His shoulders relaxed a little and he clinked glasses with everyone. "Cheers. Thank you for looking after me."

"Aren't your bridesmaids coming too?" Gabe asked, glancing at the door. "Sorry, *groomsbitches.*"

Elion grinned and nodded. "Devon drove Jodi out to get more booze without Jodi and Blake's mom finding out." He shook his head. "In-laws, man." But he smiled and sank down on the couch, taking a gulp of his drink. As much as he rolled his eyes discussing Blake's mom, Ashby got the impression he was so hyper about the wedding he was willing to forgive his future mother-in-law's ways. "So it's just us husbands and fiancés and boyfriends for now – oh my!" he said bouncing up and down. "So, when does the stripper get here?"

"No stripper," Gabe said firmly from Elion's side. "This is a *mini*-bachelor party. You still need to make it down the aisle tomorrow."

"Partner," Levi corrected belatedly.

The blond guy was sitting on the edge of the bed next to Ashby. He glanced Ashby's way. Levi was quite scary when his face was in repose. Ashby got a vague military vibe from the way he held himself. But then he smiled and his blue eyes dazzled.

"Not that there's anything wrong with being boyfriends," he said, addressing Ashby. "Raiden and I just aren't keen on the term ourselves."

Ashby blinked and realized all three of them were looking at him. "Oh, no," he said quickly, spluttering on his Champagne. Then he laughed before his panic could make him sweat. "Trent and I are just friends. We only met this week," he added with a nervous giggle.

Levi leaned back against the pillows as Elion crossed his feet underneath himself.

"Really?" Gabe said with a frown. "Sorry, Joey and I just assumed."

He stood again, fetching the bottle of fizz to top them all up. The first glass of bubbly was going down a little too easily, but Ashby was nervous and needed the Dutch courage.

Elion knocked back the rest of his drink, then held up his glass for a refresh. He too was frowning. "So," he said while Gabe played waiter. "You're *not* here as TJ's date?" He didn't sound convinced.

Ashby waved his hand and smiled despite his apprehension. "Oh no," he insisted. "We're just friends. It's a funny story, though." He skipped over the slightly rocky start and explained how Trent had offered to teach him some snowboarding, then rescued him from that creep Kiefer. "Seeing as there's going to be a bit of press coverage here, Trent and I thought it best to keep up the charade just in case Kiefer went prying. Besides, this way I don't have to spend the weekend alone hiding in my room so I didn't risk seeing him. I get to go to a lovely wedding instead!"

He grinned and took another glug of bubbly. But the three curious faces looking at him told him that he was missing something.

"Um," Ashby began. "Doesn't Trent normally make new friends?" It probably wasn't the exact question he wanted to ask. But it was the easiest and safest.

"It's not that…" Elion said slowly.

"Well, yeah," said Gabe, bobbing his head. "He normally doesn't make friends unless he, um…"

"Unless he's got his mind on fucking," drawled Levi, looking at Ashby through his golden eyelashes.

Ashby choked on his drink, slopping it down his T-shirt. "Oh, bugger," he said as he coughed. He brushed at the liquid, embarrassed. "No, no, Trent is straight. I know that."

He could feel his eyes were wide as he looked around the room, imploring them to believe him. Elion had already jumped up to grab him some tissues and Gabe leaned forward to replace the Champagne he had lost. Levi shook his head and patted Ashby's knee. His face was kind.

"I wasn't being a prick," he murmured. His manner was very intense. "I was simply stating a fact. Why? Aren't you interested?"

Ashby wasted a few seconds mopping up his T-shirt. It was already almost dried. "Trent's *straight*," he said again for emphasis.

Elion waved his hands, risking spilling his own drink. "But what if he weren't?" He regarded Ashby for a moment as he struggled for words. He desperately didn't want to incriminate himself. But Elion hopped up and nestled himself between Ashby and Levi, putting his arm around Ashby's shoulders. "I thought Blake was straight, too," he said warmly. "Levi was so convinced Raiden was straight Rai had to practically jump him before he would take him seriously."

"Hey," Levi growled, nudging Elion's leg with his foot. But his smile showed he wasn't really offended.

"My point is," Elion continued, "have you told him how you feel?"

"What makes you think I feel something for him beyond friendship?" Ashby stammered. "Can't we just be friends? I know he's deliriously hot and talented and successful, but, well, I just got out of a long-term relationship, actually, and I'm quite happy being friends."

He was met with three sets of raised eyebrows.

Ashby dropped his shoulders and let his head fall back as he cried out in frustration. Fine. If these almost-strangers wanted to play at being his therapist, so be it.

"All *right*," he conceded. "I've told him numerous times that I think he's gorgeous and one night I actually invited him into my room. But he politely declined and I'm grateful we're still friends after all that."

Elion bounced on the bed and squeezed his shoulder. "You hit on him and he *still* invited you to a wedding?"

"Uhh," Ashby said. "Look, please don't read too much into it." *Please don't get my hopes up.*

Gabe smiled sympathetically at Ashby. "Sorry," he said, his gaze flicking to the other two on the bed. "It's just, well, Joey and I must have mistaken your body language earlier. You seemed very coupley."

"I've known TJ for almost three years now," Elion said. He still had his arm around Ashby's back. It was comforting. "And Levi's right. He doesn't really *make* new guy friends. Not one he would bring to a wedding if there wasn't something romantic lurking there. I'm sure of it."

"He'd just fly solo and force everyone to drink tequila until they couldn't feel their legs anymore," Levi said dryly, then sipped his Champagne. "Ask me how I know."

"Yeah, we were putting pressure on him to bring a date to this wedding," Gabe explained. "But that was because we thought he was hiding someone special from us."

Elion squeezed Ashby's arm again and wiggled his eyebrows at him.

But Ashby shook his head. "We only met this week," he said again. "And if it weren't for the whole Kiefer business, he would have just come alone. Like you said." He toyed with the hem of his T-shirt. "I'm not special." He tried to laugh, but it came out a little sad.

Elion scoffed and looked Ashby dead in the eye. "You seem absolutely charming to me."

Gabe smiled and even blushed a little. "That accent," he said, shaking his head.

"You're a regular James Bond," Levi agreed.

It was Ashby's turn to scoff. "More like Miss Moneypenny," he said. He figured a joke might make Trent's friends less intense. And they did all laugh. But Elion still had his arm around Ashby.

"Maybe Miss Moneypenny is his type," he said gently. "TJ is helpless to a beautiful face. But…well, it's unusual for him to introduce someone to his best friends. Practically unheard of."

"Just think about it, Moneypenny," Gabe added with a wink.

A knock at the door brought the conversation to a close. Ashby didn't mind. He had a lot to think about.

He was introduced to the two bridesmaids. Blake's younger sister Jodi, who was on a baseball scholarship at university, and Devon, who used to work with Elion. Technically, Jodi was Blake's bridesmaid (or 'groomsbitch' as Jodi had dubbed them) but she didn't fancy hanging with her brother. "You know what those guys are like when they get the band back together," she said with an eyeroll.

They had returned with enough Champagne to keep all of them entertained until the early hours of the morning. They laughed and drank and listened to music while making Elion answer all sorts of invasive questions about his and Blake's sex life. Jodi stuck her fingers in her ears and squealed at some of the more salacious details.

By the time Ashby headed back to his room, his stomach and face ached from so much laughing. But he had successfully distracted himself from overthinking everything the guys had said to him. Until now.

Could he really have a shot with Trent?

He eased the door open into their darkened room as quietly as he could. But he was immediately disappointed to see that Trent had made a bed on the sofa, just like he had said he would. He was also fast asleep. So much for a mutual drunken fumble like Ashby had fantasized many times about, inhibitions thrown to the wind.

Ashby shook his head. It was probably for the best. He

was dreaming if he let those guys convince him there was anything romantic going on between them. Better not to raise his hopes up again.

It was a while before he got to sleep, knowing Trent was so close by.

Eighteen

TRENT

TRENT IMPRESSED HIMSELF BY MANAGING TO DEFLECT JOEY'S probing questions for most of the night before the wedding. Sure, Joey had pulled out the puppy dog eyes several times and asked a few leading questions about Ashby. But Trent wasn't Gabe. He didn't have to give in to that sort of act to make sure he kept getting sex.

So he brushed Joey off as nicely as he could each time, usually by buying more drinks from the bar for them, Raiden and the groom-to-be, Blake. Being a fulltime dancer, Blake wasn't used to so much booze and Trent was aware he was playing with fire the night before the big day. But at the time, it seemed better than indulging Joey and his all-knowing glances.

Trent already felt enough of a dick for not reciprocating Ashby's feelings. He didn't need Joey acting like they were on the verge of true love or some shit. Yeah, Trent really liked the guy. It was strange how much his thoughts were preoccupied by Ashby. But that was just because he wasn't used to clicking with new friends.

Besides, even if he *did* feel like he could experiment with another guy, that guy couldn't be Ashby. Trent would hate to abuse his trust like that. So what if he had indulged in one… or two private sessions with his cock and his hand with Ashby in mind. It was just a weird thing, it would pass.

When Trent woke up with a mild hangover the next morning he did feel a twinge of guilt that the other guys must be feeling ten times as bad. They didn't have his stamina. But then he heard Ashby whimpering from the bed and it drew his full attention. "Heavy night?" Trent asked, sitting up and grinning over at Ashby curled up in bed.

"I can't even blame the altitude this time," Ashby cried, covering his face. He was cute when he got all dramatic.

Trent chuckled and threw off his blankets, heading for the phone. He realized belatedly that he was only wearing his boxer-briefs. But Ashby had seen most of it before in the sauna, and Trent had *definitely* seen more of Ashby at the pool. So he dismissed any inhibitions he might have had.

"Yeah," he said once the operator picked up. "Could I order some room service?"

He felt Ashby watching him as he ordered half the menu. His pale pink mouth was hanging slightly open and he glanced away every time Trent looked in his direction. It was getting kind of tense, so the next time Trent caught his eye, he winked, hoping to turn the mood silly. As he hoped, Ashby grinned and rolled his eyes, like it was no big deal.

While they waited for their food, Trent jumped in the shower. He was going to be getting ready in Blake's room with Joey and Raiden, so Ashby would have plenty of time to get ready once he was gone. Trent sat in a robe as they devoured pastries and fruit and pancakes, washing it all down with tea and coffee. Ashby seemed strangely touched that Trent remembered he didn't drink coffee, but it was just manners.

Ashby chatted away about his night before, recounting

several funny stories. It made Trent pleased to think of him getting along with his friends. From the sounds of it, those guys hadn't given him the same grilling Joey had tried to give Trent. He was glad. He didn't want Ashby feeling awkward.

"So, I'll see you soon," he said as he paused at their door. "You okay heading down alone?"

Ashby gave him a beaming smile. "Oh, no. I'm meeting Gabe and the others first. They're being so kind in looking after me."

Trent winked and touched Ashby's elbow through his robe. "They probably just like you, man. You're an easy guy to like."

Ashby blinked owlishly at him and swallowed, his Adam's apple bobbing.

Trent realized his words could be seen as maybe a little misleading. But only if he got awkward. So he grinned and shrugged. "Bet you I look the prettiest when we get down there," he said.

Ashby scoffed, all tension gone. "I think not, sir," he said, affronted. "I'll be so pretty no one will even notice the grooms."

"Is that so?" Trent asked, arching an eyebrow. "Okay, loser buys the other a drink."

"Who'll decide?" Ashby asked impishly.

"We'll take a vote," Trent promised.

It was the natural point at which to break off the conversation and head out the door. But a wild impulse took over Trent.

He wanted to lean over and kiss Ashby on the cheek.

Nothing ravishing. It just struck him as the obvious way to say goodbye. Instead, he cleared his throat and reached for the door, pulling it open. "I'll, um, catch you down there, then," he grunted.

He was out the door before he could gauge if Ashby had

noticed him being so fucking weird. What the hell? He was taking advantage of Ashby's crush and it needed to stop.

He muttered to himself the whole way to Blake's room. He was a piece of shit friend who needed to keep his cock in check. He was too old to be a slave to his fucking hormones.

Blake's room was a riot as soon as Trent stepped inside. Blake's mom was already there, a slim, perfectly polished woman who was determined to inflict her beauty standards on everyone in the room. She was dressed head to toe in lavender and wore an enormous flowered hat on her blonde hair, even though the ceremony wasn't due to start for another two hours. Wherever she moved, it became a risk to the eyes and throats of whoever was next to her.

As soon as Trent closed the door, Mrs. Jackson bustled over. Joey ducked to avoid the killer hat as he fussed with his cravat.

"TJ, there you are," she cried breathlessly, like he was late. He was actually a few minutes early. "Quick, here's your suit. We haven't got much time."

Trent met Blake's gaze before Blake looked at the ceiling and muttered something under his breath.

As Trent moved his way further into the room, he greeted Joey and Raiden. The groomsbitches, Jodi and Devon, were getting ready in Devon's room. Trent wouldn't have been surprised if Jodi had locked the door on her mom so they could get some peace. Blake had no such luck. His mom was already attacking the blond hair he'd inherited from her with several different products.

"How do you feel about using straighteners, dear?" she asked.

"Mom," he growled.

But she merely tutted. "There won't be just our usual camera crew today, hon," she said, like this was normal.

"There are the people from Us Weekly and several blogs. You have to impress them!"

He batted her hand away but managed to accompany the action with a smile. "The only person I want to impress is Elion," he said patiently.

His mom just hummed and started rolling a fruity-scented wax paste between her fingers.

Trent sighed and kicked off his sneakers. He'd been trying to forget that there would be camera crews capturing the whole ceremony on film. Blake had promised them they would be shooed away after the first dance, but knowing Blake's mom, Trent wouldn't be surprised if they stuck around until the bitter end, invited or not.

He was stuck wondering how much attention he should pay to Ashby. They were friends, and he was Trent's plus one, so he wasn't going to ignore him. But did he want to make it obvious to anyone watching that they were supposed to be more?

That was how Elion and Blake had gotten together, after all. Faking it for the cameras.

And now they were getting married.

No, no. Ashby was not Elion. Trent was not Blake. He would just be friendly, and if that shithead Kiefer saw and wasn't convinced, Trent could calmly explain that Ashby was wary of public displays of affection. Not that it was any of Kiefer's business. Ashby should just be able to say no because he wasn't interested, not because he wasn't available. Trent felt he wouldn't need much prompting to explain that properly to Kiefer.

"So. How's your not-boyfriend this morning?"

Trent looked over to see Raiden had slunk up next to him while he fiddled with his cufflinks. He looked from his wrists back over at Trent with an expression of pure innocence. He was almost as tall as Trent but about half the size. He knew full well that Trent could beat the crap out of him if he felt like it.

"If you're talking about Ashby," Trent said curtly, "he was a little worse for wear. He's not a fucking ox like your partner. They could have encouraged him to drink some water."

Raiden's dark eyebrows rose under the black bangs that swept across his forehead. "Maybe he needed his big, bad not-boyfriend to come look after him?"

He had a devilish look in his eyes. Trent's stomach dropped and he tried not to feel sick. He was glad there was music playing from a laptop, so at least the others couldn't hear. "Did…did Ashby say I was his boyfriend?" he asked.

Raiden grinned, finally sorting his first cufflink, then moving to the second one. "No, the opposite apparently. Levi said he was a great guy who kept defending you and your straightness."

Trent's panic lessened. What had he really been worrying about? That Ashby was lying, pretending there was something more about them? Or that he was so heartbroken he had made their fake relationship sound real to indulge himself for a minute?

Trent ground his teeth. "Why are you calling him my boyfriend then?" he asked, going back to his shirt buttons.

"I said not-boyfriend," Raiden corrected. "Wasn't that who Joey was trying to talk to you about last night, too?"

Damn. Trent had hoped he'd kept that from the others. "We're just friends," he said, sick of repeating himself. "Just leave it."

Raiden cocked an eyebrow. "Like you 'left it' with Levi and me?"

He had a point. Trent had sensed that eye fucking from a mile off. "That was different," he pointed out. He had just been helping Raiden to help himself. He and Levi had already slept together a couple of time by then. It wasn't like that with Ashby.

But Raiden's expression turned sincere. He leaned in and looked at Trent with those beautiful dark eyes of his. "Take it from someone who knows," he murmured. "It's okay to take a chance. Life's too short to live in a box."

Before Trent could say anything, Raiden moved aside and the conversation turned to plans for the rest of the day. Elion had taken care of most of it, but Blake was starting to show signs of nerves. He had to stand up and go through with everything in front of everyone. Worse, in front of the cameras.

Trent was reminded that this day wasn't about him and Ashby. It was about Blake and Elion.

The first chance he got, he pulled Blake to one side. "Are you okay, man?" he asked. Someone had to ask. Getting married was a big fucking deal. "You still want to go through with this?"

Blake looked startled. "Oh, sure," he said a little breathlessly. "No, I'm not having second thoughts," he added earnestly. "I just want this to be absolutely perfect for Elion."

Trent smiled, relieved, then wrapped his arms around his friend. "It's going to be fucking awesome," he promised.

Blake nodded into his neck, then pulled back to look at him and the other guys. His mom was hovering, admiring her handiwork. "Let's do this," Blake said.

CHAPTER
Nineteen
TRENT

Trent lost the bet.

As soon as he looked out into the crowd of people and saw Ashby seated with Gabe and Levi, he had no doubt.

Ashby looked fucking gorgeous.

His suit was a shade of grey that suited his teal eyes and blond hair perfectly. Even more striking was the perfect shade of pink on his tie that he'd picked to match the wedding's color scheme immaculately. Even from where they were standing by the gazebo, Trent could see he had done some kind of clever, elaborate knot on the tie. His thick hair was tousled just right and he was smiling and chatting with whoever turned his way. He was like a people magnet, charming men and women alike.

Trent's chest tightened. If he wanted, Ashby could go back to the room of anyone who was interested. He didn't owe Trent anything. He was beautiful and single and any one of these guys here today would be lucky to get to know him better.

Trent tried telling himself that would be a bad idea on camera, just in case their little ruse was blown open. But who was he kidding? He just didn't like the idea of someone taking Ashby away from him.

What kind of asshole was he? He didn't want Ashby, but no one else could have him?

It's okay to take a chance.

Raiden's words rolled around in his head all throughout the ceremony. But Trent wasn't just taking a chance for himself. He would be playing with Ashby's heart. He couldn't do that to him.

Like Blake hadn't wanted to hurt Elion? How did Trent know this wasn't the start of a real relationship that he was too afraid to take the first step with? What if he *liked* being with Ashby? They were already friends despite the odds. What if the physical intimacy was just as good? Not for the first time Trent reminded himself that he had done almost everything he could imagine with the various women he had been with. Why wouldn't he find pleasure from Ashby's touch?

He shivered and turned back to Blake and Elion taking their vows. Elion was a grinning, weeping mess who kept making the audience laugh with his comedic timing on the vows. When the time came to ask if anyone objected to the union, he glowered to the audience earning his biggest laugh yet. Trent noticed Blake's homophobic dad was the only one scowling.

Trent bit his lip. Was he so afraid of his sexuality he was going to let an amazing guy like Ashby pass him by? Did that make him just as bad as Mr. Jackson?

The remainder of the ceremony passed in something of a blur, as did the rest of the afternoon. Everyone cheered as Blake and Elion were declared husbands. The photographer took a million pictures of the wedding party under Mrs. Jackson's strict supervision and with the reporters roaming like buzzards. Trent eyed them suspiciously. He was rather proud of himself for not punching a single one of them.

Elion's mom, Mrs. Rodriguez, spent the entire shoot moving effortlessly between all the guests making sure none of them went a single minute without a full glass or tray of canapés within reach. "My beautiful boy," she kept declaring, wiping her eyes and drinking her own fair share of Champagne.

The food was very good, served to half a dozen tables standing on the grass by the colonial house. The weather was just right. Warm but not so hot or sunny as to make them uncomfortable. Trent was very aware of sitting next to Ashby the whole time. But where Trent became tongue-tied, as was usual when he had too much on his mind, Ashby held court, regaling the other guests they were seated alongside with tales of growing up in Singapore and England. Everyone commented on how lovely his accent was. Trent felt proud of him.

He reached over at one point, when Ashby was catching his breath and eating something for once, and squeezed his knee. Ashby looked at him with curiosity. "I'm glad you're here," Trent murmured, letting go of his leg. He meant it.

One of Blake's dance friends, Nessa, kept her eyes on Trent during dinner with obvious interest. Most people in attendance knew who he was but had the class not to approach him or act inappropriately when faced with a movie star. But Nessa, who was a very beautiful girl, was giving out just enough subtle body language to let Trent know the interest was there, if he were so inclined.

She was sitting with another guy from the dance studio who Trent couldn't remember the name of. He was an objectively handsome Black dude who was clearly intrigued by Ashby. Trent inched just a little bit closer to Ashby's seat and topped up his wine.

The speeches got off to a bumpy start with Mrs. Jackson giving a forty-five-minute slide show that was more a testimony to Blake's career than it was Blake and Elion's love. But then a slightly tipsy Mrs. Rodriguez stood and gave only a ten-minute toast, half of which was in Spanish, talking about how she knew her special boy would always find true love. Blake and Elion thanked the guests and everyone who had helped the wedding come together. Then they both spoke about each other. They held hands and said a few words about how they were the luckiest guys alive.

That was when Trent realized Ashby was quietly weeping.

Alarmed, Trent leaned over. "Are you okay?" he whispered.

Ashby grinned and hastily dabbed his eyes. This close, he looked like he might be wearing a shimmer on his eyelids and lips. That did strange things to Trent's heart. "Sorry, yes," he whispered back sheepishly and laughed. "I just love weddings. They look so *happy.*"

Trent nodded. They were.

Joey's best man speech was full of hilarious anecdotes about his best friend. But he ended on how Blake had courageously come out to the whole world on stage at the Nickelodeon awards, essentially declaring his love for Elion in the process. At that, Ashby leaned over to Trent.

"That moment changed my life," he admitted in little more than a rasp. "It made me brave."

Trent regarded Ashby. "You're always brave," he said automatically. He was. He was fearless.

Ashby blushed and looked back toward the front table.

As they moved on to the evening wedding reception, a live band set up in the gazebo and a light-up disco dance floor was laid on the grass. Servers moved with ease offering a never-ending supply of bubbly. But as the evening wore on, Trent needed something a little stronger.

Was he really going to do this? Was he going to see if Ashby wanted to put that one and only bed they conveniently had to good use?

He needed whiskey.

Blake and his crew were mesmerizing the crowd on the dance floor with their effortless skill. Ashby was in Elion and Joey's attentive care. So it was easy to slip away and head inside to the deserted hotel bar.

Almost deserted.

A lone figure sat at the bar, nursing a whiskey just like Trent was planning on getting. Even from behind, he looked like a work of goddamned art.

"Fuck me sideways 'til Sunday," Trent growled. It gave the guy just enough warning to turn as Trent ran and grabbed him, hugging him so hard he lifted him from his seat as he burst out laughing. "Reyse fucking Hickson, you absolute *hero.*"

The final member of Below Zero hugged him back just as fiercely. "Holy shit, TJ, is it good to see you."

"Dude," Trent enthused. He lifted Reyse up for a few seconds longer, his feet dangling while he laughed, then dropped him back down. "I didn't think you were going to make it!"

Reyse shook his head. "Me neither," he said. "But I'll never forgive myself for missing Joey's big day, so I pulled some strings to make Blake's."

He was ethereally beautiful in a boyish, charming way. Strong jaw, blond, highlighted hair and huge baby-blue eyes that could make whole civilizations drop to their knees. His frame was slim and he stood a few inches shorter than Trent. But he was built like a thoroughbred racehorse with all the muscles that made teenage girls and their mothers wail equally in delight. He was every kind of threat. Gorgeous in both masculine and feminine ways, talented at singing, dancing *and* acting, and a thoroughly nice guy to boot.

He and Trent had always been close in the band. It was therefore not surprising that Trent was the most forgiving of Reyse's phenomenally successful solo career, or the fact that the band's label dropped them to specifically focus on Reyse alone. Trent was happy for him. He deserved it all.

It didn't mean he hadn't missed him like crazy.

"Fuck, how long's it been?" he asked while looking him over. "The guys are going to lose their shit, man."

"Too long," said Reyse. He sounded weary. He turned to the barman who was doing a very good job not swallowing his own tongue at the sight of TJ Charles and Reyse Hickson alone with him in his bar. "Another two, my man," Reyse said with effortless charm, raising his tumbler to him. The guy nodded and poured the drinks while Reyse and Trent sat down on the bar stools.

"You in town just for tonight?" Trent asked.

Reyse sighed. "Sadly. I couldn't even make the ceremony. I hope the guys understand."

"Shit, yeah," Trent said without doubt.

"They all here?"

Trent scoffed and sighed. "I think you missed Raiden. He and his partner are, um, enthusiastic when it comes to public settings." They were undoubtedly already fucking in a closet somewhere. Or on their balcony. Or in their bathtub. Trent had heard it all from Rai.

"Damn," said Reyse with a sigh. "I really thought…it's been three years since we've all been in the same room, you know?"

"Have breakfast with us tomorrow," Trent said easily.

Reyse shook his head. "I'm heading back to the airport in two hours," he said, checking his hundred-thousand-dollar watch. He sounded so tired. But then he grinned and finished off his drink so he could start the next one with Trent. "So, give me the headlines, bro! Congrats on The Fixer, by the way. Joey said you've got a date with you?"

The way his words edged up in tone at the end told Trent that Joey had filled Reyse in with all the juicy gossip.

But rather than get angry and deny it, something in Trent broke. This was *Reyse.* "We said we'd come here as friends," said, running his finger around the whiskey tumbler, making it sing.

"But?" Reyse prompted.

"But…" Trent said. Fuck it. It was time to let the truth out. "He likes me and…I think I might like him."

Reyse nodded. "But you're scared?" He didn't even pause in his stride at the idea of Trent potentially dating a guy.

Trent nodded miserably. "Not like I don't wanna be queer," he clarified with a frown. "But he's too important to take the chance on breaking his heart. Because I don't know what I want."

Reyse studied him for a minute. Then, checking the bartender was a respectful distance away, he leaned in and put his lips close to Trent's ear.

"Do you want to run your hands over his skin?" he whispered, his words hot and sultry. "Do you want to kiss him and make him feel *so good?* Do you want to hold him and protect him and make him come so goddamn hard he screams your name?"

Trent didn't realize he was shaking until Reyse pulled away. Trent could feel his cock straining in his pants. He took a shaky breath, then a big gulp of whiskey. "Okay," he rasped. "When you put it like that…"

Reyse smiled kindly, then squeezed Trent's leg briefly. "Don't be me," he said. Trent caught the melancholy in his tone all of a sudden, no doubt despite Reyse's best efforts to keep it out. "Don't watch your life pass you by. Love is so fucking precious. If he makes your heart sing, don't let the 'what ifs' paralyze you. Besides," he added, lightening his mood. "If you really are queer, that makes a full Below Zero set."

Trent glanced up immediately, but the bartender was on his phone, too far away to hear their soft voices over the noise of the party through the doors outside. Reyse was too sensible to risk being overheard.

"I don't want to sound dramatic," Reyse said after downing his drink. "But…do it for me. One of us should have the choice."

It was like the floodgates opened in Trent's heart. He had permission. He would just *ask* Ashby if this was what he wanted, then go for it. If every couple agonized over what might happen down the line before they'd even tried, no one would ever get together.

"Okay," he said shakily.

He followed Reyse's example and knocked back the last of his drink, the alcohol thrumming nicely in his system. But this wasn't like Joey and Gabe's wedding, where he'd gotten blackout drunk. He still had his wits about him. His cock was still good to go.

"You coming out?" he asked.

Reyse shook his head. "You have your moment," he said. "Go get your man. I'll make an entrance in a minute."

To someone else, that might have sounded horrendously indulgent. But Trent knew it was extremely thoughtful on his friend's part. "Thanks, man," he said, stepping in for one last embrace. "It was so fucking good to see you."

"You too," Reyse said.

The party was in full swing. Trent felt bad as he approached Ashby, knowing he was going to ask him to leave. But luckily, he was lingering by the dance floor, alone. This was Trent's chance. He was sick of running away.

The dark of the night went some way to masking Trent as he slipped his hand lightly over Ashby's waist. He looked over at him, startled. "Hi," Ashby said, almost framing it like a question.

Trent was trembling again, this time with nerves. But he thought of Reyse's provocative words and found his resolve. "Hi," he said back. "Um, do you maybe want to call it a night?"

Ashby blinked several times. "Uh, sure," he said. "Do you want to say goodbye to people?"

That would blow Trent's confidence for sure. He shook his head. "We'll see them at breakfast."

Ashby nodded. "Okay," he said. He offered Trent a shaky smile, then reached down to take his hand, entwining their fingers together. It felt so good Trent's knees almost buckled. "Lead the way."

Trent kept Ashby close to him as they navigated the crowd, not making eye contact with anyone. They didn't meet a soul as they went through the front door of the manor house and up the stairs to the third floor.

"Um," said Ashby as they approached their room. He was spinning his card key between his long fingers. "Did you – uh – want to come in?" His English accent got more pronounced when he was anxious, Trent had noticed. He was obviously trying to make a joke of the situation, inviting him into their shared room. But Trent was done fooling around.

He touched the small of Ashby's back. "I'd love to," murmured.

He could see Ashby's Adam's apple bob as he gulped. "Okay," he whispered, then turned to swipe his card and let them inside.

As soon as the door closed behind them in the dimly lit room, Ashby shrugged off his suit jacket and walked over to the full-length mirror. His hands were trembling as they attempted to undo the complicated knot he'd done for his tie. Trent removed his own jacket more slowly, then moved to stand beside Ashby.

"Here," he said softly.

Ashby turned to face him so he could loosen the silk. "Thank you," Ashby said. There was a tremble to his voice too.

Trent worked silently to free Ashby from the pink tie, then let it fall to the carpet by their feet. His hands were already hovering there anyway, so Trent rested them on Ashby's chest and rubbed the tips of his collar between finger and thumb. So far, there was nothing freaking him out about putting his hands on another man.

"Thank you for coming with me today," he said, focusing on the hollow of Ashby's throat. It looked so kissable. Would Ashby like being kissed there? "It meant a lot."

"Of course," Ashby replied with a little squeak. "That's what friends do for each other, right? They help them out when they get in a pickle. We couldn't have you flying solo. 'Going stag,' as you Yanks say."

Trent laughed, a nervous response to Ashby's own unease. But he didn't want to cause him to fret. He wanted the opposite, in fact. He frowned as Ashby's face fell and he took a step away.

"Ashby," he said. He placed his hands flat on Ashby's chest to steady him. It worked. This was the point of no return. "I...I've been thinking."

"Oh?" Ashby replied, licking his lips. Fuck, Trent wanted to kiss them even more than his throat. "That sounds like that sort of thing that requires a stiff drink to accompany it," Ashby said. It sounded like he was aiming for a light, casual tone and not really achieving it. "Thinking, I mean. Always a tricky one. I think that thinking – yes – um – stiff – sorry – would you like one as well?"

Trent couldn't think of a time he'd less wanted a drink. He bit his own lip. "I'd like…" he said, his gaze lingering on Ashby's mouth. "Uh…"

Ashby surprised him by resting his own hands on top of Trent's. The action calmed him and helped clear his thoughts. He could do this. The worst Ashby could do was reject him. Knowing him, he'd even do that with kindness. But every signal Trent was getting was that he was into this, too.

So, Trent pulled one of his hands free and cupped the side of Ashby's face, making him gasp as he gently brushed his cheek with his thumb.

"What would you like, Trent?" Ashby asked, his voice sincere as he gazed up at Trent. "What do you want?" He lifted his own hand and touched his fingertips gently to the middle of Trent's forehead where he was no doubt frowning.

He wanted more of that. More hands on more skin. Less clothes. He wanted…

"I want you," Trent whispered.

Trent watched as Ashby stilled completely. Even his breathing seemed to stop. "You want…?"

"You," Trent said, feeling his confidence growing.

He closed his eyes and decided that from now on, he would have no more hesitations. When he opened them again, he was looking directly into Ashby's teal ones, full of trust and hope.

"I know what I said…before," Trent said, thinking back to the last time Ashby had invited him in. "I know you're a guy. But someone told me to stop overthinking things."

"Oh," said Ashby shakily. "That's, um, nice. Isn't it? I guess…uh, well-"

"Ashby," Trent growled and raised an eyebrow.

Ashby tilted his head and looked back at Trent. "Uh, yes?"

"Stop overthinking," Trent said gently.

He smiled and rubbed his fingers against Ashby's collarbones through his shirt.

"Okay," Ashby said, nodding. "Okay, no more thinking. Um, does that mean I can kiss you instead?"

Relief and happiness flowed through Trent so much he thought he might actually be glowing.

"Yeah," Trent said, not allowing nerves to get the better of him. "Let's try starting there."

CHAPTER

Twenty

ASHBY

ASHBY FELT LIKE TIME HAD STOPPED ALL TOGETHER.

Trent wanted to kiss him. Was waiting for Ashby to *kiss him.*

This couldn't be happening. Ashby had promised himself no men while he was away and he *especially* shouldn't be getting involved with a straight guy.

If there was the slightest possibility Trent wasn't straight, though, Ashby was willing to be the one to find out.

Housekeeping had left a couple of lamps on by the lone bed that had seemed so ominous yesterday. It was just enough for Ashby to make out everything of Trent. His perfectly trimmed stubbled jaw. His glossy, dark hair falling to his shoulders. The lines of his sculpted muscles under his white shirt.

Ashby was still dressed aside from his jacket and tie. He was too afraid to take the plunge and kiss Trent just yet. So to ease himself in, he reached up and began gently pulling at the cravat around Trent's neck, loosening the material to expose his skin.

"There," Ashby whispered. He dropped the material to the

floor where it pooled alongside his own tie, the two pink shades almost identical. "Now we're even."

He expected Trent to laugh at him or tell him to hurry up and kiss him. Instead, he watched silently as Ashby next got to work on the buttons of Trent's waistcoat. There were only three, so he was soon slipping his hands over Trent's rock-hard shoulders, pushing the silky garment off his body and onto the carpet.

Ashby exhaled slowly. He would have thought that Trent watching him would have made him feel anxious. But that was what was so different about Trent and the likes of Gordon. Trent made him feel empowered.

That was the last time Ashby would allow himself to think about Gordon. He was the past. Ashby wasn't sure what the future might hold, but his present was standing patiently in front of him. Trent. Ashby couldn't quite believe this was really happening, but it was.

He took his time tracing his fingers over Trent's body, exploring the well-defined lines hiding beneath the cotton. Every now and again he looked up to gauge Trent's reaction. He was breathing heavily. They both were. Ashby was trembling in anticipation, his pulse loud in his ears. But although he was clearly affected, Trent didn't react other than to watch Ashby work.

"Is this okay?" Ashby asked, his voice a mere rasp.

"Yes," Trent replied.

Ashby ran his hands up Trent's flanks and over his pecs. "Have you…really never done this with a man before?"

Trent shook his head. "No."

Ashby bit his lip. His hands came to rest on Trent's biceps. "And…you're sure you want to do this with me?" Ashby thought that was lunacy. He wasn't worthy of such an honor. "You could have anyone. I'm…I'm just so…" He trailed off in embarrassment.

But at that, Trent did finally move. His hands lifted immediately to cradle both sides of Ashby's face. "You're so amazing," Trent said. "I don't know why you can't see that."

Ashby couldn't help but look into his beautiful brown eyes. "You hear a thing often enough," he said, his voice trembling, "I guess you start to believe it. Shallow. Useless. Unremarkable." He cleared his throat. He hadn't meant to say those words out loud. "Uh, you know, things like that."

"How about," Trent said slowly. He leaned in so Ashby naturally closed his eyes. The kiss didn't come on his lips, though. It landed carefully on his left eyelid. "Worldly." His right eyelid. "Kind." His right cheek. "Charming." The tip of his nose. "Beautiful." He rubbed their noses gently together in an Eskimo kiss. "And sexy as hell."

Ashby laughed nervously. He was definitely not bloody sexy. He knew he was good looking. But he couldn't agree that his slim, pale body instilled any kind of sexual desire in a red-hot man like Trent.

"Oh, you don't think so?" Trent said. There was a playful tone to his voice.

Ashby risked peeking out through his eyelashes and grimaced. "No," he said, trying not to giggle again. But he felt like maybe that was what Trent wanted.

He dropped his hands from either side of Ashby's face and used one hand to expertly push the buttons on Ashby's own waistcoat through their holes. The other hand held onto Ashby's hip. Ashby begged his heart not to explode, because it would be a *dreadful* shame to kick the bucket now and miss out on this divine experience.

Trent made short work of the vest and then started on the shirt, this time using both hands to slip the many buttons free and expose Ashby's chest. In no time he was running his hands over Ashby's flesh, along his shoulders and arms to divest him of the shirt, then down his chest.

"You don't think this is gorgeous?" Trent asked as he wrapped his fingers around either side of Ashby's ribcage. The span of his hands was so large it felt like he was holding the entirety of Ashby's torso.

"Um, no," said Ashby. If he was honest, he was certainly *feeling* pretty sexy right then. But he wanted Trent to keep on convincing him some more.

It worked like a charm. Trent smiled lazily at him before dropping his head and kissing the side of Ashby's neck. "This is very sexy," he mumbled against Ashby's skin. "I was looking at this little bit earlier." He kissed his way along to the base of Ashby's throat.

Ashby moaned and dropped his head back. "Oh my god," he moaned. "This can't be happening."

"Why?" Trent asked. He kissed back up and along Ashby's jaw. His hands were exploring Ashby's stomach, tickling his tummy and making Ashby squirm in delight.

"Because," Ashby said as he desperately struggled to remember what words were. "You said you were straight and if that were true I'm definitely not the, uh-" Trent was nibbling on his earlobe "-man to change your mind."

"Oh," Trent said into his ear, licking the shell and making Ashby's whole body tremble. "I'm going to have such fun proving to you just how wrong you really are."

Ashby whimpered. Fine. If Trent really wanted to do this, Ashby needed to stop fighting it immediately. Otherwise, heaven forbid, Trent might change his mind.

His cock was really starting to strain inside his trousers now. When Ashby was brave enough to look, he realized he wasn't the only one in a bit of a bother. The bulge between Trent's legs was getting bigger, and it wasn't a small length thickening in there from what Ashby could tell.

He was too afraid to tackle that just yet. Instead, he refocused on Trent's shirt, working his fingers to undo the buttons just like Trent had done for him. Inch by inch, he exposed endless light brown skin covered with the tattoos Ashby had seen in the sauna. Except this time, he was allowed to touch them all he wanted.

"What do they all mean?" he asked.

Trent looked down at himself. "I can tell you sometime," he said. "But not now."

"No?" Ashby squeaked. "But, um, I have lots of questions."

Trent took a step closer. There was hardly any space between them now. Their cocks were so close to brushing together. "I have a lot of questions too," Trent rumbled. He nuzzled against Ashby's neck and carded his fingers through his hair. "The first is: what do you like?"

Ashby whimpered again. "Uhh," he stammered. Nobody ever asked him what he wanted. They generally just went ahead and fucked him however they wanted, and Ashby was happy to go along with it.

"I want to make you feel so good," Trent said, his voice raspy. Ashby worried he might genuinely come in his briefs before Trent even got a chance to touch his cock. "I could guess, but I'd rather hear you talk dirty."

"F-fuck," Ashby moaned.

Trent's hands were still roaming the naked upper half of his body, his lips ghosting across Ashby's face and neck, his breath making the hairs on Ashby's skin stand to attention. His cock throbbed, begging Ashby to allow Trent near it soon, *now*.

"Ashby?" Trent asked.

Ashby gulped. "I w-want," he uttered. "For you to, um, to…"

Trent closed the distance between them, hugging Ashby close while looking in his eyes. Ashby gasped at the sudden contact of skin on burning skin. Trent clung to his hair with one hand and splayed the fingers of the other across his lower back. There was no masking their lust when their cocks were rock hard and rubbing against each other.

Trent grunted, several emotions flitting across his face. He'd never felt that sensation before, Ashby surmised. Cock rutting against cock. Ashby felt flushed with pride.

"Fuck, I want you," Trent said. There was wonder in his voice. Like he couldn't quite believe it himself. "How can I make you scream my name?"

"Oh, Christ," Ashby sobbed. "I want you to bend me over that desk and fuck me senseless."

He choked back his own surprise, holding his breath to await Trent's reaction.

Trent kissed him.

'Devoured him' might have been a more accurate description. Their lips crashed together and Trent's tongue plunged into Ashby's mouth, seeking out his tongue and demanding it dance with his. He nipped at Ashby's lips and moaned as their mouths met again and again.

Ashby wasn't sure who moved first, but suddenly he was backing up until the backs of his legs met the edge of the mahogany desk he'd been admiring before. Trent reached around and swept the writing paper, pens, room service menus and telephone off, sending it all clattering magnificently to the floor. Ashby gasped for breath between kisses, feeling like he was in danger of passing out at any second.

He never did this. He liked sex in bed, all cuddled up under the blankets. Gordon had rarely had any imagination when it came to fucking, so they'd always done it with Ashby on all fours. So long as they held each other afterwards, Ashby had always told himself it was all right.

But right now he couldn't think clearly at all. All he wanted was to be ravaged within an inch of his life.

Trent grabbed him by the hips and sat him on the desk. He looked feral as he grinned at Ashby and attacked his belt buckle. "Like this?" he rasped, pressing their foreheads together as he whipped the belt free and flung it across the room. "Is this what you want, gorgeous?"

"Jesus, fuck, yes," Ashby cried.

He scrambled at Trent's belt, but his hands were shaking too much. So Trent batted them away, stepping back to shove trousers, boxers and belt down to his ankles in one swift motion. "Fucking hell," Ashby whispered. His eyes were glued to Trent's large cock, jutting thick and proud from a nest of dark curls. The tip was cut, like Ashby had heard most Americans were, and was a darker brown than the rest of his skin. It was already glistening with precum.

"I hate to alarm you," Ashby said. Trent was yanking off his shoes and kicking away the rest of his clothes to leave him gloriously naked. He was grinning so hard he was almost laughing. His delight was infectious and Ashby giggled too. "But I really don't know if that will fit."

Trent came back to him and hugged him close, inhaling deeply. "You smell like a man," he said.

Ashby inhaled too. "So do you," he muttered, shivering. Trent smelled spicy and tangy and sweaty and fucking *delicious*.

Trent's cock was rubbing on Ashby's stomach, leaking clear beads onto his happy trail. "I've gotten this cock plenty of places it shouldn't have gone," Trent said wickedly as he held the back of Ashby's head for more scorching hot kisses. "If you want me to fuck you, I'll fuck you so sweetly you'll forget your own name."

Ashby wanted to say something clever about making Trent scream it to remind him. But all he could do was surrender to the kisses and point weakly in the direction of the bathroom.

"Wash kit," he said faintly. "Lube. Condoms. Get the things. The, uh, sex things."

Trent chuckled and laid Ashby down on the cool wood. "You brought protection?" he teased as he hovered above him.

Ashby nodded earnestly. "Always. Go. Please."

Trent laughed again, kissed him, then moved away to do as he was told.

"Don't you go anywhere now," he called over his shoulder. Ashby tore his gaze away from Trent's perfect arse and nodded.

"Promise," he said hoarsely.

Within moments, Trent was striding back out towards Ashby and the desk. His giant cock was wilting slightly, but Ashby was sure they could do something about that between them.

Trent may not have been with a guy before, but he was obviously extremely experienced, sexually speaking. He no longer had any sense of hesitation about him. He was in his element.

Once he'd placed the supplies down on the desk, he leaned over Ashby again, running his hands over his skin. "Everything okay down there, beautiful?"

Ashby could only nod as Trent unzipped his trousers and pulled them and the briefs down over Ashby's still very hard cock. He lifted his hips so Trent could yank everything down, leaving them both totally naked. Trent wasted no time in stroking Ashby's length, milking the precum from the sensitive head.

"Wow," he said reverently.

"Is it okay?" Ashby asked, lifting his head a little to see. Fuck, that was an extremely hot sight.

Trent shook his head. "It's gorgeous. Just like you."

Ashby got a fit of the giggles and dropped his head back down with a thump. "You're ridiculous," he chided fondly.

"And you're sexy as fuck," Trent asked, giving his cock a firm squeeze. "Believe me yet?"

Ashby tried his best to temper his laughter. "No. Yes. Maybe," he babbled. "Jury's out. No brain function left. Only cock. Oh *shit*, Trent."

Trent had obviously got distracted and decided to have a go at a blow job. With his hand still on the shaft, he sucked on the end of Ashby's dick like a lollipop. "Always wondered what that was like," he said, before doing it again.

Ashby gasped for air and tried not to thrust himself unashamedly down Trent's gullet. This was his first attempt at giving head, so Ashby needed to be gentle, even if he desperately wanted to be deep throated.

"So good," he stuttered. He only had a certain amount of restraint, so he couldn't help but grab fistfuls of Trent's thick locks. The hair was silky to his touch. "Holy shit, just like that."

It was so tempting to consider coming then, inside Trent's hot, wet mouth with his tongue lapping against his sensitive shaft. But they had this absolutely brilliant desk and it really would be a shame to waste it.

"Stop, stop," he stammered.

"What's wrong?" Trent asked, immediately concerned.

Ashby shook his head. "Nothing," he said earnestly. "Too good. I'll come if you keep that up."

Trent grinned mischievously and stroked Ashby's throbbing cock. "But I want you to come," he said.

Ashby groaned and wriggled. "Said you'd *fuck* me," he protested like the spoiled brat he was. "Now, Trent. I *need* you."

Trent half-climbed the desk to get on top of him. His kiss was intense. Possessive. "I need you, too," he murmured.

Ashby felt like he was vibrating as he watched Trent uncap the lube and squeeze out an impressive amount. He really did know what he was doing. He stroked at Ashby's hole while he leaned over and kissed his stomach. Ashby couldn't seem to stop mumbling and hissing anything that wasn't 'fuck' or 'oh my god.'

Trent didn't hesitate as he pushed his middle finger in. Ashby concentrated really hard on relaxing and letting him in. He didn't have time to spend ages on prep. He wanted Trent inside and fucking him as soon as humanly possible.

"Fuck, yes, that's it," Trent said, adding a second finger. Ashby had experienced guys calling him a slut or a whore at this point in the proceedings for how quickly he was able to stretch out. But Trent just appeared impressed. "See. I'll fit," he said triumphantly.

As Trent stroked his prostate, Ashby scrabbled at the desk, not finding anything to grip on to as he rutted shamelessly against Trent's fingers. "Do it, yes," he gasped. "I can take it. You need to be hard again. Do you need help? I can give you help."

Trent laughed, deep and throaty. With his fingers still inside Ashby's hole, he leaned over and kissed him on the mouth. "You're so fucking cute, I could eat you."

"Next time," Ashby promised. "Cock in arse, now. Please," he added on impishly.

He raised his legs up and grabbed his knees, exposing himself for Trent to take full advantage of. Trent took the hint, slipping his fingers out and reaching for the condom. Ashby waited as patiently as he could while Trent stroked himself hard again then rolled the condom down.

As Trent pressed his thick tip to Ashby's entrance, they both gasped. Ashby was quaking and dripping with sweat. Trent was using both hands to hold Ashby's arse cheeks apart, and he squeezed and massaged the flesh as he slowly pressed in further.

"Holy fuck, Ashby," he said. "You feel so good."

Even though it burned, Ashby had to agree. Trent felt amazing. He and Gordon hadn't had sex in several months now, much to Ashby's relief. He hadn't quite appreciated how much he'd missed it.

"Yes, that's it, fucking Christ, fill me up with that giant cock," he jabbered. He didn't care what he was saying, he just needed Trent to find his prostate again and destroy him.

Together, they managed to get Ashby to take Trent, Ashby gnashing his teeth against the burn. He wanted this so badly, he just had to remind his body of that fact. Now that he was inside, Trent cradled the back of Ashby's neck and rubbed up and down his flank.

"So good," he said over and over. "So good. That's it, almost there."

When Trent bottomed out, they both shuddered and cried out as one. "Yes, yes," Ashby blathered, nodding his head. He could feel Trent rubbing up against his sweet spot once more. "Go, ride me. Want it. Want you."

Trent was cautious to begin with. It was a strangely gentlemanly consideration. But soon the carnal lust overtook them both, and they were thrusting and pounding so hard the desk was squeaking and probably in danger of coming apart.

"Fuck, fuck, fuck," Trent yelled.

At least they only had one room next to them to worry about. Ashby hoped their neighbors were still out partying at the wedding.

He was soon beyond caring, though. His orgasm was building and lights were dancing in front of his eyes. "I'm going to…" he uttered, wrapping his hand around his cock to finish the job.

At least he tried. Trent batted him away and began to jerk him mercilessly in time to his thrusts. "Wanna watch you come, gorgeous," he said. "Come for me, let go."

Ashby threw back his head and wailed. His entire body convulsed as his climax ripped through him and he spurted hot cum all over himself.

"Fuuuuck," Trent hissed, stretching out the word as he slammed the last few times into Ashby's trembling body. Then he arched his back, his fingers digging into Ashby's hips as he came. *"Ashby,"* he yelled, filling the condom with his seed.

Ashby lay panting as Trent staggered. He didn't withdraw just yet, though. He looked down at Ashby and brushed back the damp hair from his forehead.

"Are you okay?" he whispered.

Ashby blinked. "I just got shagged senseless," he managed to say with a weak smile. "You're the one who just had sex with a man for the first time. Are *you* okay?"

Trent laughed and slowly eased himself free. As they were by the desk, the wastepaper basket was right there, so he was able to peel off the condom and dispose of it effectively. They were both still sticky messes, but Ashby didn't care.

All he cared about was that Trent leaned over and gathered him up in his arms for a cuddle, just the way he liked. "I'm good," he mumbled into Ashby's hair. "You feel like sharing that bed tonight?"

Ashby's heart ached with happiness. He nodded and let himself be led away from the carnage and over to the massive four-poster bed. Trent managed to snatch a box of tissues along the way so they could mop up before slipping under the sheets.

Ashby watched Trent carefully as they turned off the lamps, plunging the room into almost total darkness. But as his eyes became accustomed to the gloom, Ashby could make out his lover's face again.

A tiny part of him worried that Trent wasn't completely okay with what they'd just done. In his experience, though, it was easier for guys to wrap their heads around doing the fucking rather than being the ones getting fucked. So, maybe he'd be all right. Ashby caressed the side of Trent's face as they lay side by side with their heads on the pillows.

Trent reached up and gently wrapped his fingers around Ashby's hand to stop him, then kissed the palm. "I'm great, I promise," he whispered. "Stop worrying. We can talk in the morning, if you want?"

Ashby did want that, very much.

With the promise of clearing a few things up, he allowed Trent to pull him close so he could rest his head on Trent's expansive chest. He could hear his heartbeat and his breathing as sleep quickly enveloped him.

Ashby's last thought before he drifted off was that he felt so very safe.

Twenty-One

ASHBY

A CLATTERING NOISE STARTLED ASHBY AWAKE. HE WAS IN AN unfamiliar bed with his heart racing as he scrambled to pull the covers around him. He was naked. He was sore.

Slowly, he released the breath he'd been holding as wonderful memories came flooding back to him. It was okay. He'd been with Trent last night. It had been beyond fantastic. The soreness he was experiencing only served as a reminder of their time together. So rather than let it bother him, Ashby squirmed his arse a little bit and enjoyed the slight stinging sensation.

He was alone in the bed. Reaching over, the sheets still felt warm. Then another clattering sound came from the adjoining bathroom where the door had been left ajar.

Trent must be in there, Ashby figured. Was he taking a shower?

Even though they were sharing the room, Ashby felt like he ought to be looking after Trent. Shame swept through him. He should have heard Trent get up, not just left him to his own devices. Ashby glanced at the clock and saw it was still early – far earlier than they needed to get up to make it back to the airport for their flight. But there was no going back to sleep now. Ashby felt awful lounging about while Trent was up and busy.

Sheepishly, he slipped out of bed and picked up the first shirt he found. It happened to be Trent's, so it was big enough to cover Ashby's more intimate areas once he'd buttoned it up. He padded over the carpet and carefully pushed the bathroom door open a little.

"Trent?" he said, standing just on the threshold rather than simply barging in. His heart was in his throat. Last night had been so amazing. The last thing he wanted was for Trent to think he was being selfish.

Within a second Trent appeared at the door, opening it all the way. His smile was like sunshine breaking through the rainclouds. He was wearing a bath towel wrapped around his hips and his hair and skin were damp. He must have just had a shower after all.

"Hey," he said softly. "I thought you were still sleeping. Did I wake you?"

Ashby swallowed. He didn't *sound* pissed off. "Um," he said, fiddling with one of the shirt buttons. "I'm sorry I overslept."

Trent frowned and stepped forward. "You didn't," he said, shaking his head. He reached out and slipped his hand behind Ashby's neck. Ashby couldn't help but melt into the touch. "Is something wrong?"

Ashby thought about the clattering. A quick glance showed several single-use toiletries on the counter and plenty of splattered water droplets. Maybe the clattering was just an accident? Ashby bit his lip. Crashing and banging was the kind of thing Gordon did to make him feel guilty all the time. He would have been mad that Ashby was asleep when it wasn't even as though they'd set their alarms and still had plenty of time to check out.

"I thought you might have thought I was being selfish," he mumbled, feeling himself blush. Was that crazy? Now he was saying it out loud, it did sound a little nuts. But Gordon had flipped out or given him the silent treatment for far less when they were together.

Trent frowned. "Selfish?" he repeated. "I was just taking a shower. I didn't want to disturb you."

Ashby tried to loosen the knot of worry in his gut. "Oh, okay," he said nodding. He pulled at the shirt cuffs as embarrassment crept over him.

"Is this about last night?" Trent asked. He raised his other hand and rubbed Ashby's arm. "Do you regret it?"

"No," Ashby blurted out. He cleared his throat and licked his lips, his gaze dropping to the white floor tiles. "I mean, not if you don't. No."

Trent leaned over and kissed his forehead. "I don't," he said. "But it is a lot. You want to have that talk?" He looked down at Ashby's bare feet. "You must be cold. Get back into bed."

Ashby realized he was shaking. So he nodded and allowed Trent to lead him out of the bathroom and back towards the bed. He crawled under the blankets and curled up, not even sneaking a peek as Trent dropped his bath sheet and slipped in after him.

Trent laid his head on the pillow and looked at Ashby with concern. Ashby blinked and looked away. He was acting like a freak and Trent was going to run for the hills.

"Can I hold you?" Trent asked.

Ashby looked back at him. He was used to guys just pulling him in when they wanted him. Trent's chivalry was borderline unnerving. But...also extremely sweet. Ashby really fucking liked being asked what *he* wanted and not having someone make assumptions.

Feeling some of that tension finally melt a little, Ashby

nodded and scooted over to let Trent slip his arms around him. Trent kissed his hair and caressed him through the shirt with little circles he was making with his fingers.

"What's on your mind?" Trent asked.

Ashby shrugged. "Don't know," he said truthfully. It was stupid of him to jump to conclusions about the noises from the bathroom. Now he felt like an idiot for making a fuss for no reason. Trent just hummed, though, and kept holding him. He sighed. "I guess my ex liked forcing me to jump through hoops and it made me nervous," he said. "When you weren't in the bed, I mean. That's not your fault. I'm just being neurotic."

Trent stroked his hair. "Guy sounds like an asshole," he said. Ashby snorted. That was one way of putting it. "I'm sorry I worried you. No one wants to wake up alone after the first time they sleep with someone."

As unsure as Ashby was, his ears couldn't help but prick up at Trent's words. *First time*? Did that mean he wanted there to be *more times?*

"I'm not made of glass," Ashby grumbled, irritated with himself. "I should be able to work out you're just in the other room and not go mental. You must think I'm like a pathetic puppy."

"No," said Trent, lengthening the 'oh' sound and rocking Ashby back and forth. "I think you're an adorable puppy. Good boy."

Ashby swatted his arm. But it felt good to smile.

"Do you want to talk about what happened last night?" Trent asked.

Nerves wiped the smile from Ashby's face pretty quickly. "Um, yes," he said. He didn't know what the hell he wanted to say, but he did want to talk. "Do you want to go first?" He figured the 'straight guy' would have more issues at this point.

"Oh, sure," Trent said. They were still cuddled close, but now their gazes were locked together. Trent took a deep breath. "I don't know what this means. About me," he clarified. "But I really like you, Ashby. I liked being with you." A smile crept onto his face. "That was *seriously* hot sex. But... well, I like you as a person too."

"I like you too," Ashby said, making himself be brave. "And, um, yeah. Fantastic sex. Ten out of ten."

Trent snorted. "I'm pretty sure fucking isn't an Olympic sport."

"Well, it should be," said Ashby sincerely. "That was one hell of a workout."

Trent laughed again and kissed Ashby lightly on the lips. "You're so cute," he said. "So...everything's okay?"

He clearly wasn't convinced about Ashby's freak-out being unrelated to having sex last night. If he was being honest, Ashby couldn't one hundred percent say it wasn't. Had he perhaps transferred some of his anxiety about Trent being supposedly straight into his worries just now?

"Yes," he said firmly. "I suppose..." He played with the edge of his pillow, then traced a finger along the word written over Trent's heart: *Bulletproof.* "I suppose I was maybe a tiny bit worried you were just using me for kicks. For an experiment. And, well, I know this is just a holiday thing or whatever. But I'd rather not be dumped on my arse just yet."

Because he had to face facts. He was heading back to London in two weeks. So there was always going to be an expiration date on whatever this was. But he so desperately didn't want to feel used by Trent.

"I'd never use anyone," Trent said with a frown toward the ceiling. "I guess there have been times where I've been with someone and it started out as no strings then one of us got attached. But not on purpose." He blew out a lungful of air and looked back down at Ashby. "I'd like to make use of the time we have. If that's what you want," he added.

Was it Ashby's imagination or did he sound nervous? Like he was afraid that *Ashby* wouldn't want *him?*

"It is," said Ashby carefully. "But…it doesn't bother you that I have a cock?"

Trent nibbled his lip and frowned in thought. "I'm aware of the fact," he admitted. "And it is kind of strange if I think about it too much." That was fair. Ashby could understand that. It didn't mean he could stop his heart from tightening in his chest just a little. "But," Trent continued, "is it okay if I just *don't* think about it?"

"In what way?" Ashby asked.

Trent shrugged. "I just know I like hanging out with you, and last night was amazing. Can we just keep on doing that, for now? And not get ourselves wrapped up in other things."

"Like," said Ashby slowly. "No labels?"

"Is that a total dick move?" Trent asked. He looked Ashby in the eye, not flinching away as Ashby stroked his hair.

"No," said Ashby honestly.

He didn't want to be anyone's boyfriend right now. Who knew if they would even keep in touch once Ashby went home to London and Trent went back to making movies? He also didn't care if Trent didn't want to name his sexuality. That was entirely his business. So, actually, continuing like this sounded blissful.

"Friends can be a label, though," Ashby added shyly. "Can't it?"

Trent smiled and kissed the tip of his nose. "Definitely friends. Good friends," he said. He looked down at the shirt Ashby was wearing. "Maybe…naked friends again?" He wiggled his eyebrows.

Ashby laughed, the last remnants of the morning's stress finally leaving him. "Sounds marvelous," he said. He glanced at the clock. "You know, we still have a few hours before we have to head to the airport."

Trent hummed. "Yeah," he said. "I was supposed to get brunch with the boys."

"Oh, of course," Ashby said quickly. But Trent shook his head.

"I'm thinking we get room service," he said as his hands slipped under his shirt and began to roam over Ashby's body, making him quiver. "Just you, me, maybe some cream of some kind?"

Ashby pretended to scoff even as his cock came to life. "I don't know what you're suggesting, sir," he said in his best uppity voice. "But it doesn't sound hygienic in the slightest."

"That's what the shower's for," Trent mumbled as he began kissing down Ashby's neck and chest, heading under the covers.

How could Ashby argue with that?

———

In the end, they were too busy kissing and giving each other hand jobs to order food. But they still had time to shower, pack and meet the guys for a late breakfast. Not everyone was there, though. Apparently, Elion was too hungover to drag himself out of bed, and Levi and Raiden had already left to head back to Kentucky. Blake looked to still be on a post-wedding high though, and Gabe and Joey were their usual cheery selves.

They were also still the two most observant people in the room, apparently. Ashby was fully aware of the way their eyes traveled between him and Trent as they sat down at their table. Ashby panicked. Had they been walking too close together? He usually tried to be so careful of such things. You never knew what homophobic arsehole was watching.

But it seemed Joey was just eager for gossip. Luckily, though, he was in between Gabe and Blake, so that apparently made him behave. But he clearly wanted to ask where Ashby and Trent had gotten to last night.

Gabe and Blake held up most of the conversation as they ordered, then ate brunch. Trent was unusually quiet, even for him. He had barely said two words after they left the hotel room, which worried Ashby. It was all well and good saying labels didn't matter and they shouldn't over-think things when they were naked and fucking. But the real world didn't stop existing.

Trent was no doubt questioning a lot of things about himself. How he felt, what did this mean for the future? It wouldn't be the first time Ashby had let a straight guy fuck him only to have him go back to his dude-bro ways immediately after. But before Ashby hadn't cared.

He cared now.

But what was he really hoping to happen? This was a holiday romance at best, but more than likely just a one-night-stand. He needed to draw back, protect his heart. He'd promised faithfully that he would take a break from men and work on himself. Yet here he was, pining over a guy who was probably already passionately regretting what they did.

Ashby was so lost in thought he didn't realize his name was being called. He looked up to see Blake smiling at him. "Sorry, man. You hungover, too?"

Ashby tried equally not to blush nor to look at Trent. "Yes," he said with a laugh and sipped some orange juice.

"I just asked if you were enjoying your vacation?" Blake asked. "TJ said you met at the resort. That's pretty awesome you were able to come here as well when you weren't prepared."

"Oh, no," said Ashby with a wave of his hand. "I travel all

the time. Trent hadn't booked his flights yet, so it was all very easy."

"Is that with work?" Gabe asked. Ashby blinked at him. "The travel," Gabe explained with a smile. "What is it you do?"

Fuck. Ashby had almost made it through the whole weekend as well. "Uh, I'm…between projects right now," he said evasively. "But I'm lucky that my family is well off, so I'm just seeing some new places for a while. 'Finding myself,'" he added with air quotes and an eye roll to show he knew how stupid he sounded.

But the guys didn't sneer at him. "That's great," Joey said, nodding at Blake and Trent. "Traveling definitely helped me work out who I wanted to be." He looked at Gabe and slipped his fingers between his husband's. "It's a big wide world out there."

They had been traveling for work, though. They were touring and doing all sorts of exciting things. Ashby was just bored and running away from his awful ex-boyfriend. He didn't say that, however. He just smiled and finished his eggs.

Blake, Joey and Gabe managed to chat enough to keep the rest of brunch from becoming awkward, but it was like a black cloud was hovering over Trent and Ashby's anxiety was eating him up. Ashby had ruined this for Trent. He'd just wanted to spend some quality time with his friends, and yet here he was no doubt worrying himself sick over what Ashby had encouraged him to do last night.

He knew this would be a mistake. And now he had lost what small, budding friendship they'd had together.

Eventually, Ashby was relieved to bid the other guys farewell. At least they all hugged him and made noises about seeing him again soon. Like that would ever happen.

He dared to ask if Trent was okay on the cab ride to the airport. To be fair, Trent blinked like he was coming out of a trance, then smiled at Ashby. There was a tightness to it, but Trent still reached out and wrapped his hand around Ashby's where it was resting on the seat between them. "Tired," he grunted. But his smile twitched again as he squeezed Ashby's hand once more and rubbed his thumb against the back of Ashby's knuckles.

Little butterflies of hope unfurled in Ashby's chest. Maybe Trent didn't hate him. But he was clearly disturbed by what had happened.

Ashby wouldn't push him again. What they'd shared had been incredible for him, unforgettable. But he was leaving to go back to England in two weeks anyway. At best, he and Trent could remain friends, leaving Ashby the memory of their time together to cherish.

It would have to do.

CHAPTER
Twenty-Two

TRENT

WHAT THE ACTUAL FUCK WAS TRENT DOING?

He was weird with Ashby the whole way back from Ohio and couldn't seem to think of a single thing to talk about. Give him a script and he'd act the shit out of anything. But trying to pretend he was fine when he wasn't had turned him into a grunting gorilla.

He felt awful. Ashby was clearly freaking out and Trent should have just told him everything was okay.

But it *wasn't.* Trent had no idea what their night together meant. Yes, he'd loved it. And Ashby wasn't putting any pressure on him to label himself or commit in any way. But Trent knew something seismic had shifted within him and he didn't know what to do about it.

Why was this so hard for him? Raiden had been through a similar thing last year, realizing he was pansexual. But pan, bi, gay – none of those words seemed right for Trent. Despite Ashby assuring him no labels were needed, Trent was having a hard time coping without one.

What made matters worse was that he knew he was hurting Ashby. On the way back to Ohio he'd commented twice how the next time he would be flying was when he went home to London. It was like he was determined to put on a brave face and remind them both that he wouldn't be here long.

That made Trent feel worse. He wanted Ashby to like him still, but how could he when Trent was acting like a goddamned freak? Marble statues had better personalities than he did currently.

He wasn't surprised that they went back to their own accommodation on Sunday night when they returned to the resort. He tried writing several different texts to Ashby over the evening, but in the end, he deleted them all. He had no idea what he wanted to say.

I really like you but I have no idea what this means.

I miss you already but I feel like admitting that means I'm losing who I am.

You're incredible. Please don't hate me.

I'm sorry I'm being such a dick.

Can I come over?

They all got deleted one by one without being sent. Trent was a fucking coward. Why was it so hard to just admit he was queer? Joey had lectured him and the others on the Kinsey scale so many times Trent knew all about it. How zero was straight, six was gay and three was bi. That left him two whole numbers in between straight and bi he could explore. Why couldn't he accept he was probably a one and get over it?

So much of his life – especially his brand as a singer and an actor – was built around his lady-killer ways. But he'd always been too afraid to commit to those women, some of whom had been downright phenomenal. If he couldn't find happiness with them, what made him think he could be happy with Ashby?

That he could make Ashby happy?

Fucking hell. He was going to drive himself insane. He woke up Monday morning in his snowy cabin with a raging hardon and so close to coming, of course dreaming about his and Ashby's night together. He angrily took himself off for a cold shower and refused to jerk off. Until he could sort out his fucking head, he didn't get to masturbate over his friend. That was gross.

He came to the rather pitiful realization that in that moment, he would have given anything to talk to his mom. He never wanted to sugarcoat the past and pretend they were best friends. But at least she understood matters of the heart. She always listened to him, even if he called out of the blue after weeks or even months of no contact.

But she was gone.

Trent sighed as he stood in his open-plan cabin and watched the snow drifting down on the other side of the window. It was a gray day with heavy cloud cover, matching his mood perfectly.

Well, fuck it. He'd promised he would go talk to his dad anyway about a memorial. If that went well, maybe he'd feel better about this Ashby thing. Maybe it would go so well Trent would actually have the courage to ask his dad about what he should do. He couldn't really see that happening, but it was enough to get him out the door.

Monday was change-over day at the resort. Most people booked their vacations to arrive and leave then. So the main lodge was a bit hectic when Trent arrived. He had to push his way through a lot of people with even more luggage. One of the reasons he liked snowboarding was that skis were just so enormous to lug around with you. He almost got smashed over the head a couple of times as he shouldered his way toward the gift shop.

At least this would mean the resort was even quieter now. This close to the end of the season meant more people would likely be leaving than arriving. Trent looked forward to a bit more peace and quiet, even if it did mean there was no longer enough snow to board on.

Eventually, he made it to the gift store where a newly arrived family were taking their time picking out a fridge magnet. Trent's dad saw him from behind the counter and nodded. At least it was an acknowledgment. Trent hung back while the family debated over a snowy mountain and a cartoon wolf character.

Merlin realized Trent was in the shop and came clattering out from behind the counter. At least he wasn't attached to his leash, so he managed not to knock anything off the shelves as he tore down the aisle to greet Trent, who chuckled as he dropped to his knees and ruffled the little guy's fur. He was so excited he was slobbering all over Trent's hands.

"I swear you've already grown," he murmured, grinning in spite of his black mood. It was hard to be upset when such a happy ball of fluff was hopping around as if seeing you was The Best Thing Ever.

"Can I pet your puppy?" Trent looked up to see a pair of big hazel eyes. The girl was about three or four with poker-straight brown hair and bangs that looked to have been cut using a ruler. She was so entranced by the dog she hardly even glanced at Trent.

"Sure," he said, looking up to make sure it was okay with Mom and Dad. Their son would have been around eight and he turned to them to see if he could join in too. With their permission, he cautiously came over. Miraculously, Merlin calmed a little, letting the kids stroke his fur.

They were a classic nuclear family. Mom, dad, son and daughter. Picture perfect. Trent felt a wave of hurt and confusion roll over him again. At least when his mom had been alive, they had tried to be a regular family. But that had never been good enough for Trent. He'd been ungrateful in his desperation to escape and make a life for himself in the big wide world. And now his mom was gone.

Did he even want kids? Was what he was looking at a possibility for his future? Or was he doomed to keep throwing away relationship after relationship?

If he was losing touch with his past and had no idea where his future was going, what chance did he really have with the present?

He did his best to smile and waved the family off once they'd bought their mountain magnet. The kids called their goodbyes to Merlin, who strained against Trent holding him back by his collar. Finally, it was just him and his dad in the shop, alone.

"How was the wedding?" his dad asked.

He didn't quite look at Trent over his smudged glasses. Instead, he rearranged the colorful cigarette lighters standing up in a cardboard display box. He wasn't putting them in any order. Just swapping one random arrangement for another.

Of course he remembered it was Blake and Elion's big day. He was always good like that, reminding Trent to get cards for his mom's birthday and Mother's Day. He was caring. But he still didn't smile at Trent or show him any affection. He was still just as pissed as the day Trent had returned home.

Trent didn't know what to do. He felt like he was about to reach a breaking point. Slowly, he approached the counter with Merlin surprisingly obedient by his feet.

"I don't know how I can make this better," Trent said. His throat was tight. "I know you're mad I wasn't there for you when…two years ago. But, Dad. What could I have done? She was gone in an instant."

"You could have visited more than twice a year!" his dad snapped. He turned his blazing eyes to Trent and held his gaze unflinchingly. For such a small guy, he was suddenly shaking with rage that seemed to make him grow in stature. "You could have called more than every other month! You could have made sure your mom knew you loved her before she *died*."

Trent stood staring at his dad, frozen. As much as his dad gave the impression of suddenly growing, Trent felt like he'd radically shrunk. He was a dumb little kid again with his head in the clouds, selfishly shunning hard work and a real career in pursuit of fame and fortune.

He wanted to argue that it wasn't true. That his mom knew he loved her. But how could he really be sure?

"I'm sorry," he mumbled thickly. "I – I can't change the past. I didn't know how to handle it."

"So you ran away," his dad said bitterly. "Big surprise. It's what you always do."

"Dad," Trent ground out, a pleading tone to his voice. "I'm not running away now." There was a pause while they stared at one another. "Can I come to your place later? We can talk." Trent really wanted to try and do this somewhere they weren't at continual risk of an audience.

"Talk about what?" his dad demanded. "Like you said. We can't change the past."

"About how we feel," Trent said, trying to remember what Barry had told him. He had offered to fly a shrink down for both the Charles men. As much as Trent hated the idea of spilling his guts like that, he'd do it for certain if it made things better. But he knew his dad would never go for it, not in a million years. Real men handled their own problems. But if they couldn't use a therapist, the best Trent could do would be to try and get them both to open up. Even if it was a can of worms.

His dad gritted his teeth in anger, though. Merlin pawed anxiously at Trent's feet, gnawing at the laces on his boots.

"Trent," his dad said, shaking his head and finally looking away. "I can't help you with your guilt. I'm sorry."

"So, what then?" Trent exploded. Merlin flinched away from him and Trent felt awful. "That's it? You're just not going to talk to me anymore? You're done with me?"

"I'm not sure what we have left in common." His dad's voice broke as he spoke, tearing a ragged shred from Trent's heart. He sounded so broken. "I needed you and you were too scared to come home. I don't think there's much we can repair of that now."

Trent wanted to argue that he *would* have come home. But the longer they left it, the worse it got. Then his dad had let old Lancelot be put to sleep without telling Trent, and Trent had been so hurt and angry he had left the wound between them to fester. But standing there now, god damn it, he wanted to *try*.

Merlin suddenly yelped, jumping back to his feet and making both Trent and his dad visibly jerk. Growling and yelping, Merlin tore through the shop, taking out a tray of thimbles and scattering them noisily to the wooden floor.

"Oh, hello!" A familiar voice called from out in the hall where the puppy was sprinting off to.

Trent's heart plummeted down into his boots. Great. If it didn't rain, it poured.

Ashby looked immaculate as he stepped over the shop entrance threshold. His blond hair was swooped in that perfect way that made Trent's stomach flip. He wore skinny jeans, a low V-neck shirt and a stone-gray cardigan that was so long it swished around his knees. He was as beautiful as ever and Trent felt his heart contract. What the fuck was he afraid of here?

But then Ashby looked up from petting Merlin and saw Trent was watching. His pale face lost what little color there was in his cheeks and his eyes went wide. "Oh, I'm sorry," he stammered.

"No, it's fine," Trent said quickly. He half-reached out with his hand. "Don't go."

Ashby smiled awkwardly and stood, despite Merlin's protests. "No, I didn't mean to interrupt you. I'll, um, see you later."

"Yeah?" Trent said hopefully. But Ashby just gave him a ghost of a smile and turned away.

Trent hadn't thought it was possible to feel worse than he had a minute ago. He'd ruined everything. Then he looked back at his dad.

Trent Sr. was shaking his head in disgust as he stooped down and began picking up the thimbles. "You broke that poor boy's heart," he said, glancing up and raising his eyebrows. "Jesus, Trent. I really wanted to believe you'd treat this one right. Don't you care about *anyone* but yourself?"

If Trent hadn't been feeling like he was crumbling apart from all sides, he might have been impressed that his dad hadn't even batted an eyelid at the idea of Trent being involved with another man. As it was, he could only hear yet another disappointment in a long list of his failures.

"I'll go," Trent managed to say. "You don't want me here. I'll just go."

His dad clenched his jaw and shook his head. He pulled his glasses off and finally cleaned them on his sleeve. "I don't *want* you to go," he whispered. "But if this is how things are, I think it might be for the best."

Trent's eyes blurred with tears as he looked down at his feet. Fuck. He was not going to cry *now*. He didn't fucking cry, let alone in front of his dad.

He didn't want to leave, though. He wasn't even sure if Barry would let him. But it was clear they weren't going to achieve anything today. "I'll give you some space," he mumbled, walking out of the shop before anyone could come in and see him looking like shit. He heard Merlin whimpering as he left, but the pup didn't follow.

If Trent didn't do something with himself, he was going to start drinking, even though it was only midday. He could feel the kind of bender upon him where he didn't usually stop until the world disappeared entirely and he woke up in some woman's bed with a three-day hangover. He was damned if he was going to give in to those urges right now. He only had the resort bar at his disposal, for one thing. But more than that, he didn't want to end up in some strange girl's bed.

He only wanted one person.

But Ashby obviously didn't want him, and with good reason. Trent had ghosted him quite spectacularly to his face. So for a few hours, Trent went back to his cabin and worked with the weights he'd got himself. Then he threw himself down the slopes on his board with increasing disregard for his safety. When it was just him and the burn in his muscles, he hurt less.

But his luck ran out when he took a corner too sharply and sent himself flying head over heels, narrowly avoiding breaking his neck. As he lay in the snow, panting and trying to calm his heart down, he stared up at the ominous gray sky and allowed reality to sink in.

His mom had died just like that. It didn't matter that she was an experienced skier. One day, she had just lost control for whatever reason and then everything was gone in an instant.

Trent wasn't ready to lose everything.

He sat up and detached his feet from the board. At least there weren't many people around to witness his fuck up. Not this particular fuckup, anyway.

Trent's dad was right. He did run away from too many

things. He skirted around the big issues and treated life like a goddamned party. Well, at some point, someone had to flick on the lights and clear up all the mess.

Trent didn't know how he was going to do it. But he *had* to make things right.

Starting with Ashby.

CHAPTER
Twenty~Three

ASHBY

ASHBY LAY ON HIS BED AMONG HIS SCATTERED CLOTHES AND open suitcases. He was flicking between different screens on his phone, trying to decide where was best to fly to. He didn't really want to go home, but he didn't feel like going on holiday anywhere else either. Not when it was obvious wherever he went he couldn't keep his dick in his pants.

His mum had said he was welcome to come visit them in Dubai, but they were working. Besides, he was not comfortable going there as someone so openly queer. They were only supposed to be staying there for eighteen months, so Ashby would wait until they were stationed somewhere most hospitable to go visit them.

Several of his friends back in London were begging him to come see them. But he was so ashamed he didn't think he could face anyone right now. He was more heartbroken over a one-night-stand than he was a two-year relationship. They all thought he was cut up about Gordon, when he didn't give a damn about that manipulative, cheating twat. He cared about Trent, though. Deeply.

Which was insane because they hardly knew each other. He needed to get over himself and get far away before he embarrassed himself or Trent any further. He just couldn't bring himself to commit and book any flights, despite having them loaded up on his phone, good to go.

Maybe he should try and talk to him one last time? Things had been fine before they left the hotel room. And yet the second they hit reality, Trent had folded like a house of cards.

If he couldn't deal with being queer, it wasn't Ashby's place to force him. No matter how much he wanted to. No matter how much it made him want to cry at the thought he was walking away from the only decent man he'd ever loved.

Shagged. He didn't love Trent, that was ridiculous. They had fucked, once. Twice. Yes, it had been *truly* spectacular. But it wasn't love. The gaping hole in Ashby's chest was just that pain of being rejected, yet again.

Home, he decided abruptly. He wanted to go home. He wanted his flat in Chelsea and his local pub and his lovely friends. He wanted to taste the polluted but familiar spring air of the city. He wanted a proper cup of tea.

Battling down a sob, he went to open his phone where it had gone dark and locked. But a knock at the door stopped him.

With a wet chuckle, he figured it was probably Maeve. She always seemed to know when he was feeling down so she could appear with her particular brand of brutal honesty. He'd miss her. Maybe she would want to stay in touch? He'd already seen she had a Facebook account filled with cats and pictures of hot men. He felt like they would have a lot to chat about.

He rubbed his eyes and sighed as he approached the door, doing his best to keep ahold of his smile.

It wasn't Maeve on the other side.

Trent looked broken. He was still obviously a large, hot, muscular man. But his shoulders were slumped and his eyes looked wary as he regarded Ashby. He swallowed, his Adam's apple bobbing in his throat.

"Can I come in?"

Ashby had sworn he would do everything in his power to walk away from this disastrous not-relationship. But Trent looked so bloody sad he couldn't stand it.

"Okay," he said quietly. He stepped inside and allowed Trent to follow. The door swung shut behind him.

As he turned to face him, Ashby caught the horrified expression light up on Trent's face as he took in the debris littered across Ashby's room. "You're leaving," he croaked.

"Uh," said Ashby. He looked down at the phone he'd left on his bed. "Maybe?"

"Fuck," Trent cried, grabbing his hair. His sad eyes had turned wild as his gaze darted about the room before settling on Ashby. "Please," he said. "Please don't go. Oh my god, I've been such a prick to you. But give me a chance to unfuck this. I don't have the right, but I'm begging you, please let me try."

Ashby took in a couple of shallow breaths. "I'm not going to ever be a woman," he said. He knew that wasn't the whole truth, but it was what Trent needed to hear at that moment. His cock certainly wasn't going anywhere, and he didn't have boobs. "I like you, Trent. I really do. But if you can't cope with me not being a woman-"

"I don't give a shit about you being a dude," Trent growled, dropping his hands from his hair and looked Ashby in the eye. "I'm not scared of that, and...fuck it, I'm not scared of coming out. It's a big deal, but I'd do it. I'm...scared to death of committing to someone for the first time in my fucking life. And I know you don't even live in this country.

But Ashby…I…don't want to let you go. I can't. Not if there's any chance you'll have me."

Ashby could hardly trust himself to breathe. "Do you mean that?" he asked in barely more than a whisper.

Trent balled up his fists, but he nodded. "I don't have the right words to work out how I'm feeling. Other than…god, I want to hold you and never fucking let you go."

A small part of Ashby's mind tried to warn him that they were very nice words, but it might not change anything. However, most of his thoughts were telling him that Trent was *here*. He was *trying*.

Ashby reached out his hand.

Trent crossed the room in two strides, swooping Ashby into a bone-crushing hug. He buried his face into Ashby's neck while Ashby took his turn jamming his fingers through Trent's gorgeous hair and holding tight. The sob Ashby had been fighting earlier broke free as their bodies pressed together.

"I'm so sorry," Trent growled. "I should never have freaked out. My head's a mess. You deserve much better than that."

"Shh, shh," Ashby said. Normally it was him, the emotionally excitable one, being consoled by whichever alpha male he'd picked to cry on. Soothing Trent didn't feel like an imbalance of power, though. It felt right. Like Trent really did trust him. "I'll stay. We can talk. I…I don't want to let you go either."

Trent cradled his face with his large hands and rested their foreheads together, taking several breaths in and out that gradually slowed down, getting deeper. Ashby rested his hands on Trent's chest, just under the open leather jacket he loved so much. He could feel Trent's heartbeat through the cotton of his T-shirt.

"Come here," he said softly. He took hold of Trent's hands

and walked the short distance back to his bed. He swept the few items of clothing loitering there to the floor and placed his phone carefully on the dresser. He sat down, pulling Trent with him, until they were laying down together.

Trent wrapped Ashby in his arms and kissed his hair. He certainly wasn't being hesitant to put his hands on a guy again. To put his hands on Ashby.

When Ashby had been moping, he hadn't bothered to turn on any lights as the evening faded into night. He was glad now, as it gave them a certain amount of intimacy as they held one another in the growing darkness. Trent inhaled deeply, rubbing his nose against Ashby's hair. Ashby finally felt some of the tension easing from his many muscles.

Ashby brushed his fingertips over Trent's jawline. "We could talk," he said, trying to be reasonable. "But I'm quite desperate to kiss you. And if I kiss you, I think I might have to encourage you to take off your clothes. Just for a little while." He licked his lips and was pleased when Trent responded to his smile with one of his own. "I'm trying very hard to be a grownup about this," he said sincerely. "But certain parts of me aren't agreeing with my brain."

The truth was he knew Trent was shit at talking. It seemed logical to Ashby that he'd be able to communicate his feelings better to Ashby by touch. Also, Ashby was turned on to all hell and only had so much self-discipline.

"We can talk afterwards?" he suggested.

Trent leaned in and nuzzled his nose against Ashby's. Ashby's heart was going to beat right out of his chest. Blood was thumping in his ears. He hadn't honestly let himself believe for the past twenty-four hours that he was ever going to get another chance at this.

"Talk later," Trent murmured before his lips met Ashby's.

The hunger from their first night together was a distant

memory, as was the playfulness of their brief morning tryst. Every kiss now was filled with tenderness. They undressed slowly, stopping after every garment to touch and caress and kiss. While they were still in their underwear, Trent encouraged Ashby to stand for a moment so he could pull the bedsheets back and snuggle them both under side-by-side.

When they finally lost their boxers, all Ashby could feel was Trent's hot skin covering every inch of his body. His breath was cool and his mouth tasted minty where he'd obviously brushed his teeth before coming over. It was a small but thoughtful act that made Ashby smile.

"What?" Trent asked as their bodies rubbed together. He already had his hand around both their cocks, creating delicious pressure as they slid together, lubricated with precum. He definitely wasn't holding back when it came to acknowledging he was in bed with a guy again.

Ashby smiled wider and kissed his cheek, loving the way his stubble scratched against his jaw. "I'm just so glad you're here."

"Me too," Trent said.

Ashby shimmied his hips. "Get on top of me," he suggested.

He wanted to feel Trent's weight pressing down on him. Trent complied, lying lengthways over him, grinning as he took their cocks back in hand. Good. As sweet as this was, Ashby wanted them to bloody well have fun while they were shagging. If they were going to have a go at being together, he didn't want it to start all weepy.

He gripped the back of Trent's head and the side of his throat. "I want you to make me come like you did last time," he rasped, then bit his lip and fluttered his eyelashes. "Make me forget my own name."

Trent leaned down and also gave Ashby's lip a nip, running the flesh slowly between his teeth. "No problem."

Before Ashby could do anything else, Trent disappeared below the sheets, kissing his way down Ashby's stomach. He'd started doing that the morning after the wedding, but then he'd come back up again and jerked Ashby off instead. This time, he kept going.

His minty breath was hot and tingly against the fleshy part of Ashby's tummy as he trailed his mouth down toward his cock. Ashby groaned as Trent dug his fingers into his arse cheek with one hand and gripped the base of his prick with the other. He wasted no time wrapping his lips around the tip and sucking firmly, his teeth sheathed as if he'd done this dozens of times before.

"Trent," Ashby moaned as he tried not to writhe and thrust too much. "Holy fuck, yes. Like that."

He thought Trent would just suck him for a few seconds like he had last time, then come back up so they could frot. But he got stuck in, bobbing his head up and down, working Ashby's cock with his tongue and lips. His hand left Ashby's arse and began massaging his balls and stroking his taint.

"Fuck, shit," Ashby garbled. "Trent, I'm going to come if you keep that up. No, I'm serious, *ngh!*" Trent didn't let up. In fact, he increased his pace, working harder and sending Ashby crazy. "Trent, I'm not kidding, *oh my god.*"

Ashby was spurting his load down Trent's throat hard and fast. His body was a quivering wreck as his orgasm rippled through him, lifting him high and snatching his breath away.

He covered his face with his hands. "Oh no," he moaned shakily. "I tried to warn you. I'm so sorry."

He felt Trent crawl up his body. Then strong hands were prying his fingers away from his eyes. Ashby blinked and saw Trent grinning. "I wanted to," he said, his voice husky from Ashby's cock working its way down his throat. Ashby blushed but couldn't help but be delighted as Trent kissed him. Ashby tasted his own intimate flavor.

"I can," Ashby said vaguely, gesturing down to Trent's hardon. He absolutely wanted to return the favor, but he was exhausted.

Luckily, Trent just grinned at him some more. "Can I come on you?" he asked, already taking himself in hand and stroking leisurely.

"Oh fuck, yes," Ashby said, nodding. He normally hated guys trying to mark him. It made him feel like a dirty beast, nothing but a bit of property. But he wanted Trent to claim him.

Trent bent down and kissed him as he began jerking off. Ashby moaned and kissed down his throat, running his hands up and down his chest and arms as Trent gnashed his teeth, obviously close. "You're so beautiful," Trent murmured, gasping. "Ashby!"

He shuddered as he found his release, hot, thick cum shooting up Ashby's chest. Some even hit his chin and hair. Ashby couldn't help but giggle as Trent groaned and took several breaths as his climax passed.

"Feel better?" Ashby asked.

Trent smiled sleepily and leaned down to kiss the cum from Ashby's face. Then he slowly kissed down his neck and chest, lapping up his own mess from Ashby's body.

"Fuck, that's *hot*," Ashby whimpered. He was so tired, but he couldn't stop watching Trent as he carefully cleaned Ashby with his tongue and lips, swallowing down his own seed. Ashby hummed and ran his fingers through Trent's thick hair while he worked.

When Trent was done, he flopped down beside Ashby and flung his arm over him. Ashby wriggled until they were cuddled together better.

"Talk in the morning," Trent grunted. He picked up

Ashby's hand and kissed the palm. "Promise. Won't go shower."

Ashby managed a weak chuckle. "In the morning."

As he slipped fully into unconsciousness, Ashby couldn't help but feel the smallest bit hopeful.

Twenty~Four

TRENT

TRENT WAS EXCESSIVELY USED TO WAKING UP IN UNUSUAL beds. He moved around so much (and slept around so much) he was familiar with that lurch of disorientation. Ordinarily, it took him no time at all to get his head together and figure out what he had to do. Was he due somewhere for work? What time zone was he in? Did he want to wake the girl or let her sleep? Was he looking to leave as soon as he could or hang around? Did he even remember her name?

He remembered Ashby's name.

Sex was definitely not the problem here. Another night with Ashby had convinced Trent he had no hang-ups what-soever about being with this gorgeous person. Just because he hadn't felt like putting another cock in his mouth before didn't stop him from wanting Ashby's. Like how girls had different pussies and breasts, probably. Just because they came in different shapes and sizes didn't make them any less desirable.

Something about Ashby had unlocked a corner of Trent's desire he hadn't been aware existed before. He realized how glad he was for that as he stroked back his sleeping lover's blond hair.

Ashby hummed and squirmed a little against Trent. The sun was up and the morning light was spilling through the windows where they hadn't pulled the curtains. Ashby blinked his pretty teal eyes and looked around before settling them on Trent.

"Morning, gorgeous," Trent said.

Ashby's face split into a warm smile. "Hi," he said softly.

Guilt and worry threatened to creep around Trent's heart. But he took a slow breath and concentrated on not panicking. Everything was fine between them. Although he did feel the need to apologize again.

"I'm sorry," he said, chewing on his lip.

Ashby frowned. "For what?"

"Messing you around," Trent said. He shrugged and moved more onto his side so he could see Ashby properly. He was trailing his fingers over the back of Ashby's arm lying between them.

Ashby tutted. "Stop apologizing," he said briskly. "I get you freaked out. It's a lot to take on."

It was Trent's turn to frown. "It shouldn't be, though," he said. "It's the twenty-first century. I like you, big deal. I shouldn't have noped out on you like I did."

Ashby moved his hand and linked it with Trent's, stopping him from moving around. Ashby kissed the fingers through his own, then held Trent's hand up to his heart. "You're reassessing a big part of your identity," he said seriously. "I'm not going to tell you it didn't hurt, that I wasn't worried. But I understand."

"You do?" Trent asked dubiously.

"It's the commitment thing, right?"

Trent frowned. He had said something about that last

night, hadn't he? But Ashby lifted both their hands so he could touch a finger above Trent's heart.

"Mr. Bulletproof," he said, lowering their hands back down.

Trent raised his eyebrows. "You spotted that, huh?" he said, looking down at the tattoo. He'd never allowed himself to think much about why he'd got that specific ink, other than it had felt right.

"Don't worry," Ashby said with a little laugh. "I'm not asking you to marry me."

The words didn't send the usual jolt of panic down Trent's insides. But it also wasn't really what had been bothering him, although that was what he'd said last night. Fuck, his thoughts were such a mess.

"I want to try and commit to this," he said honestly, refusing to allow his mind to wander off into the infinite 'what ifs' that might conjure up for the future. "We can take it slow, day by day."

"So…it's the queer thing?" Ashby said.

"Kind of," Trent said. "I wish I could keep it simple. But it's not."

Ashby bit his lip. "If you were freaked out by cocks, I think that might have come up last night."

Trent grinned and made himself be mature and not quip about other things coming instead. "I was just thinking that," he agreed. "But…" He sighed. This was the thorny part he'd been coming to the conclusion about, gradually. But he didn't know how to phase it. "It's only…your cock. I've not been attracted to another guy like this before."

Ashby snuggled up closer to him. "It doesn't bother me if you don't want to put a name to how you're feeling," he said. "I mean about…not being as straight as you thought you were. I'm happy being the 'special' one who turned your head." He fluttered his lashes. "But did you want to talk about some of the available words out there? It might help."

Trent rubbed his thumb against the back of Ashby's hand. "The guys have talked to me enough about their labels," he said. "Gay, bi, pan, demi. I get all those the way they describe it for them. But...I don't know." He bit his lip, unsure if he should say what was floating about in his brain.

"Yes, you do," said Ashby. He had a slight devilment to his tone. "I mean, I think you really do know. Say it however best you can. I'm pretty hard to shock."

Trent wasn't convinced. "I'm worried what I want to say is going to come across as offensive. But I don't mean it like that, at all."

Ashby considered him seriously for a second. "Well," he said. "If I'm offended, we can talk through why. I'm a grownup, I promise. Despite evidence to the contrary."

The small joke helped to ease Trent's anxieties a little. "Okay," he said after a few moments. "I guess...I guess I feel like I'm attracted to you because you're...well, you're not, um..."

"Very masculine?" Ashby suggested. His tone was bright and he didn't sound pissed off at all.

"Um, yeah," said Trent. "Is that okay?"

Ashby's smile was a huge relief. "Of course it is," he said kindly. "I'm *not* very masculine. I like being effeminate." He chewed his lip. "If we're being honest and talking about labels, I could explain that a bit more. If you like?"

"Sure," said Trent. "Go ahead, shoot." The idea that he wasn't the only complicated one made him feel a bit better.

Ashby seemed to think about his words for a moment. "So, you know how you're not quite straight? Well...I'm not quite a man."

Trent couldn't help but flick his gaze down to where

Ashby's cock was under the covers and think about how he'd sucked it twice now.

Ashby poked his chest. "Biologically, yes. I'm a guy. And I'm fine with male pronouns and all that. But sometimes, not all the time, I don't feel like I'm either. Male or female."

Trent was very keen on not fucking up and using the wrong words now. He chewed his tongue for a second. "Is that, um, trans?"

Ashby smiled at him. Relief swirled inside Trent. He so wanted to understand Ashby and have him look at him with pride like that as much as he could.

"Yes," Ashby said, becoming more animated. "It comes under the umbrella of trans. I'm nonbinary. You might have heard the term androgynous, but I like nonbinary. Or, more accurately, there are times when I'm happy to feel and present more male. Then there are times, when I feel comfortable and safe, that I love blurring the lines between genders." He let go of Trent and waved his hand about before linking their fingers again. "I won't get on my soapbox, I promise. But what I'm trying to explain is that I don't feel like gender is any more binary than sexuality. Like...you know you're definitely a man, but you're now attracted to me. I assume?"

Trent laughed and kissed him. "Yes, I'm definitely attracted to you."

"Right, good, that's nice," Ashby said, bouncing a little on the bed. "So, I know I'm always attracted to men. But sometimes I love things that are seen as being for women. Like wearing lacy blouses or heels or painting my nails."

"Or makeup?" Trent asked, remembering the wedding.

Ashby nodded. "Yes. So, I don't feel I'm a woman trapped in a man's body, like a trans woman. And I'm not performing as a woman, like a drag queen. I just see gender as this blurry thing that I'd rather not be tied down to."

Trent frowned. He wasn't sure he entirely got it, but he didn't necessarily have to. As long as Ashby was comfortable in his own skin, he liked Ashby just the way he was. He liked him a lot.

"So," he said. "It's okay that I like you because you're not entirely male?" He winced. "I'm sorry, that sounds like an insult."

Ashby shook his head. "No, it's not. I think it's very accurate and, well, no one's ever said that to me so directly before. It's oddly validating."

"Really?" Trent felt that burst of pride again. Ashby nodded. "So, you're saying the parts of us that aren't quite a man and aren't straight have…overlapped?"

Ashby's eyebrows rose. "Ooh, I like that," he said nodding. "Like those circle graphs that overlap to show, um, science stuff." He let go of Trent and wriggled his other arm free so he could make two circles with his fingers and created a figure eight with a tiny overlapping area in the middle. "A Venn diagram!"

Trent touched the space in the center. "We're the Venn diagram," he murmured.

Ashby nodded, clearly pleased. "Does that help?" he asked with genuine concern. He dropped his hands and rubbed Trent's thigh. "I quite like the sound of that, myself."

Trent let out a breath. "I think so," he said. "It's…quite a bit to think about. But there's probably more answers than questions floating around in my head now." He raised an eyebrow and hugged Ashby to him. "You don't feel like…I don't know. Don't you want to be with a proper gay guy?"

Ashby pondered his words for a moment. "You know," he said. "I always go for these hyper masculine alpha dudes. And…I think they're the type that kind of wish they were straight. But guys like me are the closest they can get to a girlfriend. So…they end up resenting me?" He shrugged. "It's just a theory, one I've only just now considered. But maybe what I needed was a straight dude who likes the girly side of me *as well* as my cock."

Trent arched an eyebrow. "I don't have a lot of experience," he said, lifting the covers and peering down, "but it is a pretty great cock."

Ashby's peels of laugher echoed around the beige hotel room, filling it with life. "Why thank you," he said, pretending to swish his hair back.

Trent considered him. It didn't seem unusual to him that Ashby 'blended gender styles' like he said. It seemed natural. Some guys wore makeup and it looked uncomfortable. Hell, Trent wore makeup on set all day and the stuff still got in his eyes and bothered him. But Ashby just made it seem effortless.

"What?" Ashby asked. Before Trent could answer, he leaned forward and kissed the tip of Trent's nose, making him laugh. Ashby seemed so much happier. It made Trent's chest burst with joy.

"Did you know my mom was Arapaho?" Trent said. At Ashby's blank face, he remembered he was English and might not know the term. "Native American," Trent supplied. Sure enough, Ashby made an 'ohh' sound and nodded. "We didn't always talk much about it. But she said something cool once that I committed to memory for Joey." Trent frowned and racked his brains for the right pronunciation. "Her people had – or have – a third gender. They call them *haxu'xan*. They're guys who live as women and they marry guys and are respected by the tribe."

Ashby blinked at him. "Seriously?" he said. Trent couldn't blame him. He knew how much queer people had been persecuted throughout history. Especially trans people.

"I know it's not exactly like you," Trent said. "But it's kind of cool, I think."

Ashby nodded. "Very," he said shyly. "Thank you."

Trent looked around at all the clothes still scattered around the room from where Ashby had obviously emptied out his closet. Fuck, Trent was so glad he caught him before he made any serious plans to leave. It got him thinking though.

"Did you bring any of your more nonbinary-"

"Enby," Ashby said. Trent frowned. "You know," Ashby explained, "like as in the letters N-B."

"Enby," said Trent, nodding. "It's cute."

Ashby gasped in delight. "I know, right?"

Trent chuckled. "Okay, so. Did you bring any of your enby clothes with you?"

Ashby blinked and looked around the carnage. "Well, um, yes," he said. "It's just, well...I don't tend to wear them places I don't know. Especially if I'm by myself."

He tried to keep his voice light, but there was a flicker of sadness in his eyes. Trent could only imagine the hurt he'd experienced while looking different. Even violence. Trent would never let anybody touch Ashby while they were together. He knew that for certain.

He was feeling so freed after their talk, though. Like an enormous burden had been lifted. Or better, like he'd had a box full of puzzle pieces and now they had all slotted together the way they were meant to.

He smiled at Ashby and ran his hand up and down his arm. He could feel his desire flickering to life again. "Would you, uh, put something on for me?" he asked. "Something you feel pretty in?"

Ashby looked at him for a moment, his expression slowly turning into complete joy. "Um, okay," he said, nodding as he slipped out of the bed. "Are you sure?"

Trent grinned. "Absolutely," he said.

Ashby licked his lips, considering everything that was

thrown about the room. Carefully, he began to pick up items one by one, seemingly unaffected that Trent was watching him walk about naked.

"I'll be right back," he said once he had everything he apparently wanted, then dashed into the bathroom.

Trent laid back in the bed and touched his fingers to the 'Bulletproof' insignia over his heart. Had he really been that hellbent on keeping people away from him? Not the boys from the band. He'd always had love for them. But Trent tried to think of a time he had ever let another friend get particularly close to him, let alone a girlfriend. He'd always kept everyone at arm's length.

Even his own parents. It had felt good to talk about his mom. He hadn't told Ashby the whole truth, how she wasn't here anymore. But they could get to that.

Trent felt he could talk to Ashby about anything. That he would be patient and help Trent find the words. Together, they could tackle anything.

A knock at the door made him jump. *"Housekeeping!"*

"Come back later," Trent called back. The door was in direct line of sight of the bed.

The voice cackled through the wood. "Oh, nice try with that accent, Ashby."

Before Trent could think of what to say, the door swung open to reveal one of the women from the housekeeping staff, judging by her uniform. She was middle-aged with curly brown hair and colorful horn-rimmed glasses. Or so Trent saw before he gasped and yanked the covers over his head.

"Jesus, Mary and Joseph!" the woman cried in delight. "Ashby Wilcott, you get out here this instant!"

"Maeve!" Ashby shrieked. Trent peeked out from under the covers to his left, just enough to see a dressed Ashby

burst out of the bathroom. "What are you doing? Go on, shoo!"

Maeve, the housekeeper, cackled some more. "Oh, sweetie, don't you look pretty? Okay, all right, I'm going. *Bye TJ!*" she cooed. Trent heard the door close.

After a few seconds, Trent dared to look above the covers. Ashby had his hands in his hair, staring in mortification at the closed door. "She seemed friendly," Trent commented. There was no sense getting upset. He wasn't going to be ashamed about Ashby, so why not come out of the closet right now?

Ashby turned to him. Trent felt the humor drop from his face as he took in Ashby's outfit.

It was simple. The same stonewashed skinny jeans he'd been wearing yesterday, but now matched with a pair of black boots with a small heel that disappeared under the denim. The top was a Chinese-looking black tunic, silky, with a gold and jade pattern of hummingbirds and flowers embroidered on it.

The ensemble was elegant, though neither wholly feminine nor masculine. Even without makeup and last night's bed hair, Ashby looked totally stunning.

"Fuck me," Trent murmured in surprise.

It looked like Ashby took a moment to register the lust in Trent's eyes. He spun and smiled. "I'd rather you fucked me," he said with a wink.

Trent crooked his finger, beckoning Ashby to him.

"That can be arranged, gorgeous," he said.

CHAPTER
Twenty~Five

ASHBY

ASHBY WAS DOING HIS BEST NOT TO GET SWEPT UP IN THE romance and intoxication of such incredible and regular fucking. But it was difficult. Now Trent had been given 'permission' (as Ashby saw it) to crush on Ashby, he was having the time of his life. He fancied Ashby no matter what he was wearing. But even when they were lying around naked, he seemed captivated by Ashby's body, always running his hands over it and kissing every inch.

So it wasn't just the makeup or pretty clothes that Trent liked. It was everything about Ashby. It eased the worry that Trent was confusing him for a girl, although since their chat that hadn't really been a concern.

What was an issue was their very separate lives. Ashby had made a home for himself in London. Not that he had a job, but he had friends and a community there. Trent's home was LA and his movie career sent him all over the globe while he was working. But he was already making noises about 'making it work.' After all, they both had money, they could travel. But could a relationship really work with so many thousands of miles between them?

Was this even a relationship? Sure, the sexual chemistry was off the charts. As Ashby sat in the bar and stirred sugar into his tea, he looked out the window at the outdoor pool, steaming like usual as the cold air hit the warm water. Late last night, after a couple of glasses of wine, he had strongly encouraged Trent to put a robe on with him and run out naked to the pool after hours when the lights were off. They had frotted and jerked each other off and kissed until they'd come under the stars in the dead of night.

Ashby shifted in his seat and glanced around. He had a table to himself and there weren't that many people around. Still, he would have been mortified if the nice grandparents with their grandkid in the big glasses caught him getting hot and bothered in the middle of the day. But bloody hell, just thinking about Trent's muscular body made Ashby want to climb him like a tree. Again.

A quiet yowl by his feet made him look down. He was surprised to see Merlin the St. Bernard puppy lying down by his shoes. Ashby looked up in surprise. But when he caught eyes with Darnell at the bar, he gave Ashby a thumbs-up. Then Darnell turned to the entrance of the bar where Kadie from reception was hovering. She followed Darnell's line of sight to see where Merlin was, pointed toward the dog, then called something like 'he's here' down the corridor. Ashby realized she was probably telling Trent's dad where his dog was and that everything was okay.

Ashby figured Mr. Charles didn't want him back for the moment, so he bent down and scratched the dog behind his ears. "Good boy," he murmured. He did love this little fellow a lot. He was so sweet, if not at times a little too exuberant. Mr. Charles was probably glad to get a break from him for a while, unfortunately.

Trent kept skirting around the issue of his dad. Ashby knew things weren't right between them, but he wasn't sure what the exact issue was. He had pieced together himself that Trent had got Merlin as a present for his dad and it possibly hadn't gone down as well as he had hoped.

Ashby felt sad he might not be around to see them patch things up. It was in his nature to want everybody to get along and help achieve that in any way possible. Perhaps he could extend his stay here?

But where would it end if he did that? He and Trent couldn't stay on holiday indefinitely. They had to go back to the real world at some point. Would their budding relationship survive when they did?

"Oh my gawd," a voice squeaked.

It pulled Ashby from his reverie and his gaze away from the swimming pool beyond the window. He turned to see a slim guy in glasses with thick black rims and a navy baseball cap standing by his table. His scraggly goatee was in need of a proper trim, but the way he was looking down in delight at Merlin made Ashby think kinder of him.

"Is that your dog?" the guy asked. He looked up at Ashby and placed his hand on his chest. Gay, Ashby immediately identified. The guy gasped and smiled. "Do you mind if I pet him? I just love puppies so much."

"Sure," said Ashby. "He's not my dog, sadly. He belongs to someone on the staff, but he seems to like me."

Mr. Goatee looked up at him from where he was crouched with Merlin on the floor. For once, Merlin didn't seem too interested to say hello.

"Oh," Mr. Goatee said. "Wow, I love your accent. You from England? You sound like Harry Potter."

"I'm a Hufflepuff," Ashby said like he did whenever people mentioned the famous book series. As usual, it created an immediate bond with whoever he was talking to.

"No way, me too," Mr. Goatee said, jumping back to his

feet. He held out his hand toward Ashby. "Dez. Nice to meet you."

"Ashby," he replied.

"Hey, you want some company?" Dez asked. He gestured toward Ashby's eReader. He had been so lost in his thoughts he'd not even opened up a book.

"Sure," he said automatically. Then he realized how that might look. Gordon would flip his fucking lid if he caught Ashby talking with another guy without him. Trent wasn't like that, but Ashby wanted his cards on the table from the start. "I, um, have a boyfriend," he said. He and Trent hadn't specified relationship labels yet, but it was the easiest way to say he was with someone and not looking.

Dez waved a hand at him. "Oh, no, me too," he said with a scoff. "But he's not here yet and I get bored so quickly. If I buy you a drink would you tell me about England for a while?"

Ashby nodded as Darnell came over to them. Seeing as it was midafternoon, the bar wasn't that busy, so he could serve them himself. Trent was working out for a couple of hours, then had a call scheduled with his manager, so Ashby had given him some space for the day.

"Can I get you guys something?" Darnell asked as Dez slipped into the seat opposite Ashby. Darnell glanced about to check Bob wasn't around, then winked at Ashby. "I've been working on my cocktails," he said excitedly.

"Ohh," Ashby said with genuine enthusiasm. "Well done, you. I'm so happy to hear that! Surprise me. I'll take something fruity."

"Me too," said Dez, smiling sweetly. They watched Darnell make his way back to the bar and begin flipping bottles again, much to the delight of the three middle-aged women drinking cosmos at the counter. "So," said Dez, swinging his feet under the table. "You here with your boyfriend, huh?"

Ashby bit his lip. His heart fluttered whenever he thought of Trent, but he had hardly gotten to speak about him to anybody apart from Maeve yet (who had demanded to hear *everything*) so he couldn't help but be enthusiastic.

"We met here, actually," he said. "So, it's new and exciting. But…he's special. I think it could be going somewhere." He tried not to blush, but he couldn't help but be happy. "What about you and your boyfriend?"

"Oh," Dez said dismissively. "High school sweethearts. Not new or that exciting, but, you know, true love, yada yada." He smiled, then leaned back as Darnell came back with their drinks. "Oh, yummy!"

Ashby felt a little sorry for Dez and his lackluster interest in his boyfriend, but they moved on to talking about London and the cool places to go. Dez had never been but always wanted to visit. Ashby was more than happy to talk about Soho, Carnaby Street, Shoreditch and the best Indian restaurants on Brick Lane. "Honestly, you've never had curry until you go there," he said with a giggle. The drinks were kind of strong on an empty stomach, but Dez was already waving at Darnell to get two more. They *were* delicious.

Dez was so impressed when Ashby talked about the kind of parties he usually went to. He wondered if that didn't make Dez a little shallow for being impressed because Ashby brushed shoulders with C-list celebrities. But it was nice to have someone think what he did was cool for a change. And Dez seemed sweet and harmless.

"So, this is your ex Gordon, huh?" Dez asked when they were on their third cocktail.

He was thumbing through Ashby's Instagram. A lot of people followed him, he was ashamed to admit. Just because he was pretty and went to places with people who were vaguely famous. Ashby didn't like seeing Gordon's face again, but he wasn't going to delete the photos from his feed. He needed to remember not to let himself get in that kind of relationship again.

"Or does he know he's an ex yet?" Dez asked, wiggling his eyebrows.

"Urgh, no, he's gone, out, bleurgh," Ashby said pulling a face. "Trent is a million times better than him."

Dez sighed, then looked at the clock on his phone. "Oh, shit! Is that the time? Oh, sweetie, I have to go! I'm so sorry. But I'll message you on Insta, okay?" He made noisy air kisses and hopped down from his seat. "See you soon, okay?"

Ashby barely had time to wave goodbye before Dez had run out of the bar. Ashby frowned and looked down at Merlin. "Weird," he said to the puppy, who grumbled and rolled onto his side to continue sleeping.

Ashby didn't really mind, though. He had another drink to keep him company and he skimmed through his various social media accounts, catching up with people. Darnell was kind enough to bring him some water and a bowl of pretzels, so he sobered up a little bit.

Which was a good thing, considering a flustered-looking Skye from the beauty spa rushed in about an hour later. She spied Ashby and made a beeline for him. "Oh, hon," she said breathlessly. "I'm so glad I've found you. Have you *seen* the news?"

Ashby's stomach dropped. "No?" he said cautiously. "Why?" His mind instantly thought something bad might have happened back in London.

Skye pulled her phone out of her tightly fitting uniform and brought up a screen. "I have certain words flagged, so they ping up on my newsfeed when there's a story, you know?" Ashby did, so he nodded. "Well…uh…"

She showed Ashby a story from a Hollywood blog site, one of those celebrity gossip ones.

His heart dropped through his boots.

"Can you..." he stammered, getting to his feet. He gestured between Merlin and Darnell, who was looking at him with concern as he almost tripped getting out of the chair. "Merlin needs to, I – oh my god. I have to find Trent. I'm sorry. Darnell, can you take Merlin?"

Ashby didn't wait for an answer. His eyes were blurred with tears as he fumbled his way out of the bar, trying to get his own phone out of his jeans. He should have known this was all too good to be true.

He had to find Trent *now*.

Twenty-Six

TRENT

AS MUCH TRENT HADN'T WANTED TO LET ASHBY OUT OF HIS sight, after two days near constant fucking and lazing about in his cabin, they had both agreed a few hours apart would be a good thing. Ashby had gone back to his own room to freshen up and Trent had taken the time to do a much-needed work out.

Barry had threatened to check in with him later. He probably had news for him about the next Fixer contract. Trent wasn't ready to go back to the real world just yet. But he would be willing to pop his head back in for half an hour knowing that Ashby was waiting for him to have dinner together later at the resort.

Although they had shared dinner together before, this would be their first time out in public as a real couple. They hadn't used the word 'boyfriends' yet, but Trent felt they were going that way. At least he hoped so. A small, mostly empty restaurant would be the perfect place to test how it felt to be seen together.

Mostly, though, Trent just felt excited. He'd asked Ashby to wear whatever he felt comfortable in and he hoped he might experiment a little and wear something just a bit flamboyant. Trent wanted to prove he could be at ease around him, however he wanted to present himself.

It felt like by working things out with Ashby he had accomplished something huge. Could this be the start of a relationship that would actually stick? Trent's heart ached with hope that it might. He rubbed his chest. It wasn't so bulletproof anymore.

He knew it was a bit early for dinner, but Ashby had messaged a while ago to say he was having tea at the bar. Seeing as Barry hadn't called when he was supposed to, nor responded to Trent's text chasing him, Trent decided he would just go meet Ashby and could step out if he got a call.

His mind was preoccupied with the thought that if they had dinner early, that left them the rest of the evening to play. Trent wished he had his motorcycle here. He wanted to take Ashby on a long, fast ride, then make love on a blanket under the stars somewhere. A beach preferably. Trent had always been partial to a bit of public fucking. Not like Raiden and Levi who were always dashing into closets and spare rooms, the horny bastards. But to be out in the open with someone, to feel the elements and them on your skin, it was something else.

Trent couldn't believe it when Ashby had dragged him out to fuck in the pool, wearing even less than the first time Trent had seen him there. It ticked all Trent's boxes. He was starting to appreciate that Ashby did that a lot. He was perfect in so many ways.

Trent was already getting carried away with ideas of how they could stay in touch when they both had to go back to their homes. All he knew was, the more time he spent with Ashby, the harder it was going to be to say goodbye.

He was so caught up in his thoughts, he almost didn't notice when he bumped shoulders with someone in the hall on the way to the restaurant. The white Stetson really should have given it away.

"Well, look who it is," Kiefer drawled. "Lover boy, in the flesh. Guess you decided to come crashing out of that there closet after all," he said with a snicker.

Trent took a step back and shook his head. "What do you want, Burton?" he asked. "Why are you even still here?"

Kiefer smiled, although it was more like a sneer. "Oh, I had business. It's almost taken care of now. I really should thank you."

Trent frowned. "For what?"

Kiefer grinned, showing off his perfect pearly whites. "Well, I thought I had a decision to make. But…" He shrugged and leaned in closer to Trent. "You took something of mine, I took something of yours."

"Take?" Trent repeated, not understanding. "You mean Ashby?" His rage flared. "He was never yours and I didn't *take* him, asshole."

"Oh," Kiefer scoffed. "It looks to me like you've been taking him quite spectacularly. In all kinds of places." Kiefer shivered, that shark-like grin still loitering on his smug face. "You see, I don't deal with public humiliation very well, TJ. Now you've flaunted that piece of ass for the whole world to see, I don't want him anymore. But," he added, "I still felt like getting even."

Trent was angry and confused. He and Ashby hadn't even had dinner together yet. Where had they been flaunting things? At the wedding? Had Kiefer stalked the photographs of that weekend just like they feared he would?

"I don't give a fuck what you do," Trent growled, stepping to move past Kiefer. "Neither does Ashby. Nothing you do matters."

"Oh?" said Kiefer from behind Trent's back. "Like selling

this pitiful excuse for a resort? You mean things like that don't matter?"

Trent stopped walking. Slowly, he turned back around. "Sold it to who?" he asked.

Kiefer laughed, hooking his thumbs over his leather belt and angling the gold buckle so it glimmered in the hall lights. "See, I was looking for a new owner, someone who didn't care about sinking cash into this money pit. Hard work, as you can imagine." His eyes flashed their first true look of hatred. "It's a real shit hole, if you hadn't noticed."

Trent clenched his fists. He knew the Grand Resort wasn't as nice as it was in its glory days. But hearing him talk like that was like hearing him insult Trent's parents directly.

"So I sold the land instead," Kiefer said. He bit his lower lip and looked very pleased with himself. "Much easier. In three months this place will be flattened and in three years it'll be a shiny nuclear power plant."

The air rushed out of Trent's lungs. "W-what?" he couldn't help but stammer. "You can't do that."

"I can and I have," Kiefer snapped. "You should have remembered what real power looks like before you fucked with me, boy," he snarled. "When your pops and all his buddies start crying about their jobs and their homes, you can tell them it's all your fault. You and that pretty piece of English ass. Oh, look! Speak of the devil."

Trent turned toward the direction of the restaurant. Ashby was furiously rubbing tears from his eyes as he stormed toward Trent and Kiefer. He barely seemed to notice Kiefer as he marched up to Trent. "Can we talk?" he asked, his voice clipped. He came to a halt, his arms folded and his phone gripped so hard in his right hand his knuckles were going white.

Trent blinked. He was reeling from the news that what

was essentially his family home was going to be demolished out of pure spite and now Ashby looked livid with him.

"Of course," he said, bewildered. "Can I meet you back at my cabin? I've just got to – something's come up."

"Damn fucking *right* something's come up!" Ashby shrieked. He whipped his arms apart and unlocked his phone with shaking hands. Before Trent could work out what was happening, the screen was thrust into his face, showing a blog article.

British socialite tempts TJ Charles away from pregnant fiancée, the headline read. *Heartbroken boyfriend Gordon Pritchard tells all from London. Distraught Elsie Hadden contemplates life as a single mom.* There were photos of Trent and Ashby at the wedding and one of Ashby drinking a green cocktail in the resort's own bar, laughing.

Then there was a photo of them fucking in the swimming pool last night.

Trent had to take a step back. He was dizzy from so much bullshit.

"Pregnant fiancée!" Ashby yelled. Tears were streaming down his face. "No wonder you were so conflicted!"

"No, Ashby," Trent shouted over him. "It's all lies, it's-"

The camera flash startled him so much the words died in his throat. They'd attracted a few people in a crowd.

One of whom was Dez Starr.

"TJ!" he called out. "Was one home not enough? You had to wreck two?"

The light went again and again. Ashby staggered backward. "You?" he said. Trent's head snapped between them. How did Ashby know this paparazzi scumbag? What the hell was he doing here, in Wyoming? "What happened to your accent, Dez?"

Dez ignored him. "He must be a magnificent fuck, TJ, to turn you gay and wreck so many lives."

"Oh, Ashby here's a real cannonball," Kiefer drawled, clearly delighted with what was going on. Trent had forgotten he was there. *Flash! Flash! Flash!* Guests had their cameras out, filming everything.

"You piece of shit," Trent raged at Dez. "You made all that up, all of it!"

"Not the photos," Dez said, grinning and snapping some more. "Isn't this where your mom died? You decide to piss on her memory some more?"

Trent raised his fist before he knew what he was doing.

But then hands were grabbing him and hauling him back. His dad was shouting in his ear. Darnell, the bartender, was using his surprising strength to help. Bob, the resort manager, was shouting at everyone. Dez was still rattling off his disgusting questions as people pressed in from all sides, his camera snap, snap, snapping away.

Trent shrugged everyone off him and turned from Dez to look for Ashby. He was pushing his way out from the crowd, his phone still in his hand as he sobbed and rushed for the door.

Trent didn't give a shit about anything else right then. Barry could fix the lies like he did before. There still had to be time for them to do something before the sale of the resort was finalized. Right then, Trent had to get to Ashby and explain. Everything else could wait.

Dez kept hollering after him, but Trent figured someone must have held him back because he didn't follow as Trent sprinted after Ashby.

He wasn't going to throw a relationship away. Not again.

Not with Ashby.

CHAPTER
Twenty~Seven

ASHBY

It was fucking *freezing* outside. The wind had picked up something fierce, flinging snow in every direction.

Ashby didn't care. He wanted to hurt.

How could Trent do this to him? He should have known there was more to his freak-out than being afraid of commitment. He was just another lying, cheating-

"Ashby!"

The voice carried over the storm, but Ashby didn't turn around. But he realized too late he had automatically been heading toward Trent's cabin. He didn't want to go there. He didn't want to go back into the resort and face that zoo. He just wanted to disappear.

He was only wearing jeans and a sweater. Not enough to keep the icy cold out as he sunk to his knees in the snow and covered his face with his hands, the screen of his phone pressing against his face. His fingers and ears were already burning. He let out a wail and sobbed. He was such a fool.

"Ashby!" Trent bellowed again. Within seconds, those strong arms that Ashby had come to adore threw themselves around his body. The scent of Trent's leather jacket filled Ashby's lungs.

He shoved him away.

"Fuck *off,* you *liar!*" Ashby screamed, hiccuping as he cried. "You *bastard!*"

But Trent came right back, kneeling in the snow with him. "None of it's true, Ashby, I swear on my fucking life! There's no baby. Elsie and I hooked up *years* ago, and there is absolutely *no one* now but you!" His hands fluttered uselessly like he wanted to grab Ashby's shoulders or face but didn't know if he should.

Ashby swallowed, not daring to trust him. "Why should I believe you?" He was shivering so violently he could barely talk.

Trent pushed his snow-dusted hair away from his face. He was so gorgeous it broke Ashby's heart. "Did you leave your boyfriend behind in England and cheat on him with me?" Trent asked.

Ashby saw red. *"No!"* he yelled over the wind. "No, I fucking did not. He cheated on *me.* We're done, over. I came here to get away from him!"

Trent took a shaky breath and held his arms open. "Please come here," he begged. "That's what Dez does. He lies and he hurts people and he says gross stuff about my mom so I'll punch him and give him another scandal."

Ashby licked his lips. He was so cold now he couldn't think straight. There was so much snow whirling around them he struggled to make out anything aside from Trent. He looked so pained. Ashby wanted to believe him so badly.

"You swear," he said, hating how pathetic he sounded. "You swear there isn't a secret baby and a jilted girlfriend."

"On my mother's *grave,*" Trent said. Were there tears in his eyes too? Trent didn't cry. But his chest shuddered and he rubbed his eyes. "On my mother's grave, Ashby. I have never and will never lie to you."

His mother's grave? Fuck, Dez had said something about Trent's mother's memory, too. Ashby could feel the pieces falling into place. Trent's mum was gone. That was the rift between him and his dad.

"Oh, Trent," he said. It felt like his heart cracked for him. "I'm so sorry." He was sorry for his mum. He was sorry for jumping to conclusions. Why would he believe Trent had a pregnant girlfriend when he knew the part about cheating on Gordon was a lie? He should have taken a breath and thought before losing his shit.

Trent shivered. "I'll explain everything. Please, just let me take you inside." Trent shook his head. "I'm fighting for you, Ashby," Trent said through gritted teeth. "I'm not letting that asshole take you from me. I won't let that other asshole take my home, either."

"What?" Ashby asked, confused. He couldn't stop shaking. The wet snow was seeping through his jeans.

Trent held his arms open again, and this time Ashby gave in and threw himself into them. "Come on," Trent grunted, hauling him off the ground and walking them, tripping and fumbling, to his cabin. Ashby was still shivering and hiccuping. Trent rubbed his arms and hugged him to him tightly. "It's okay," he murmured over and over. "It's okay, Ashby. I've got you."

The second they were inside, Trent wrapped his arms around Ashby again and hugged him with his entire body. The cabin was only illuminated by a couple of lamps Trent had evidently left on when he'd left the place earlier. It was blissfully warm. Ashby trembled and cried.

"I'm so sorry," he said.

"No," Trent said firmly. He stood back and scowled at Ashby. For a second, he was scared. But then Trent shook his head and ground his teeth. "You should be mad. My life's a fucking circus. *I'm* sorry."

Ashby swiped angrily at the tears on his face. "I'm fucking *done* with arseholes controlling my life!" he shouted.

Trent broke into a smile. "Yes," he said. "Fuck those bastards."

Ashby was still quivering, but he was laughing as well now. The fury was still there, but he was through with being scared and letting other people make choices for him. He'd also had enough of crying already.

"I'll have my family's lawyers eat them alive," he snarled. "I'm going back in there and giving that dickhead a piece of my mind."

Trent cupped his face. "As much as I would love to see that," he said, "the best thing we can do is be calm, happy, and not give douchebags like Dez the satisfaction of getting a rise out of us."

Ashby took a long deep breath in and out. Then he cupped his hands over Trent's. "You're the expert."

"Unfortunately," Trent agreed. "Though I've not been very good at this recently."

Ashby shook his head. "I'll follow your lead. We'll be a united front. Much harder to break that way."

Trent nodded. "I'll stand by you anywhere," he murmured.

Ashby bit his lip, staring into his brown eyes. Then he placed his hand over Trent's bulletproof heart. "Why me?" he asked.

A smile twitched at the corner of Trent's mouth. "You're one in a million," he said. "And…I think I'm finally ready to stop running." He closed his eyes and took in a breath, then opened them and smiled. It changed his whole face. He was no longer scary or intimidating. He was warm and caring. "We're the Venn diagram, remember? Ain't nobody like us."

Ashby had to laugh at that. "Now *that* is the truth."

Trent gently pulled him closer to him, allowing their lips to meet for a sweet kiss. Ashby still felt awful, though. "I shouldn't have jumped to conclusions," he said. "I was too ready to believe the worst about you."

Trent cocked his head. "I think you were too ready to believe someone would do the worst *to* you," he said. "You need to stop dating fuckheads."

Ashby spluttered out a laugh. "Bloody hell, Trent Charles," he said. "You don't talk much, but when you do, you make a lot of sense."

Trent nodded. "True."

"Besides," Ashby said. "I don't plan on dating anyone else for a *very* long time."

"Is that so?" Trent asked, leaning in for a more heated kiss.

"Take me to bed and I'll show you how much I mean it," Ashby said, grabbing his leather jacket.

But Trent sighed. "As much as I would love to," he said. "Dez Starr was only part of the awfulness that's gone on tonight." He stepped back and pinched the bridge of his nose. "Kiefer was gloating how he's sold the resort."

Ashby glanced back toward the door they had just come through, like that might give him answers. "Isn't that a good thing?" he asked. "Won't another owner actually take care of the place?"

"The new owner is going to level the resort and build a nuclear power plant."

"Motherfucker!" Ashby cried before he could help himself. "No! Everyone will lose their jobs. What will happen to the community?"

What would happen to Maeve and Darnell and Kadie and Skye? Ashby was even worried about Bob, the hopeless manager. His kid may have been on the mend now, but

Ashby knew about American medical bills. He'd probably be paying those off for years. He needed this job, just as much as Maeve and her cats, Trent's dad and Merlin.

But Ashby was surprised to see Trent looking just as upset as he felt. "This place *is* my folks," he said gruffly. "It's all my dad has. It's…it's all we have left of my mom."

Ashby swallowed the lump that had risen in his throat. He grabbed Trent's hand and squeezed it. He understood now. "Then we fight for it," he said. "We stop letting these bastards dictate our lives. Come on. There has to be something we can do. If there isn't a manager here to talk to, I'll find one elsewhere." He sniffed. "I'm very good at speaking to managers."

Trent laughed and pulled him in for a passionate kiss. "I love you," he murmured.

Ashby blinked. But Trent didn't look shocked or like he was scrambling to take it back. If anything, he looked a little dazed.

"I-" Ashby said. "I think I might love you too."

Trent kissed him softly. "Good," he said. "A lover *and* a fighter. I knew you were perfect." Ashby could only stare as Trent leaned over to the coat rack and offered him his ski jacket. "Sorry, it's not pink," he said.

Ashby put the black jacket on even though it was too big. "I'll wear anything into battle," he said, his confidence growing by the minute. "You should see me in a dress. I'm a fucking Valkyrie."

Trent licked his lips. "I bet. Come on. Let's go see what kind of carnage we left in that place."

Together, hand in hand, they marched through the snow. Several times, Ashby almost allowed himself to feel guilty about overreacting to the article. But then he came to the sudden epiphany that his rage had been a *good* thing. He hadn't rolled over and taken it. He hadn't slunk away weeping. He had come out swinging.

Which is what he needed to do now for Trent, Maeve, Mr. Charles Sr. and all the other new friends he had made over the past week and a half. He wasn't sure how, but there had to be something they could do to stand up to that douchebag Kiefer.

He expected there to be some activity in the main lodge when they returned. Perhaps Dez still stirring up trouble with the crowd, or Kiefer handing out last paychecks to everyone. Instead, when they reached the main lobby, several people were running around frantically.

Ashby blinked as they whistled and checked behind the sofas and underneath the front desk. When Kadie spotted him, he raised his eyebrows at her. She ran over to him awkwardly in her bulky clerk's uniform.

"Ashby, Trent," she gasped. "Have you seen Merlin?"

"Merlin?" Ashby repeated, immediately concerned. "No – I – I mean I left him with Darnell when…" When he first saw that terrible article full of lies about him and Trent.

Kadie clutched her chest. "Darnell thought Skye had him, but she thought *Darnell* had him."

"What are you saying?" Trent asked. His gaze was darting around the room.

"Uh," Kadie said. "Merlin is missing. And your dad is a *wreck.*"

Twenty~Eight

TRENT

"WHERE IS HE?" TRENT DEMANDED, IMMEDIATELY IN CRISIS mode. "Where's my dad? Who saw Merlin last?"

"Darnell," Kadie said, wringing her hands. "He's so upset, poor love. He threw that hideous reporter man out the front door. Then by the time he came back to the bar, Skye was already looking for him."

"Merlin's probably just in the kitchen or something," Ashby said, reaching out to rub her arm. It was only then Trent realized he and Ashby were still holding hands. Well, fuck it. He wasn't letting go now. He needed his boyfriend's strength.

If Merlin was missing because of the shithead paparazzi Trent had brought to the resort, he'd never forgive himself.

"He normally turns up by now," Kadie insisted, shaking her head. "Maeve got us checking all the usual places. I think she's with your dad now at the bar. He's worried someone walked off with him or something."

"Dez didn't take him?" Trent asked, already marching toward the bar with Ashby right next to him.

Kadie scuttled along beside them. "No, definitely not," she

232

said. "Darnell put that guy in a cab and told him if he came back Darnell would call the cops." She sounded proud of him.

Trent glanced at her pushing her short blonde bob back again and again behind her ears as they walked. She was clearly upset. He had no idea Merlin meant so much to her or anyone else. Or that his dad did, for that matter. His heart ached.

"He's somewhere," Ashby said resolutely. "He's small and fat, he won't have gotten far."

Trent nodded. If he was honest, he was stunned his dad was upset enough to whip the whole resort into a frenzy. Even guests were joining in whistling for Merlin. As they entered the bar, Trent spotted the little girl with the hazel eyes from the gift store and her family, the grandparents with their bespectacled grandkid, and the three middle-aged cosmo-drinking women, all in their own little search parties.

Trent's dad was sitting in the deserted restaurant with Maeve the housekeeper rubbing his back. A woman with curly chestnut hair in a beautician's blouse and Darnell, the bartender, were sitting at the same table. Trent stopped walking when his dad looked up at him.

He was crying.

Trent thought he was going to be the only Charles man to break down today. He'd been wrong.

"Dad," Trent said. Ashby naturally let his hand go as Trent dashed over to pull his dad in for a hug. To his astonishment, his dad hugged him back, just as fiercely. "Hey, it's okay, what's going on?"

"Merlin ran off in all the upset," his dad grunted.

He was trying his best to keep it together. His voice was reasonably steady, but tears were streaming down his leathery face from under his glasses. He never looked so old as he did in that moment.

"Is it true they're demolishing the resort?" the beautician asked. Beneath her heavy makeup, she looked very pale.

"One thing at a time," Trent said firmly. "You guys last saw Merlin here?"

They nodded. Trent felt Ashby come stand beside him as Kadie positioned herself standing between where Darnell and Maeve were sitting. Trent noticed that when his dad sat again, his shoulders hunched in defeat, Maeve began rubbing his back once more.

"I'm so sorry," Darnell said shaking his head. "I thought Skye had him. It's my fault. I should have made sure."

"I *should* have had him," Skye, the beautician insisted.

"No, no, it's no one's fault," Kadie said. She went to awkwardly touch Darnell's arm, then apparently thought the better of it.

Trent scowled. "It's my fault," he said. "Dez was here because of me, and Kiefer is punishing the resort to get back at me."

"Oh bugger them both sideways," snapped Ashby, quivering with rage. "We'll deal with those little scumbags *after* we've found our puppy. Maeve, you said you've checked his usual hiding places?" The older woman nodded, her eyes wide behind her colorful glasses. "Right. You and Mr. Charles check the ground floor. Knock on every door if you have to. Darnell, you and Kadie double-check with the kitchen staff. He could very well be searching for food. Then you can go through the lobby again. Skye, can you go through the spa and make sure he's not asleep in a nice warm cupboard of towels?"

The faces around the table were a little taken aback, but they all nodded. Trent's heart swelled with pride as he turned to Ashby. "Where do you want us to look?"

Ashby's face was grim. "The second floor," he said. "We'll also go door to door." He turned back to the group. "I'm sure he's fine. But the real concern here is that he got outside. There's a real blizzard gaining force out there and he's too young to survive for long on his own. I'm *sure* he's fine. But let's get him reunited with Mr. Charles sooner rather than later."

Kadie looked scared. "He'd know not to go outside alone, wouldn't he?"

Trent's dad shook his head as he hurriedly got to his feet. "He's nothing but trouble. He'll run out in traffic or get lost in the snow. *Goddamn* it." His voice choked with worry. Trent had known all along that deep down, of course, his dad loved his new dog, no matter how naughty he was.

Trent rested his hand on his dad's shoulder, making him pause. "We'll find him," he told him. "We won't lose anyone else."

His dad clasped his hand over Trent's. "No," he said determinedly. "We won't."

Then Trenton Sr. turned and looked directly at Ashby. For a second, Trent's heart threatened to stop. There was probably no mistaking their body language. His dad had already intimated he knew Trent had been close to breaking Ashby's heart. How would he react now they were actually together?

Trent's dad clasped Ashby's shoulder, bulky with Trent's coat. "Thank you, son," he said. "You boys stick together."

Ashby blinked, then smiled. "We will, sir," he said.

"Okay," Maeve said loudly as they began to spread out. "Whoever finds that little scamp first, brings him back here to the bar for a spanked bottom."

"You're not fooling anyone," Kadie said with a tut. "He'll get nothing less than half a chicken and a cuddle if you find him first."

Maeve raised an eyebrow at her. "I don't know what

you're talking about," she said as she bustled after Trent's dad.

"Thank you," Trent said as they left the others and began to climb the stairs. Ashby glanced over at him, a questioning look in his eyes. "For taking charge," Trent elaborated. "For understanding that he's not just a dog."

Ashby scoffed. "Of course he's not *just a dog*," he said. Like there could ever be such a thing.

"You boys aren't talking about that adorable little fellow with the floppy ears, are you?"

Trent came to an abrupt halt with Ashby and tried not to grind his teeth too hard. They turned to see Kiefer behind them in the hallway on the second floor. No doubt he had followed them up the stairs. He must have been loitering around the bar.

For once, he wasn't wearing his Stetson, so he became immediately that much more forgettable. Objectively speaking, he really wasn't as handsome as Trent had first given him credit for. He was pretty plain despite his dazzling teeth and expensive clothes.

"Fuck off, Burton," Trent growled at him.

But Ashby raised his hand up to Trent, his eyes trained on Kiefer. "Why do you ask?" he enquired sweetly.

Kiefer's gaze swept disgustingly up and down Ashby. Trent could just imagine him undressing Ashby mentally and wanted to smack that smug look off Kiefer's face. But then he remembered what he'd told Ashby back at his cabin and reined in his temper. He wouldn't give Kiefer the satisfaction of seeing him lose his temper again.

"Well," Kiefer said. He rocked on his cowboy boots and imitated concern. "Only there was a chubby pup who was awful keen to be let outside by the pool a while back. He obviously needed to do his business, so I opened the door for him. I do hope that's not a problem?"

Trent really did almost lunge for the asshole. But Ashby was already hauling him past the slimebag, back down the stairs. "No, no problem at all," Ashby called back. "Thank you *so* much, darling!"

"Why would he tell us what he did?" Trent snarled as they made it back to the first floor and ran toward the pool.

"Because he's a sociopath who needs everyone to know how clever he is and just how much power he has over them," Ashby said, quite succinctly considering how fast they were sprinting. "I can't wait to deal with him. I'm going to *disembowel* him. It'll be fun."

Trent glanced at his lover as they burst out into the snowstorm, unable to stop himself smiling despite the dire circumstances. "I really do love you," he said.

Ashby smiled bashfully back at him.

CHAPTER

Twenty-Nine

ASHBY

THE WEATHER HAD RAPIDLY DETERIORATED. CONSIDERING IT had almost frozen Ashby's balls off twice in the last hour, he couldn't say he was thrilled as he and Trent stepped back out into the howling wind and thick, heavy snow.

"Merlin!" Trent bellowed.

The door to the resort slammed shut behind them. Ashby couldn't really make anything out in the flurry. It was too early in the day for the lights to be on around the pool. The sky was a dark iron gray, hardly letting any sunshine through to help with visibility.

"Merlin!" Ashby also yelled at the top of his lungs. "Shit, Trent," he said, trying not to become panicked. "We're never going to find him in this weather."

"Yes, we will," Trent said. "We have to."

He reached out and took Ashby's hand so they could slowly move through the snow together. Ashby could just about make out the sauna building to the left, but it was difficult to see where the swimming pool was.

"Should we text the others and let them know he's definitely outside?" Ashby called over the wind.

"Let's just look a minute," Trent called back.

Fuck Kiefer. What kind of bastard put a puppy in danger just to spite someone? The old Ashby might have fallen into a pit of guilt that Kiefer was essentially doing this because Trent stopped him from 'having' Ashby. But the new Ashby didn't have a single fuck to give about that. He absolutely should not have shagged Kiefer for any reason when he didn't want to. It definitely wasn't his fault that the twisted psycho was now trying to hurt him, Trent and Trent's family anyway he could. He was a maniac and deserved to be behind bars.

Ashby's ears just caught something that made him stop. He tugged Trent so he would pause too. "Did you hear that?" he asked.

"What?" Trent asked, shaking his head. The wind was roaring and howling like a wounded beast. Or...was that whimpering Ashby could just make out?

"I think he's close," Ashby cried, trying not to get emotional. He needed to concentrate, not panic. "Merlin? Merlin! Good boy, come here!"

Trent shook his head. "I don't hear anything?"

But Ashby knew there was something drifting on the violent winds. He lifted his arm up to try and stop the snow from flinging into his eyes as he moved to the left where he thought the sound might have come from. He wished he had his ski goggles on.

"Merlin? Good boy, come here, sweetie!"

Both he and Trent froze at the same time. "There!" Trent cried, pointing. Ashby had to agree. There was definitely a yowling sort of whimper coming from in front of them. They hurried forward. Trent only just pulled Ashby back before he ran over the lip at the edge of the pool.

"Oh, shit!" Ashby said, clinging to Trent to stop himself

from falling. Then he gasped in realization. "You don't think...?" he said, looking up at Trent.

The yelps came again. This time, Ashby could make out a faint sound of splashing.

"He's in the pool!" they cried together.

Ashby didn't even think. He let go of Trent, unzipping the big coat he'd borrowed and throwing it to the ground. "Wait, Ashby," Trent said. But Ashby was already running down the steps into the heated water.

"Merlin!" he yelled, dragging him and his saturated clothes further into the pool. The steam and snow made it impossible to make anything out. "Merlin, baby, come here!"

Splashes from behind told Ashby that Trent had followed after him. Ashby waded on, only able to see about a foot in front of him in any direction. The warmth of the water was a sharp contrast to the evil, icy winds cutting through the top half of his body. Where the water splashed up and made his clothes and skin damp, the air was even more biting. Ashby sunk down further to try and stop his teeth from chattering.

The splashes in front of him were getting louder. Ashby lifted his feet and swam blindly toward the noise. Then the steam parted to reveal poor Merlin, soaked to the skin, struggling desperately to keep his head above water.

"I've got him!" Ashby screamed. He lunged forward, kicking and thrashing until he scooped the little guy into his arms, holding him to his chest and taking his weight.

Within seconds, Trent's muscular arms were wrapped around Ashby and Merlin both, supporting them as they huddled together in the rippling water sloshing around their shoulders.

"Oh, good boy! Good boy!" Ashby said. He allowed himself a little sob as the puppy wriggled in his grip, whimpering and licking his and Trent's faces.

Trent kissed Ashby's temple, pressing his lips to his skin for several seconds. "Well done," he said. "Let's get inside."

They began the difficult task of pushing their way back through the water. Merlin wasn't exactly convinced about venturing back out into the biting cold and begin squirming, trying to stay in the warm water.

"Come here, dude," Trent said affectionately as Ashby almost lost his hold on him. Trent easily cradled the fat puppy against his chest as they hurried up the pool steps.

Immediately, Ashby was so cold he saw stars. But Trent didn't pause as he marched back toward the lodge door. Ashby only hesitated long enough to pick up Trent's leather jacket as well as his ski jacket that they'd discarded in the snow.

It felt like an eternity to get through the frenzied snow. But eventually, Ashby was following Trent and Merlin through the door into the side corridor that led back into the belly of the lodge. "F-fuck me," Ashby stammered. It was undeniably warmer inside, but the chill from the wind clung to their sodden clothes and Merlin's thick fur. He was yowling and grousing in distress. Poor thing was probably going to be averse to baths his whole life now.

"Bar, go," Trent grunted. "Phone, in pocket."

Luckily, Trent had left his important possessions in his leather jacket, just like Ashby had moved his stuff to the coat pockets when he'd put it on. Neither of them had destroyed their phones by jumping in the pool. As they squelched their way down the hall, Ashby fumbled with trembling hands to remove Trent's phone, presumably so he could call his dad.

He didn't need to, though. As they rounded the corner, they were met with several gasps. Maeve and Trent's dad were crossing the lobby toward the bar. As the guests nearest Trent and Ashby cried out, Maeve and Mr. Charles turned their heads to see them.

"Jesus, Mary and Joseph!" Maeve shrieked. She grabbed Mr. Charles's hand and the two of them joined the small crowd thronging around Ashby, Trent and Merlin as they shivered.

"He was in the pool," Trent managed to grunt as he handed the puppy over to his dad. Mr. Charles apparently couldn't care less that he was getting wet. He looked so happy, laughing with tears of relief in his eyes. "That asshole Kiefer Burton let him outside on purpose."

"No!" Maeve gasped, scandalized.

"Here, boys, here." Ashby looked around as he realized Skye had appeared from nowhere with an armful of towels from the spa. "We saw you coming in from the bar window," she explained as she wrapped them both and Merlin in thick, fluffy towels. "I can't believe you got in the pool in this weather!"

"What else would we have done?" Ashby said with a laugh.

Before he knew what was happening, Trent pulled him into a fierce, sodden hug and kissed his damp hair. People around them stilled in surprise.

"My *boyfriend*," Trent said with emphasis to no one in particular as he looked Ashby in the eyes, "was the one who jumped in and saved Merlin. He's a hero."

Ashby could feel the blush rising on his face, a sharp contrast to his still-freezing skin. "Oh, uh, no, not really," he stammered.

"Of course he is," Maeve said. She wagged her finger in Trent's face. "And don't you forget it."

"No, ma'am," Trent said with a huge grin on his face.

"Thank you," said Mr. Charles, nodding at Ashby. Merlin was subdued in his arms, probably finally feeling tired from his stressful ordeal. He glanced at Trent, his son. "For everything," he added to Ashby.

Kadie and Darnell had joined the crowd. Darnell reached out and shook Ashby's hand, then Trent's. "Man, you guys saved the day."

Kadie waved her hands in distress. "You need to get out of those clothes. You'll catch your deaths!"

"I agree," Maeve said shooing them back. "We'll sort out this pup. You two go get yourselves *warmed* up." Ashby didn't miss the way she wiggled her eyebrows at him and he backed away before he could die of mortification.

"What about Burton?" Trent asked.

His dad shook his head. "We'll deal with him later. This resort isn't going down without a fight, I'll tell you that much."

"We can talk about it tomorrow," Kadie fretted. "Go, go, before you ruin the carpets totally!"

Ashby laughed and let Trent lead him through the crowd that seemed to just keep getting bigger as people leaned in to pet Merlin's head and coo over what a lucky boy he was to be safe and sound.

Ashby allowed Trent to walk him back to his room. Once the door was closed, Trent wrapped him in his big strong arms. "You're amazing," he said. "I'm so lucky."

"Oh, shut up," Ashby said, swatting his firm chest lightly.

"No," Trent said simply with a grin. "Please get changed into something warm. I have to get you back to my cabin immediately."

Ashby licked his lips and pulled at Trent's shirt. "We could get naked right here," he suggested, desire stirring in his belly.

But Trent shook his head. "My place has a log fire," he said.

Ashby blinked. "Give me one minute," he said.

Thirty

TRENT

THE RUG WAS SOFT AND FLUFFY UNDERNEATH TRENT'S BACK. His burning skin was slick with perspiration and tingled all over. He looked up at Ashby straddling him in the flickering firelight and felt full to overflowing with joy and love.

He couldn't stop his hands from roaming up and down Ashby's naked thighs, around his slim waist, across his chest. Ashby gripped Trent's shoulders as he rode him, their heavy breaths mingling as Ashby leaned down for a kiss.

"You're so beautiful," Trent murmured with wonder against his mouth. "All mine."

"All yours," Ashby agreed with a gorgeous smile. He sat up again, dropping his head back as he ground down on Trent's cock. "Fuck, you feel so good. Holy shit."

Trent reached up and touched his fingers to Ashby's exposed throat, feeling his Adam's apple move as he swallowed. He traced his hand down the middle of his chest, brushing his knuckles against Ashby's flat, soft stomach, then circling his fingers around his stiff, leaking cock.

Joined together, completely naked, it couldn't be more

obvious how different they were. Yet Trent had never felt so perfect with anyone.

"Come on me, gorgeous," Trent said as he jerked Ashby off and made him cry out. "You're so pretty when you come."

Ashby bit his lip as his grin got bigger. "I'm pretty all the time," he managed to gasp. "I'm going to come all over you and show you that you're mine. Fuck, yes, like that, don't stop."

Trent had never been come on before. He loved marking his partners when he felt close with them, but it felt so right that Ashby should be the only one able to mark him back in the same way. Everything about him was right: right place, right time. As Trent's climax built, he felt like the luckiest guy in the world.

If he had met Ashby before now, there was every chance Trent would have missed this opportunity completely. He would have never known how happy he could be with another person. He clung to Ashby's hip and knew he would put everything into this relationship. He never wanted to let this precious man go.

Ashby managed to bend over and steal a passionate kiss before his orgasm hit him. He wailed as his body shuddered, his cum painting thick stripes up Trent's chest. Seeing him climax and the pure bliss drawn all over his face tipped Trent over the edge. He bucked, filling the condom deep within Ashby.

For several seconds they clung to each other, riding out the aftershocks of their lovemaking. But eventually Trent regained the use of his limbs enough to reach up and cup the side of Ashby's face in his palm. Ashby smiled, still panting, and gently eased himself off Trent's softening cock.

"All warmed up now," he declared, flopping to Trent's side by the fire. "Thank you very much."

"Anytime," Trent assured him. He turned to kiss him

softly on the lips before removing the condom and discarding it on the wooden floor beyond the plush rug. Darkness was falling outside, so only the dancing flames illuminated Ashby's face. It was enough for Trent to make out all his features, though.

Ashby linked their hands together. "Do you want me to, um…?" he said, glancing down at the mess he'd made over Trent's chest.

Trent shook his head. "Not if you don't want to," he said. He knew his kink for eating his own cum was a bit feral. He was thrilled Ashby had been so into it. But Trent wasn't so concerned about Ashby doing the same, especially if it wasn't to his liking.

"Not really my cup of tea," Ashby said, wrinkling his nose. "Sorry."

"Don't be," Trent said. "Maybe you could help me clean off in the shower in a bit?"

Ashby's eyes lit up. "Ohh, now that I would be into."

"Awesome," Trent said, kissing his lips. "I was thinking," he said, cuddling Ashby to his side. Ashby looked up from where his cheek was resting on Trent's bulletproof tattoo.

"Oh?" he said.

Trent played with his blond hair for a second. "Well, uh," he said. He was more nervous than he wanted to admit. But he had never asked anyone this before. "Seeing as you're going to be here for a while, I thought. Well, we could go into town and get tested. If you like?" He hadn't ever not used a condom in his life and was almost certain he wasn't carrying anything. But even if Ashby thought he was fine too, it was sensible to be sure. Besides, there was something official about committing to getting tested together as a couple.

Thankfully, Ashby's face lit up. "I'd love to," he said. He nibbled on his lip. "So, about what you said…in the lobby."

Trent raised an eyebrow. "Are you...am I...can I be your boyfriend? Please?"

Trent laughed and leaned down to kiss Ashby's forehead. "Sorry, I should have asked first. I got carried away."

Ashby was flushed from the sex and the warmth of the fire, but Trent could have sworn in the dim light that he blushed even deeper. "I loved it," he said quietly. "I – I love you."

Something raw and wonderful unfurled in Trent's chest. "Yeah?" Ashby nodded. Trent hugged him tighter and buried his face in his soft blond hair. "I love you too, gorgeous," he said. Then he laughed. "How unlikely are we?"

But Ashby shook his head. "We feel inevitable," he said.

"Really?" Trent said. "Even though I'm...well, I don't know what I am."

Ashby tapped his chest. "Actually, I was thinking about this. How do you feel about calling yourself questioning? It's what a lot of baby gays call themselves when they're not quite sure."

Trent considered that. "No," he said slowly. "There's nothing I'm unsure of here. How about plain old queer? Do I have to be more specific, or will that do?"

To his relief, Ashby looked thrilled. "It's good enough for this enby's Venn diagram," he said playfully.

Trent ran his fingers up and down Ashby's arm. "While I'm working on saying what's on my mind," he said, aware that his communication skills weren't always great, "I wanted to ask you about sex."

"Oh, fabulous," Ashby said. "Anything in particular?"

Trent nodded. "Obviously, I'm new to doing it with a dude. But, we don't always have to do it that way round." He bit his lip. "Just because you're smaller, and fem." He paused checking that was the right word. Ashby didn't correct him, so he went on. "It doesn't mean I feel like I should be the one doing the fucking every time. We can switch."

Ashby blinked and looked at him for a few moments. "That's one of the sweetest and most considerate things anyone's ever said to me," he said softly. He picked up Trent's hand and kissed his fingers. "But I don't like to do that," he said. He swallowed and Trent worried he was upset. "It's a dysphoria thing. I like my cock very much. But topping…it makes me feel disconnected with my body. I don't…it jolts something in my brain. Sorry."

"Hey, no," Trent said, taking his turn to kiss Ashby's hand. "I'm happy doing whatever. I just wanted to offer it and not make assumptions."

Ashby shook his head. "I can't believe I ever thought you were scary," he said with a giggle. "You're the loveliest teddy bear. Oh!" Excitement brightened his face. "We could play with toys, though, if you wanted to try something new?"

Trent shivered, surprised by how turned on he was by the idea. He drew Ashby to him so they could kiss. "I'd love you to fuck me with a toy," he rasped. Ashby moaned and kissed him harder.

"Good thing I'm sticking around, then," he said. "We'll have lots of time to experiment."

They made out for a while, but they were still too wrung out from fucking to get all that hot and heavy. "Does that mean you're not taking that flight back to London?" Trent asked.

Ashby ran his fingers through Trent's hair, caressing the back of his neck. "You said you were here for three months before you were going back to work?" Trent nodded. "Then yes, I'm sticking around." He licked his lips and sighed. But a smile tugged at the corner of his mouth. "I love London, but home is where the heart is. And…I feel like my heart belongs near you."

Trent closed his eyes and rested their foreheads together. "I couldn't agree more," he murmured. "I want to make this work."

"Me too," Ashby said. "I don't really feel like putting an ocean between us just yet."

"How long is your current visa?" Trent asked. "Three months, right?"

A mischievous glint sparkled in Ashby's eyes. "I was actually thinking of something a little more permanent," he said. "I told you my mum is from the States, didn't I?"

"Yeah," said Trent. He didn't want to get his hopes up too much, but he couldn't help it.

Ashby Bit his lip. "Well, my parents never applied for dual citizenship for me. But because my mum and grandparents are American, it will make things easier to get a green card and become a permanent resident. Then I'd be eligible to become a citizen for good."

Trent's heart skipped a beat. "You'd really move here?" he said. "For us?"

Ashby looked upward, thinking. "As much as I want this to work, I know it's only early stages still. I do think a relationship stands a better chance if the people in it actually *see* each other. But that isn't my main reason for considering moving so soon. It's part of it, but I don't think I'd change my whole life after a week with someone. I hope you're not disappointed?"

Trent shook his head. "That's very sensible," he said honestly. As much as he would have supported Ashby moving closer so their love could stand a better chance of flourishing, it was a relief to know it wasn't the only drive behind it. "What's the other reason?"

That devilment was back on Ashby's face. "I've had the *most* delicious idea," he said.

CHAPTER
Thirty~One
ASHBY

"Well, look what the cat dragged in."

Ashby smiled at Kiefer as he and Trent entered one of the resort's only conference rooms. Like the rest of the place, the walls were beige and the carpet a faded and threadbare brown. A sad-looking potted fern sat drooping in the corner. Poorly painted watercolors of the mountains hung in frames on the walls.

A cream oval table with eight chairs dominated most of the space in the room. Kiefer sat toward one end with two other guys, all still wearing their Stetsons. One was large, the other tall and lanky. Ashby's English sensibilities were offended by the bad manners of wearing hats indoors, let alone to a meeting, but he smiled and ignored the cultural clash. Let them think this was their meeting.

"Mr. Burton," Ashby said cheerfully. "How lovely to see you again. You'll be delighted to know Mr. Charles Sr. was reunited with his beloved dog Merlin. I know you must have been terribly worried after your faux-pas the other day."

Kiefer took a sip of whiskey from the tumbler he had in front of him, as did the two men flanking him. "Of course,"

250

he said dryly and licked his lips. "You seen any more reporters on the premises? I'd hate for you boys to have been bothered any further."

Ashby hummed as he and Trent took their seats down at the other end of the table. He wouldn't have been surprised if Kiefer was inviting the paparazzi in with open arms to harass him and Trent some more. Luckily, there hadn't been any other incidents so far.

"Oh, we've got far more important things to worry about than some silly photographers," Ashby said with a wave of his hand, his bangles chinking quietly together. He placed the file he held down on the table and offered the other men a sweet smile. Trent sat in silent support beside him.

Ashby had thought very carefully about what he wanted to wear today. He knew first hand it was tricky to come across with authority to people who were narrow minded if he presented as too feminine. But he also knew he was more confident when he looked like himself. With Trent beside him, he had decided to push his gender boundaries as much as he felt able to for this occasion.

He had on his favorite black boots with the small heel and black leggings with a white shirt loosely tucked in. But he finished the look with a beaded necklace under the collar, one of his flowing cardigans in teal that reached down to his knees, and had slicked on a little eyeliner. He could feel the other men in the room casting suspicious gazes over him. But this was a conservative look to Ashby. Just enough to make him feel like a bloody warrior.

Opposite the Texans was Bob, the resort's down-and-out manager. He looked absolutely shattered and more than a little wary of the men to his right. Ashby noticed that Bob did not have a drink.

It was fine. Ashby didn't anticipate they would be here for all that long.

"So, what's this all about, princess?" Kiefer asked, sounding amused. "I was most surprised when my secretary informed me you had requested this meeting." He laughed and looked to his buddies for approval. "I do hope I'm not in trouble," he said as they forced out chuckles.

"Quite the opposite, Mr. Burton," Ashby said in delight. "I'm very happy to inform you that I'm here to help."

"Right," Kiefer said slowly. "Mr. Willoughby, was it? Or should I call you Miss?"

"Mr. Wilcott will do nicely," Ashby corrected cheerfully. Kiefer could play all the games he liked. He wasn't going to ruffle Ashby's feathers that easily today.

"Sure," Kiefer said, his tone suggesting he couldn't care less. "Well, I'm not sure what you could possibly help me with."

The way his eyes traveled up and down Ashby's body suggested he knew *exactly* how he would like Ashby to help him out. Ashby was impressed he managed not to gag. The idea of letting that asshole anywhere near him was beyond repulsive.

"It's simple," he said, opening the file in front of him. He took two identical documents out and slid one toward Kiefer and the other to Bob.

"What's this?" Kiefer asked, tapping the top sheet of stapled paper without bothering to look at it.

Ashby beamed, excitement fizzing in his guts. He couldn't believe he was actually doing this. "Oh, that's just my proposal to buy the resort outright for twice what the nuclear power plant people were willing to pay for the land. In cash."

The three Texans stilled. Bob's tired eyes suddenly popped wide open and he snatched up the papers in front of him to flip eagerly through them.

"Cute," Kiefer said, his tone clipped. "But it's a done deal, son."

"Actually, no it's not," Ashby said, enjoying himself probably a little bit too much. "I had my team of lawyers check. And according to them, any proposal to buy the resort has to be considered as to whether it's regarded as the best option for the employees and community at large. You see," he said leaning forward, "when *I'm* the owner and not you, I will be committed to restoring this business to the standard it should be. I'll invest in it like an owner should and see that it starts turning a profit again. Quite a substantial one." He waved his hand and leaned back in his seat again. "It's all there in the proposal," he said.

Trent's hand snuck over to squeeze Ashby's knee. It wasn't even for a second, but Ashby appreciated it.

"As the owner," Kiefer said with a tight smile, "I ultimately get to decide what happens with this dump. And I would personally love nothing more than to see it razed to the ground."

"Now hold on there a minute, Burton," one of the older Texans said, the large one. He had the proposal open and pushed it over to the other skinny guy, stabbing a finger at what Ashby guessed was the bottom line. "This is a ridiculously good offer. If this boy wants to throw his money at this shithole, I say let him."

"Me too," the lanky guy said. Ashby could see the greed in his eyes even from where he was sitting across the room. "It's not like we have anything to lose. This place is a money pit."

Ashby didn't look away from Kiefer as he stared at him. He knew the point here was how much Kiefer wanted to hurt him and Trent for 'beating' him, as he saw it. But that wasn't going to happen. Anyone could see that selling the resort as a fixer-upper was the far preferable option to bull-dozing it. Ashby could see the dollar signs in Kiefer's colleagues' eyes. As stakeholders, they had just as much to gain as Kiefer did.

"Um, excuse me?" Bob's timid voice floated across the room. "This, uh, means no one would have to lose their jobs, right?"

"Actually," Ashby said. He clasped his hands in front of him and turned so Bob had his full attention. "It says that within nine months, that is, by the middle of next ski season, we should be able not only to offer pay rises for all current staff, but we should also be in the position to hire a number of new employees." He looked back at Kiefer with a sweet smile. "You see, when you invest in things like remodeling, updating staff training, expanding services and proper marketing, it means more customers come and spend their lovely money. Like I said at the start. Simple."

"Right, okay," Bob said, nodding eagerly. "That. I want to do that."

"On behalf of the resort's employees," Trent said. He pulled a folded piece of paper from inside his leather jacket pocket and opened it to reveal all the signatures they had collected. "I can confirm this is what they want as well."

"Let's do it," said the large Texan on the left. "Where do we sign?"

Kiefer wasn't quite done yet though. "We can't do anything without informing our current business partners at the energy company," he said irritably. "I say we still go with them."

"And I say I'll tell them myself that they have been outbid," said the skinny Texan on the right. He pulled a gold pen out from his breast pocket and clicked it open. "You're outnumbered, Kimmy. We'd be fools to turn down this offer."

"It *is* a ludicrous amount of money," Ashby said with a sigh, shaking his head.

Both the Texans had already signed the contract. The big

one pushed the papers in front of Kiefer and raised his eyebrows.

The vein on the side of Kiefer's head was visibly popping out. He ground his teeth and glowered at Ashby and Trent. "Fuck it," he snarled, snatching up the pen and scrawling down his signature. "I hope it makes you bankrupt."

"Oh, I don't know," said Ashby as he reached over and pulled the papers back to him. "I am obscenely rich and I'm not an idiot." He batted his eyelashes at Kiefer as he downed the last of his whiskey. "Or an arsehole. I'm prepared to actually do some work and make this place flourish. It was a pleasure doing business with you. Now, please leave my resort. We have certain standards to maintain."

Without another word, Kiefer rose to his feet, buttoned up his blazer, and stormed out of the conference room. The other two Texans seemed to pick up that the insult wasn't directed at them, as they took the time to come around and shake Ashby's hand before they left. Bob watched them go with an open mouth.

"Right, Bob," Ashby said, catching his attention. "Would you like to go over some more of the proposal? I've got so many ideas that I'm very excited about discussing with you. I'll give Darnell a call and see about having some refreshments brought over. We're celebrating after all."

Bob looked at him, then giggled, like a child. He clapped his hand over his mouth, but it didn't stop the mirth from shining out of his eyes. "I can't believe you saved us," he said once he found some of his composure. He looked like the weight that had been sitting on his shoulders had finally lifted, and he appeared years younger for it.

Trent took Ashby's hand and smiled at him. "That's what he does," he said. Ashby saw the pride in his eyes and could have died from happiness there and then. "He's a hero." Trent leaned over and kissed Ashby softly on the cheek. "I'll leave you guys to discuss business. I'll see you at home."

Because of course Ashby had bought Trent's cabin for them as part of the agreement. He had plans to expand on it and make it a real home.

"Bye," he said softly, watching his boyfriend leave and close the door. He couldn't stop smiling.

Finally, he'd done something of real value with his life. And he had the man he loved by his side as he did it.

CHAPTER

Thirty~Two

TRENT

Trent stood on the side of the mountain and looked down at the spectacular view below. Snow-dusted pine trees rose out from the pristine white landscape that glowed in the midday sunshine. The sky was a clear cobalt blue, the air fresh and cold. Down below, he could see all of the Grand Resort in all its glory.

The new construction work was already coming along nicely. The interiors were all getting makeovers, but Ashby and Bob had already given the go-ahead for the new gym being built and a children's play area. It was like the resort was coming to life after a long time in hibernation.

"It's perfect," his dad said beside him.

Trent turned and looked at his dad as he stared out over the vista. They had been hunting for a quiet spot on the resort grounds, the perfect place to put a memorial bench.

"Your mom would be very proud of you," his dad said, still looking out at the view. "She knew you loved her. I know she did."

Trent swallowed and looked down at Merlin, who was being a very good boy for once at their feet. His tongue lolled out and he wagged his tail as Trent leaned down to scratch between his ears. He'd calmed down a fair bit since his adventure in the pool. Or, Trent privately suspected, since he and his dad had stopped fighting.

"Thank you," he said around the lump in his throat. "I…I miss her."

"I know, son. Me too," his dad said with a sigh. "But sometimes things don't go as planned. I'm just so grateful for the time we had together. She was my one in a million. But… she's still with us." He turned to Trent, his smudged glasses glinting in the sunshine. "She would want us to be friends again. To be a family. I know she would bend my ear for everything I put you through."

Trent shook his head and clasped his dad's shoulder. "I'm still sorry for the way I acted," he said, dropping his hand.

His dad shrugged. "Me too," he said heavily. "Grief makes us do dumb things, I think."

Trent nodded in agreement. "I needed someone smarter than me to help me get my head out of my ass," he said.

His dad chuckled. "That Ashby is a great boy," he said. Trent loved his dad so much for not once batting an eyelid at the fact Trent was dating another guy. One who didn't always look very much like a guy. He just seemed so happy that Trent had settled down. "Love looks good on you, son," he said.

Trent smiled and tried not to blush. "He's my one in a million," he said. He'd forgotten when he'd told Ashby those words that it had been his parents' saying.

"And that's how you treat him," his dad said sagely. "Everything else falls into place if you make sure to remember that, every day."

"You sound like Maeve," Trent told him with a chuckle. It had not escaped his notice that every time he saw his dad now, Maeve always seemed to be by his side. Either telling him off for not doing his books properly or fussing that he wasn't eating enough. She told anyone who would listen, loudly, that she was just looking after Merlin. But Trent saw how his dad was dressing a bit smarter these days.

He was happy for them. His dad deserved someone special in his life.

"Maeve is a wise woman," he said to Trent. "And she loves Ashby like her own son, I think."

It was Trent's turn to laugh. Ashby had been complaining that he'd got himself an American 'mom.' But Trent suspected he was secretly thrilled to have her fussing over him and caring so much.

"I won't let her down," he said in all seriousness. "I'm going to treat Ashby right. I promise."

His dad nodded, apparently satisfied. "You decided what you're going to do yet?"

Trent took in a deep breath of fresh, cold air. "Yes," he said. "I'm going to cut back and only take on projects that I really want to do. And when I'm not working...I'll come home. Here."

His dad blinked rapidly, but his mouth quirked into a smile. "You sure your old man won't cramp your style?"

"Oh, I'm buying a place in town," Trent said with a laugh. "Now that Ashby has a job he's crazy about, someone will need to drag him away from it every now and again. We'll keep out of your hair. What's left of it."

His dad scoffed and batted Trent's arm. "I still got plenty of hair," he said.

Merlin woofed in agreement.

Trent never thought he would feel at home in Nowhere, Wyoming. But home was indeed where your heart was. He had his dad back. And he had Ashby. This was where he wanted to lay his hat.

The world would still be out there, waiting for him to

explore. He never thought his wanderlust would fade. But he would travel with Ashby by his side now. Then they could come back to their little corner of the globe, a place they could carve out just for themselves.

He couldn't wait.

Epilogue

TWO MONTHS LATER - ASHBY

"Guinevere, no! Sit!" Ashby said sternly to the St. Bernard puppy at his feet. She looked up at him with a doggy grin and wagged her tail. "Merlin's been teaching you bad habits again, hasn't he?" Ashby grumbled as he got back to work. He wasn't really mad at his and Trent's rambunctious puppy, though. He never could be.

He still didn't want her and Merlin running around the bar and wrecking everything before Trent arrived. Ashby would hate for all his and his team's hard work to go to waste.

It was a double event tonight. The bar and restaurant were having their grand reopenings and all the staff would be in attendance as well as guests from the local towns and further afield. Ashby didn't need to be there, setting up himself. The events team were perfectly capable. But he was so proud, he wanted to have his boots on the ground, mucking in with the others.

He'd finished tweaking the table with all their new brochures on display, then smoothed down his skirt as he moved through the crowd over to the floral display.

He had leggings on under the skirt as well as his fluffy boots. But there was no mistaking his lacy blouse, lip gloss and eye makeup as anything other than ladylike. But, as he'd explained to Trent before, he wasn't trying to look like a woman. He wasn't wearing a bra or trying to alter his body shape in any way. He just felt like being pretty for the resort's big party. And so far, the staff and guests had responded with overwhelming positivity.

Part of the relaunch and new marketing campaign had been because Ashby had proposed to Bob and the other managers that they make it known that the Grand Resort was now a rainbow-friendly vacation spot. Not exclusively LGBT, but somewhere which welcomed all guests, no matter their orientation. Bob had been very nervous thinking it would drive other customers away to begin with and Ashby couldn't blame him. But ultimately, they decided that any guests that had a problem with a queer-friendly space could go on holiday elsewhere.

So Ashby wanted to feel free from gender constraints for the big opening. The way he felt free in so many aspects of his life now. He was liberated by his new job, thriving in a way he never thought possible. He was also completely, almost painfully, in love.

He sighed down at Guinevere, his thoughts turning bittersweet. Because this wasn't just a party for the reopening.

It was also Trent's farewell party.

He wouldn't be gone for long. His next film was only scheduled to keep him away for six weeks and then he would be back until October. Ashby knew he would miss him like crazy, but it was fine. He had so much occupying his time now, he wouldn't be bored. Trent promised they would talk every day, and Ashby thought he might fly out and visit him in Monaco halfway through the production.

He could tack it onto his trip back to London. He needed to finalize the sale of his flat and see some of his friends. There were a couple of them who were convinced he'd lost his mind. He needed to assure them he had never been happier in his whole life.

He had purpose. He was in love. He was living and expressing himself authentically. Now, if he could just wrap his head around this damn visa business he'd be all set.

Even though his mum was American, it still wasn't easy. He was nearing the end of his tourism visa, and he had to leave the country. But he couldn't leave Trent. He could extend it to a business visa for another three months, but then he *would* have to leave the country before he could come back on another visa. If the State Department saw any reason to ban him, they had the right to keep him out of the country for five whole *years.* There was no way Ashby could stand that. If his green card application would just hurry up…

He shook his head. This wasn't the day to be worrying about that. In any case, he wasn't allowed to wallow in his thoughts for long. Partygoers continuously came up and fussed over Guinevere. Some eyed Ashby's outfit warily. Others were brave enough to compliment him on it. Ashby felt content in a whirlwind of people.

The bar was packed and the restaurant had been re-arranged to have a buffet for the guests. The new décor was a slick and sophisticated scheme with electric blues and metallic finishes. They had officially renamed the place Summit, and Darnell was busy wowing patrons with his impressive mixology skills, making drinks from their newly revamped and extensive cocktail list.

Kadie was sitting at the bar cheering him on every time he threw up a spinning bottle or set something on fire. After a month's hard work on Ashby's part, she had finally asked Darnell out. As Ashby predicted, Darnell didn't care that she was ten years older than him. He'd been too shy to ask *her* out. By the looks of it, they were very happy together.

Bob was looking like a new man, attending the party with his son who was looking healthy and happy. Bob had lost ten pounds and got a haircut. No longer did he drown his sorrows at the bar every night. He and Ashby had worked their arses off to improve almost every aspect of the resort. Painters and decorators had been working around the clock to modernize every single room. The spa was expanding and now had several luxury suppliers that Skye had cried over when she'd tried the products. The gift shop had been cleared out and was now selling beautiful and charming items from local businesses, most of which were Arapaho.

It made Ashby's heart swell to see Trent and his dad rebuilding their relationship. Ashby had tentatively made plans with his own parents to come over and visit at Christmas so they could meet each other. It seemed crazy that he was thinking that far ahead. They had never even met Gordon in the two years Ashby had been with him. But that was the difference with Trent. He knew they had a future together. They made each other so incredibly happy.

Trent loved Ashby for exactly who he was. He never tried to change him or force him into a box. He loved Ashby no matter what he was wearing. He was helping him work through his anxieties and making sure his confidence grew every day. It didn't hurt that Ashby had never had better sex in his whole life. Their obvious chemistry in the bedroom alone was enough to give him faith that this was a long-term thing.

It wasn't just fucking, though. It was communication, and that was why it made Ashby so sure of their compatibility. Trent still wasn't all that great at using his words. But when those failed him, he used his hands, his lips, his whole body. He never took Ashby for granted, always making sure he was happy and getting what he needed, in and out of the bedroom.

"What are you smiling about?" Maeve asked. She'd snuck up on Ashby as he was fussing with the fresh flower arrangements.

He arched an eyebrow down at Guinevere. "Some guard dog you are," he said. She was already scrabbling at Maeve's legs though, looking for the treats she always carried in her pockets.

"Nah-uh," she said, wagging her finger at him. "You had goo-goo eyes. Were you thinking about your handsome man?"

"Maybe," Ashby said with a grin. "Were you thinking about *your* handsome man?"

Maeve tutted as she fed Guinevere too many treats as usual. "I don't know what you mean," she said haughtily. Ashby sniggered.

"Well, both our men just walked in, in case you're interested?" he teased. She snapped around and looked where Trent was walking into the bar with his dad who had Merlin on a leash. As much as his behavior had improved, it was better to be safe than sorry.

"Is my lipstick okay?" she asked in a whisper.

"Smile," Ashby instructed. "Yep. Nothing on your teeth. You're good. Not that you care," he added with a wink.

"Oh, shut up," she said, fluffing her hair, then smiling over at Mr. Charles Sr.

She went to go greet him while Trent made his way over to Ashby. He was stopped several times by people wanting to say hello and wish him good luck. Ashby waited patiently, though. He used the opportunity to get two glasses of Champagne for them and sit at the small table for two he'd reserved for them. Guinevere trotted by his feet and had a good sniff around the table legs while they waited for Trent to join them. Ashby reapplied his lip gloss and tried not to feel nervous. God, he was going to miss seeing Trent every day.

"Hey," Trent said. He leaned down to kiss Ashby on the cheek before shrugging off his leather jacket and sitting next to him. "Sorry to keep you."

Ashby shook his head. "You're the man of the hour," he said. He picked up the two flutes and passed one to Trent. He was looking ruggedly handsome as usual in a Henley that clung to every delicious, bulging muscle. "Cheers."

"Cheers," Trent agreed. They tapped their glasses together, the 'ting' ringing through the air. Ashby had hired a harpist for the evening and people were chatting easily over the music. It meant he and Trent didn't have to shout to hear each other.

"How are you feeling?" he asked, squashing down the apprehension in his belly. Trent might have been leaving tomorrow, but it wasn't for long and they would talk every day.

Trent bit his lip. "Nervous," he said.

Ashby tilted his head in confusion. "About flying?" he asked.

Trent smiled and shook his head. "Not about that," he said. "About you."

Ashby blinked, even more confused. "Why would I make you nervous? I mean, I know this visa thing is being more of an arse than I thought it would be, but I'll almost certainly be here when you get back." Ashby hoped. Oh, god, did he hope.

Trent licked his lips. "You know I love you, so much," he said.

Despite all the progress he had made, fear still shot through Ashby's chest. Trent was *not* breaking up with him. He needed to relax. Even if there was an ocean between them, they would still find a way to be together. "I love you, too," he said, taking Trent's bigger hand between his two.

Trent bit his lip. "I think about our future a lot," Trent said. "I…I'd like to do something to make it more certain. But only if you want. It's, well, I guess it's something I'd want to do at some point, so I figured why not now?" He lifted Ashby's hand, kissing the knuckle. "I don't want you to have any doubts about us," he said warmly.

Ashby's heart was skipping in his chest. "I don't have any doubts," he said, impressed that he managed to keep his voice steady. But it was the truth. After three months together, he couldn't imagine his life without Trent.

"I'm glad to hear it," Trent said. He exhaled in what sounded like relief and smiled.

Then he reached into his jacket pocket and pulled out a ring box.

Ashby couldn't help it. He'd always sworn he wouldn't be one of those people who gasped and covered their mouths, with tears in their eyes. But until someone asked you to marry them, he realized you never really knew.

"I know," Trent continued, "that this is soon. I'm not saying we have to act on it for a while. But…well, visas are much easier if you're engaged."

He opened the box to reveal an elegant platinum band inside.

Ashby blinked, fighting to say something as he lowered his hands. "You're proposing to get me a green card?" he asked, only half-teasing.

Trent shook his head. "I'm proposing because I can't imagine not spending the rest of my life with you. I *know* you're the one, Ashby Wilcott. You made me whole. You're my one in a million. If it will help you stay in the country, I want to do it now. Because I'm crazy about you, gorgeous. I don't want *anything* to come between us." He bit his lip. "But if it's too soon, I understand."

"Shut up and kiss me," Ashby said, flinging his arms around his *fiancé.* "Oh my god, I love you so much. Yes, yes!"

Trent hugged him close, shaking. "I love you too," he said as Guinevere scampered around their feet, barking happily.

Trent made Ashby whole, too, he knew it. He'd lifted him up and helped him become the best possible version of who he could be. Yes, it was soon. But that was because it was just the beginning. They were on this journey into the unknown, growing every day, becoming stronger. Why wait when Ashby knew he only wanted to continue on this journey one way?

Together.

———

To see Ashby and Trent's first kiss from Ashby's point of view, sign up to my newsletter here: hjwelch.com/subscribe

The next book in the Homecoming Hearts series is Reyse and Corey's story, Blaze. Turn the page to learn more…

Secret romance. Public retribution. But can anyone really stand in the way of true love?

After his meteoric rise to fame with boy band Below Zero, international pop sensation Reyse Hickson has it all. Or so it seems. Thanks to his homophobic label, he never expects to find love. But when he's saved from a mugging by a gorgeous stranger, the chemistry between them is undeniable. Reyse can't help but fall into his savior's arms...or his bed.

Corey Sheppard is nobody's hero. He got himself out of the foster system and stands on his own two feet. He could never be anyone's closeted lover. But there's so much more to Reyse Hickson than the world sees. Corey just can't stay away.

When Reyse's dad suffers a stroke, Reyse insists on going home. In desperate need of a friend, he asks Corey to join him. A short time together is better than none. With Reyse's hectic schedule and bullying manager, they know it's the best they can do. But for the first time in his life, Corey finds a family with Reyse. And Reyse doesn't think he can hide how feels for Corey, even though his label threatens to drop him if he ever comes out.

Can Reyse and Corey walk away from the best thing that's ever happened to either of them? Or is this love worth going down in a blaze of glory?

Blaze is a high heat, low angst standalone MM romance. It's the fifth and final book in the **Homecoming Hearts** series, where these former (and current) pop stars swap the limelight for happy ever afters. This book features a pizza-based rescue, the most fabulous wine aunt and her even more fabulous dog, sunset beach kisses, a shocking TV interview, an epic reunion for the ages, and a guaranteed HEA with absolutely no cliffhanger.

Acknowledgments

There are so many people who I have to thank in helping me complete my first series in MM romance. Heck, my first ever book series! It's been a fair old journey and whether you've been here since the start or have only just discovered Below Zero and Homecoming Hearts, I couldn't have done this without you.

Thank you to the people who have been here all the way, behind the scenes, keeping me going and bringing these books to life with me: Ed Davies, Amelia Faulkner, Conrad Rivers, Meg Cooper, Cate Ashwood, Aria Tan, Tanja Ongkiehong, Leslie Copeland and LesCourt Author Services.

Thank you to my incredible husband, whose support I simply couldn't have done without. You believed in me when I didn't believe in myself and cheered on every milestone and accomplishment. Thank you for giving me my own happy ever after.

Thank you to my friends who make *me* feel like an international pop star!

Thank you to my fur babies for keeping Mummy company in her writing cave.

And finally, thank you to every single one of *you* who has enjoyed Blake, Joey, Raiden, Trent and Reyse's stories. Thank you for all the loving reviews, for the encouragement in our Facebook Group, <u>Helen's Jewels</u>, the emails you've sent saying how moved you were by a book, the excitement for each new release, everything. Without you this series wouldn't have come to life. You're the best and I have so much love for each and every one of you.

PINE COVE BOX SET BY HJ WELCH

Welcome to Pine Cove, where true love lives happily ever after! **This 2000 page box set contains all six novels as well as all five companion short stories.**

Safe Harbor

Robin Coal needs a fake boyfriend for his high school reunion. He asks his housemate: a gorgeous, totally straight ex-Marine. What could go wrong? There's only one bed, and Dair might not be so straight after all... When Robin's past threatens their future, only Dair can save him.

Sweet Spot

It's Halloween and Robin has prepared a sexy little surprise for his boyfriend Dair when he gets home from work. Hold on to your horses, Marine!

Troubled Waters

Bodyguard Scout Duffy doesn't know what's worse: the fact that his scorching one-night-stand, Emery Klein, is his bratty new client, or the fact that he doesn't even remember Scout. But Emery's life is in danger thanks to his out and proud charity work, and once he finally recognizes Scout, their chemistry in undeniable.

Homeward Bound

Swift Coal just found out he's a father, and his daughter (and her cranky cat) are coming to stay. His best friend's younger brother, Micha Perkins, has nowhere to go and a wrongfully tattered reputation. He's relieved when Swift asks him to be a live-in babysitter. He just has to hide his lifelong crush. Easy, because Swift is straight—right?

Bright Horizon

With sixteen years between them, baker Ben Turner and lawyer Elias Solomon have no idea their crush is mutual. But when Ben inherits his long-lost family's estate and becomes an overnight millionaire, Elias swears to protect the innocent younger man from the vultures circling him. To unravel the mystery of the inheritance, they must go to England to confront Ben's estranged relatives…and their feelings for each other.

Crossed Paths

Raj Bhat is done living in the shadows. It's time for him to take charge of his own destiny and tell the man he's fallen for how he really feels.

––––––––

Midnight Sky

It's the night before New Year's Eve. Taylan Demir is all alone, and he's just lost his dog. Except when his handsome customer, Hudson Perkins, comes to his rescue, Taylan doesn't just get his dog back. He's suddenly got a hot date, and maybe someone to kiss when the clock strikes midnight.

––––––––

Memory Lane

Angel Shields saved Jay Coal's life in high school, and Jay has secretly loved his straight best friend ever since. Now Angel's back in town with amnesia after a suspicious work accident and it's Jay's turn to rescue him. He pretends to be Angel's fiancé to see him in the hospital, but with his scrambled-up memory, Angel's not sure it's fictional after all. He just knows he loves Jay more than ever.

––––––––

Thin Ice

Kamran's ex broke his heart, tricked him into aiding a bank robbery, and now he wants him to do one last job. There's only one way to say no: seek the protective custody of the biggest, grumpiest FBI agent ever, Lee Marshall. And pretend to be his boyfriend for a week-long family reunion in their giant mansion. Wait, what?

––––––––

Calm Shores

Gorgeous, sophisticated Dante walks into Oliver's bar and orders…a boyfriend?! Dante needs a man to keep his mother from setting him back up with his awful, cheating ex, and Oliver is up for the challenge.

————

Fresh Snow

Emery Klein is throwing the best Christmas party ever, but his fiancé, Scout Duffy, and all their friends have something more exciting in mind.

————

Each Pine Cove book can be read as a stand alone and has its own happy ever after. But if you read the whole series, you'll see a lot of familiar faces!

Available as an ebook or audiobook.

I've spent almost four years trying to get my captain Seth to notice me. He's hot as hell and knows how to boss a guy around, even one as big as me. To him, though, I'm just the team clown. But when he drags me into this graduation bet, it's no laughing matter. So why shouldn't this little cherub Gabe tutor me as well? In fact, I don't see why we can't share him in all *kinds* of ways. Seth is clearly a natural Daddy, Gabe thrives being doted on, and I'm happy to Daddy *and* be Daddied. Win-win, right?

GABE

Somehow, I've found myself standing up to the guy whose family pretty much owns Paddle Creek and put my neck on the line for two of the college's star players. Now we're spending every day together as I try and save their grades, and I don't know if I'm crazy but it's like they both *want* me. I've never had a boyfriend. I'm not even out to my overbearing parents. How could I choose between them…or do I actually have to when they *both* want to be my Daddies? After my life comes crashing down, it's their turn to come to my rescue. Maybe what me and these god-like men have isn't just a fling after all?

__Heaven Sent__ is a steamy, standalone MMM romance. It's the first book in the __Paddle Creek College__ series, where it's always the quiet ones who get up to the best kind of trouble. This book features a geek tutoring two hot jocks, two hot jocks tutoring a geek in a completely different way, a trash panda with a heart of gold, a human ice cream sundae, a revenge curse, and a guaranteed HEA with absolutely no cliffhanger.

though, so in a way it's safe to flirt with him and see him lose that stiff upper lip. It's not like he'd be interested in me anyway if he ever discovered what I love wearing under my clothes. Tough guys like me shouldn't like satin and lace. They shouldn't want to feel pretty. But Sir makes me feel gorgeous, and I want to be *such* a good boy for him.

__Yes, Sir__ is a steamy, standalone MM romance. It's the second book in the __Paddle Creek College__ series, where it's always the quiet ones who get up to the best kind of trouble. This book features two people learning they don't have to be ashamed of who they are, a sassy brat who really wants to behave, a master in the bedroom who's a caring Daddy at heart, role playing so good it could win an Oscar, and a guaranteed HEA with absolutely no cliffhanger.

PADDLE CREEK #3: LITTLE PLEASURES BY HJ WELCH

One jaded Daddy. One brand new boy. A fake relationship that becomes all too real.

XANDER

It's bad enough I have to move back to Paddle Creek with my awful stepmom, but now my half-brother's best friend has decided he has to look after me—even pretending to be my new boyfriend for a family wedding to keep my stepmother off my back. What Ruben doesn't know is that I've been in love with him for as long as I can remember and spending so much time with him is torture. Until it isn't. I can't believe that he's interested in me and even wants to be my Daddy, unlocking something in me I never knew was there. But when my stepmom goes too far, can I rely on Ruben to be there for me seeing as no one else in my life ever has?

RUBEN

When my life-long best friend asks me to keep an eye on his half-brother, of course I agree. Except he's a young man now, not a kid, and he's tugging at every single one of my Daddy heartstrings. Xander has just moved back into town and between finishing his degree, part-time work, and hellish stepmother, he's stressing himself into knots. It's a long time since a boy interested me, but I just want to protect Xander from the whole world. No matter the cost.

Little Pleasures is a steamy, standalone MM romance. It's the third book in the **Paddle Creek College** series, where it's always the quiet ones who get up to the best kind of trouble. This book features a Daddy introducing a boy to his inner little, the most loyal doggy best friend, a lot of dinosaurs, a heart-stopping rescue, and a guaranteed HEA with absolutely no cliffhanger. CW: Age play but no ABDL.

PADDLE CREEK #4: FOUR PLAY BY HJ WELCH

**Three hungry wolves. One pretty little lamb. The hunt for love
is on.**

HARPER

I'm here for a good time, not a long time. When a total cutie asks me
if I'd be interested in him and his two Daddies chasing me down and
having their way with me, it sounds fun. I'm only in this crappy
town for the summer, after all. But what we share is *intense.* I signed
on to get caught…not to catch feels. However, when I find myself
being hunted for real, can I really expect my wolf pack to come to
the rescue?

RICK

After my husband and I swapped military life for married life, we quickly met our sweet baby boy who we'll do anything for. When Brady says he's found a sassy little lamb for the three of us to stalk, I'm happy to indulge him. But this broken young man swiftly captures all of our hearts, even though he says he can walk away any time. There's a difference between walking and being taken, however. Now I have the scent of a fool who's about to discover what happens when he's stolen what's *mine*.

__Four Play__ is a super steamy, standalone MMMM romance. It's the fourth book in the __Paddle Creek College__ series, where it's always the quiet ones who get up to the best kind of trouble. This book features exhilarating primal play, one hell of a paint ball match, an underwater themed motel, so many smooches, an obsessive ex-boyfriend, and a guaranteed HEA with absolutely no cliffhanger.

BEARS-4-U (MULTI-AUTHOR SHARED UNIVERSE): KEEP ME BY HJ WELCH

Snowed in for a second chance at love...

BECKETT

It's been over two years since I lost my darling husband, and my best friend is taking matters into her own hands. She's signed me up to a dating app for bears and those that love them, even encouraging me to attend a weekend mixer. I go to humor her, not expecting to rescue the most adorable boy…twice. But I'm not ready to open up my heart again, am I?

LAURIE

My last Daddy was bad news. It's taken a lot of courage for me to reach out on Bears-4-U and go to this mixer, only to find that the new Daddy I've been talking to is just as awful. That's when Beckett swoops into my life like a hero in a story book. I know he's not looking for love, but I want to mend his broken heart so badly. When a scary snowstorm blows in and strands us, I trust he'll keep me safe and warm. I want to be in his life, in his bed, in his heart…forever.

Bears-4-U is a MM Daddy romance multi-author series, featuring a host of delicious Daddy pairings. The Bears-4-U dating app is all about putting Bears and Teddy Bears together for their honey-sweet HEAs. Psst, no real bears involved. Each book can be read as a standalone, but why not snuggle up with all the bears?

DADDY'S FAIRY TALES BOX SET BY HELEN JULIET

Experience Goldilocks and the Three Bears, Little Red Riding Hood, The Three Little Pigs, and Puss in Boots as you've never seen them before in this box set of contemporary adaptations! Available together for the first time, each stand alone book features a caring Daddy finding his HEA with a loving boy (or boys!)

Golden

When Goldie's ex-boyfriend leaves him in serious debt with the adult entertainment company he works for, Goldie gets the chance to work off the money…in front of the camera. The idea excites him, but then his favourite throuple—Daddy, Papa, and Baby —*demand* he comes to play with them. No matter how scared he is, he can't miss this opportunity, not even when his past comes back to haunt him.

Wild Ride

When Red is chased into the woods, he seeks sanctuary at his estranged grandma's house. He doesn't expect to be rescued by his older brother's best friend, the man he was always madly in love with. Could Hunter be the Daddy of Red's wildest dreams? Especially when he unlocks a secret passion of Red's for beautiful lingerie. There's still a threat lurking in the woods, though, and Hunter realises he'll do anything to protect his beautiful boy.

Three

When three shy best friends sign up to a dating app to finally get some by the end of the year, they don't expect to all fall for the same gorgeous, slightly scary-looking Daddy. The only solution? Let him choose who he wants to bed. Except he doesn't. Daddy Wolf wants to spoil each little piggy, one after another. But when danger comes calling, will their love for each other be enough to save them all?
Includes Halloween bonus scene!

Nine Lives

When Charlie suddenly finds himself homeless and penniless, he decides to sell the only thing left he owns. Himself. For the very first time. Lucky for him he stumbles across Miller, the own of a London kink club, who saves him from those who would take advantage of him. As Miller discovers his inner Daddy, he also unlocks Charlie's kitten alter-ego. But with both their families meddling, will new love be enough to keep them together?

Available as an ebook.

About the Author

HJ Welch is an author of contemporary MM romance series, including the international bestselling Pine Cove series. She lives just outside of London with her husband and two balls of fluff that occasionally pretend to be cats. She began writing at an early age, later honing her craft online in the world of fanfiction on sites like Wattpad. Fifteen years and over half a million words later, she sought out original MM novels to read. By the end of 2016 she had written her first book of her own, and in 2017 she achieved her lifelong dream of becoming a full-time author. When she's not writing she's usually dancing, singing, filming music videos, taking long walks, working on jigsaw puzzles, drinking prosecco, or talking about Eurovision.

She also writes contemporary British MM fairy tale adaptations as Helen Juliet.

You can contact Helen via the following:
Newsletter: https://www.subscribepage.com/helenjuliet
Website – www.hjwelch.com
Facebook Group – Helen's Jewels
Instagram – @helenjwrites
Twitter – @helenjwrites
Book Bub – @HJWelchAuthor
Facebook Page – @HJWelchAuthor

9 781999 706760